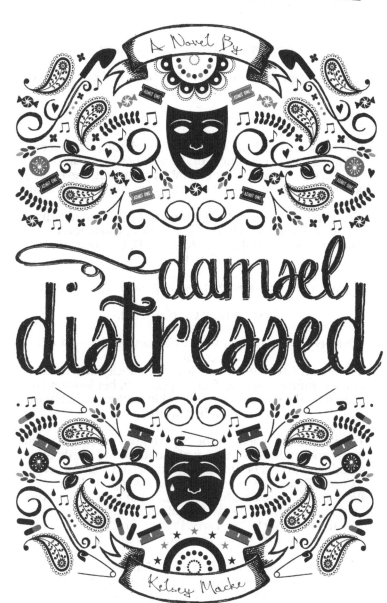

A Novel By

damsel distressed

Kelsey Macke

SPENCER HILL CONTEMPORARY

Spencer Hill Press

Please visit our website at www.spencerhillpress.com

First Edition: October 2014.
Kelsey Macke
Damsel Distressed: a novel / by Kelsey Macke – 1st ed.
p. cm.
Summary: A teen girl struggles with obesity, self-harm, and the infuriatingly perfect stepsister in her journey to overcome the stigmas put on her life, on her friendships, and on her future.

The author acknowledges the copyrighted or trademarked status and trademark owners of the following wordmarks mentioned in this fiction: Band-Aid, Barbie, The Bachelor, Chuck Taylor, Chrysler, DiGiorno, Disney, Dr. Pepper, iPod, Girl Scouts, Goodwill, Jedi, Lincoln Logs, The Little Mermaid, McDonald's, McGriddle, McMuffin, Mustang, MythBusters, Nerf, Pop-Tarts, Post-it, Prozac, Risperdal, Rolex, Sharpie, Target, Vans

Cover design and title page by Jenny Zemanek
Interior artwork by Jessica Nickerson
Interior layout by Jenny Perinovic

ISBN 978-1939392176 (paperback)
ISBN 978-1-939392-67-1 (e-book)

Printed in the United States of America

We often try to hide the parts of
ourselves that have been broken.
We work so hard to make sure other people
never see the bits that make us feel weak.
This book is dedicated to those precious,
fractured fragments,
for teaching us to grow and hope and
never, ever stop fighting.

Author's Note

This book, Damsel Distressed, is presented with Imogen Unlocked—an album of original songs performed by the band Wedding Day Rain.

If you're not into music, you can skip that piece of the puzzle.

If you are interested in the songs, they're all available for your listening pleasure at DamselDistressed.com.

You can further enhance your experience and listen to the songs while reading the book. Each illustration contains the title of the song that fits with the scene you've just read. You can scan the hidden QR code in each illustration and listen to the songs on your mobile device, or you can navigate to the corresponding page at DamselDistressed.com.

It is my hope that you will experience Damsel Distressed and Imogen Unlocked in whatever way you like.

I'm so excited to share this story with you!

Yours,
Kelsey Macke

They've been lying from the start. From the first time we read the words "once upon a time," we're fed the idea that these girls—these gorgeous, demure, singing-with-the-wildlife girls—get a happy ending. And I get it. Poor thing had to do some chores around the house, fine. But the idea that she needs a magic old lady to come down and skim off the dirt so the prince will see her beauty? That's ridiculous. Maybe she should have been working on her lockpicking skills instead of serenading squirrels. She could have busted out, hitched a ride to the castle, and impressed the prince with her safe-cracking prowess.

Sorry, magic-fairy lady. She didn't need your help. The deck's already stacked in her favor. Why? Because she's the golden girl. She's the star. No one cares about the stepsisters' stories. Those girls don't get a sweet little ending. They get a lifetime of longing.

Seriously.

Hot girls get the fairy tales.

Hot girls like my stepsister.

"Okay, Imogen. Time's up."

Therapist George is staring at his watch and straightening the cufflinks on his left sleeve. The little silver baubles are shaped like barbells. They must be new. I'm surprised, though; I never pegged him as one of *those* people. I just can't understand folks who willingly go to the gym and participate in choreographed masochism. Maybe I'd have to experience it to get it. Like, maybe if I knew what it was like to put on my jeans without doing the fat-girl, jean-buttoning rain dance, I'd understand.

I stick the end of my pen in my mouth and listen as it clicks against my front teeth and echoes inside my head.

"How did you do?" he asks.

"Fine," I say. "But..." I smile and bat my eyelashes aggressively.

"Let me guess," he says. "You didn't write about the topic I gave you?"

I look down at my sloppy writing. I press too hard. I always smear the ink as I go. "Well, no. But I wrote about something totally new!"

"Oh, really?" He smiles brightly as I twirl my pen between my fingers.

"Some girls are pretty. Some girls aren't. Some girls get attention from princely characters. The rest of us pine away and stuff ourselves with pie."

Therapist George mimics me, widening his eyes and putting his chin on his hand with exaggerated interest. "So by 'new' you mean the same Disney Princess rant you always write? I see." He smirks and shakes his head slightly as I close the spiral notebook in my lap.

I stick out my bottom lip and clasp my chubby fingers together in prayer.

"Please don't be mad I didn't write what you asked me to."

"Of course I'm not mad. In five years, have I ever been mad?"

He grins, bringing up only one side of his mouth, as he makes some notes in my file. I hate when he writes in my file. I think there should be a statute of file limitations, and after every three sessions, I get to keep his notes as a collector's item.

Therapist George scribbles as I answer, "No, TG. You've never been mad. You've also never been sad, jealous, insecure, or anxious in front of me either. You're clearly a robot."

My fifteen-cent ballpoint tastes like poison, which it probably is. George sets his six-hundred-dollar pen on the small dark table sitting to the side of his tufted leather chair. The sound of it against the wood is deep and low, as if it is a gavel he only lays down when he's made up his mind to say something heavy. I stick the pointy end of my pen through the messy, box-dyed, black bun on the top of my head and look to my right at his big wall of windows.

Therapist George follows my gaze and, as if on cue, asks, "Do you mind if I let in the light?"

A test.

When I was twelve years old, I went through weeks of testing before my psychiatrist, Dr. Rodriguez, diagnosed me with clinical depression. I spent hours and hours answering stupid questions and drawing my feelings in his overly juvenile office. "Yes, *I feel sad all the time.*" "Yes, *I understand that my mom died and she isn't coming back.*" "Yes, *sometimes my chest hurts so bad that my hands shake and I can't make myself breathe.*" Testing me was this big, complicated thing.

But Therapist George can tell how I'm feeling by simply opening his blinds.

It makes me feel obvious. Readable. I wish it were easier to throw him off.

"No problem. Let in all the light you want," I say as I cross my ankles below me.

He hesitates. I can see by the way his mouth opens slightly he doesn't believe me, but he reaches for the thin nylon cord anyway. He tugs it, sending the blinds racing to the top of the window. I force myself not to jerk at the sudden flood of light and vanish into a puff of smoke like a non-sparkly vampire. The windows in his office are tall—floor to ceiling.

I know there's glass, but in the back of my mind, it feels like an invitation. Like an outstretched hand. The blue of the sky is all I can see from my place on his sofa, and it tricks my brain into thinking it's a ledge.

Last December, the blinds were never open.

Last December, a ledge would have been far too tempting.

As TG turns to look back at me, he is silhouetted by sunlight. His shoulders are broad, and his tall form looks stronger and more handsome when the details of his features are in shadow. I imagine that's true for lots of people. We all look better when we're not really seen.

"So how about you tell me why you didn't want to write about Carmella coming to live with you?" He crosses back to his chair and sits down with his notes in his lap.

At the sound of my stepsister's name, my ears get hot and my chest tightens. "George, can't I have one more day without her in my head? Today is Happy-No-Carmella-Saturday!" I make an exaggerated smiley face. "Tomorrow is Sad-Carmella-Moves-In-Sunday." I pull the corners of my mouth down and pretend to wipe away tears. "You know the second she unpacks tomorrow, I'm going to be living with a person who decided to hate me on the very first day we met. I'm already dreading having her in my day-to-day life. Can't I at least leave her out of my sessions?"

He uncrosses his legs and leans forward in his chair. "But why is she coming now? Why not over the summer?"

"I don't know. Her dad and Evelyn had some custody spat or something. You know I could earn a gold medal in ignoring her mother completely, so I really don't care. If I had a vote, I'd never have seen her again."

I tangle my arms together over my chest and try to reclaim the calm from a few moments ago.

"Maybe it's time you told me about Christmas," he starts and pauses so his eyebrows cinch together. "I know you've said you don't want to talk about the first time you met Carmella, but I'm worried about how her moving in might affect you."

Christmas. It's hard to be festive when your dad gets engaged and insta-married to a real-life Barbie and your resulting breakdown almost earns you a two-week vacation to the Mayberry Behavioral Center. Thanks, Santa! It's just what I always wanted.

I get up from the couch and tug the waistband of my jeans up over my muffin top. I take a deep breath as TG leans back in his chair and crosses his legs again.

"You want to know about Christmas? Fine. Let me tell you a little story."

George settles in, and a grin tugs at his tanned cheeks.

I wave my arm in a high arc in front of him as I say, "Once upon a time, there was a girl. We'll call her... Imogen."

He smiles indulgently. A tiny sigh escapes his lips, but I ignore it. I know it's not the heartfelt confession he wanted, but he's gonna have to take what he can get.

"One cold December morning, Imogen's dad woke her to say he was getting married. Her dad was surprised when she went completely freaking mental at the thought, probably because her mother had died six Decembers before." I lean toward him and whisper loudly, "That's where the audience is supposed to gasp."

"Did you want your dad to stay single forever?"

The word "single" bounces between my ears.

My voice lifts higher as I pace around the couch. "When Dad met Evelyn, he tried to tell me about her, and I told him I didn't want to hear it. So he didn't *tell* me about their dates. He didn't *tell* me they fell in love. He just woke me up one morning and told me he was *marrying* her."

My stomach drops, and my brain sloshes around in my skull. I walk to the edge of the sofa and faint back on it with a dramatic sigh, holding the back of my hand against my forehead. I turn my face toward George, and with a snap of my tongue, I say, "Oh, George, isn't this just the saddest story you've ever heard? But wait, I'm getting to the good part."

The sarcasm falls over me like a shield.

George's smirk is gone, and he bites his bottom lip and holds it between his teeth as I lug myself up and continue my mockery. Guilt rises up in my chest, but I push it down. Guilt is much easier to push away than the truth.

"A few weeks later, Replacement Mom is all unpacked, and Dad tells Imogen that instead of going to see a musical on the night of the 27th, like they had every year since Mom died, they were going out for a fancy, new-family dinner. And the best part was— surprise, Imogen! You have a stepsister, too!"

I feel myself making silly fake faces as I stride around the room, but my palms have started sweating.

I check the clock on the wall, willing the hands to click over to eleven.

"Imogen, I didn't mean to push you if you're really not ready to tell me about it. We have a few minutes left. Sit. Let's revisit this some other time."

"No, George. Let's get this over with."

I sit on the left side of the leather couch as I have off and on for the past five years. I sink deeply into it as it makes a leathery creak under my weight.

"The night before our dinner, as you know, I graduated from scratching my thighs with unfolded paperclips when I found a brand-new straight razor in the garage—still in the package."

George nods his head. "That was the night you cut your arm for the first time. I remember."

"But I didn't ever tell you Carmella was there."

His eyes open wide before he can tell his brain to maintain his even and unflinching face. "She was there when you cut yourself?"

"No. Right after." I look down at my ragged fingertips and collect my thoughts. "Evelyn brought Carmella from the airport, and Dad came upstairs to tell me they'd arrived. He walked in just as I'd made the last cut."

I force myself to resist the automatic reaction of reaching for my left forearm. In my head, I can see each line.

Six scars. One for every year without her.

My sobbing echoed in my ears. I remember that. I remember trying to explain I'd barely marked the skin. I was inches from my wrist. It was the back of my arm—completely different. Right? Why couldn't my dad understand? It wasn't the worst thing. I remember worrying more about him lifting my weight than about the fact that I'd hurt myself. He clearly had that emergency situation adrenaline thing going on because he carried me downstairs through the living room.

"It was chaos," I continue. "Evelyn was screaming into the phone receiver, and I was begging for Dad to put me down. And on the couch is this gorgeous girl, my age, and she's crying because clearly this situation must have scared the crap out of her. But then our eyes met and we looked at each other for what seemed like forever, and then she sniffled, dried her eyes, set her jaw, and stomped out of the room. I haven't seen her since. She wasn't worried about me. She didn't care. I was about to get carted off to the hospital, and all she could do was scowl."

I close my eyes for a second, and I'm instantly back in that living room. I remember how grey the winter sky was. I remember the exact green of Carmella's shirt, the sound of her scoff, and her boots clanking across the floor.

My shoulders press back against the couch. I sniffle and suck air deep into my lungs and wipe under my eyes. I look around for my pen, but it must have fallen between the cushions or something, so I settle for biting at my fingernails instead.

"Well, there it is. The end. You're right George, story time *is* the best!" I force the corners of my mouth up into a sly smile, but he doesn't return it.

"Imogen, I can only imagine how humiliated you felt. I am so sorry it happened that way." He shakes his head slowly as he talks, his nose scrunches up, and his voice softens. "But this isn't last December. It's been ten months since then, and you made so much progress this summer. Why worry if you don't even know how she feels? She might have forgotten all about it."

I'm sure he wants me to sit up proud and tall because I didn't hurt myself this summer, but his pointing it out just makes me feel pathetic.

"Right. And pretending I don't exist for the ten months since Christmas is 'cause Carmella's just waiting to surprise me with her friendliness in person."

"If you're really concerned, maybe we should have a group meeting. We could have you, Carmella, and your parents—or just Evelyn, if your father is out of town."

If Dad is out of town? Right. I'm not even sure he remembers which house is ours at this point.

"It could be good to hash this out, face to face. Find out if there's even a problem in the first place." George checks his watch at the exact moment the clock strikes eleven. I've decided that looking at his watch is just something he does to remind his clients they can't stay all day because he always knows when the time is up. His internal clock is like a freaking Rolex or something.

I try to picture Evelyn, Carmella, and me—all of us together—sitting on this single leather couch. In my head, I somehow tip the couch up like a seesaw.

"It's not happening, George. I'm sorry." I drop my notebook into my bag and stand up to look in the sofa for my pen.

"You just let me know if you change your mind."

"Ugh. Where is my freaking pen?!"

He turns me by the shoulders and gestures to the top of my head.

"Oh! Right," I say as I reach up and pull my pen out of my bun and drop it into my bag. "Thanks. I gotta go get Grant. We're celebrating my last day of freedom—and also his birthday. It's a doubly joyous occasion."

"Have fun," he says as he heads around to the backside of his desk. "And, Imogen, don't worry until you have to, okay? The end of your story hasn't been written yet. You've got lots and lots of chapters left."

He puffs his chest out just slightly, and I imagine this TG quotable is going straight into my file as soon as I close the door. He should really get into the fortune cookie business.

I raise my arm and flip my hand down at the wrist. "Oh, George," I say. "Don't be so dramatic."

The sun streams in through my car's open windows. I love the feeling of a good day that's also gorgeous outside. I've run through Grant's birthday plans about fifty times, but I want it to be perfect.

As I drive down the highway, I can't help but see little memories of all the amazing times we've had at every mile marker.

That's the McDonald's where we scared the little kids by jumping out of the ball pit. There's that gas station where we sat on the curb and tried to smoke a cigarette without throwing up. And the grocery store down that road always has the best selection of cookies in the bakery. We can't settle in for an all-day *Mythbusters* marathon without our favorite cookies.

And if I were to take that exit there and take the first left and then the second right, I'd be at the cemetery where my mom is buried. And where little Grant stood by little me and held my hand while my dad cried into the ground.

I catch my reflection in the rearview mirror. I can see the signs of a few good months in the absence of dark circles under my light grey eyes. I don't like wearing makeup—other than gobs of black eyeliner. So even during bad times, when the bags under my eyes look like bruises, I never cover them up. I wear them like a warning. They're declaring the State of Imogen before I even open my mouth.

Beside me, my phone rings in the seat, and I put it on speakerphone. "Hey, I'm almost there," I say as I roll up my window with my incredibly advanced hand crank.

"Happy-No-Carmella-Saturday!" Grant shouts into the receiver.

"Wait. You can't say that—I have to say happy birthday first!"

"Too late, I win." He laughs.

"Fine. Are you ready for your day of fun? I was thinking we'd start with a movie and then a late lunch/early dinner, whatever—my treat of course—and then I was thinking we could catch the musical at Edgehill?"

"Sounds good to me."

"Brice has been trying to schedule a time for us to hang out with him and Jonathan. I could ask them to come?" I hear my voice go all nervous as I speak.

"Jonathan's cool. I don't know why you're so weird about him."

"I'm not weird about him. He just never talks to me. When Brice told me the Jonathan who's always folding paper and ignoring people in English class was *his* Jonathan, I did not believe him."

"It's not a crime to be quiet," Grant says. I can hear the smirk in his voice.

"Well, thank God." My heart flutters in my chest.

I hear his electric toothbrush buzz to life and it's probably the most precious thing ever when he mumbles, "Whassashows?"

I smile so hard I'm afraid he'll hear my blushing cheeks right through the phone. "I was thinking we could go see whatever old horror movie is playing at the dollar theatre, and then tonight, the Edgehill show is *Dirty Rotten Scoundrels*. It's supposed to be really funny."

He spits.

How is that cute?

"Sounds perfect," he says. "When will you be here?"

"I should pull up in five minutes."

"Perfect, see you soon."

I press the button to end the call, and just as I do, my phone rings again. I answer it and tap the speakerphone button without even looking at the screen. "What did you forget, weirdo?"

"Immy?"

My dad's voice squeaks out of my tiny phone speaker.

I wish he hadn't called and I'm so glad he did all at once.

"Hey, Dad. I guess you landed?"

"I did. Evelyn told me you wouldn't be there for Carmella's arrival tomorrow. Something about theatre?"

I roll my eyes at the sound of Evelyn's name and grind my teeth at the sound of Carmella's. I'm instantly defensive.

"Yeah, Dad. It's required for all techies to be there on Sunday workday. And it's been on the calendar since school started six weeks ago."

The phone goes quiet for a few seconds, and I wonder if I've dropped his call.

"Be nice to her, okay, kiddo?"

Right, because I'm a horrible bully and she's going to just skip around being precious. I reach into my purse and pull out a fun-size candy bar and pop it in my mouth.

"I've gotta go, Dad."

"And, Immy, promise you'll call if something happens, okay?"

I pull up to a stoplight and wait for him to say something. I don't want to acknowledge that he thinks I'm going to fall apart at the first sign of anything.

He clears his throat. "Up or down, you call me. Promise."

I pause as long as I can. "I promise, Dad. I've gotta go. Be safe."

"You, too, baby girl."

Before he has the chance to clarify what "safe" means for an overweight, clinically depressed seventeen-year-old girl with an anxiety disorder, I reach down and hang up the call.

I pull up to Grant's house, and he's waiting for me on the curb. He springs to life before I come to a complete stop.

I scream "Happy Birthday!" at the top of my lungs as he throws himself into the car, leans over, and tries to smother my squeals.

"You crazy girl! My neighbors are going to think I'm kidnapping you."

I laugh. "If they haven't ratted us out to the police after a dozen years of our shenanigans, they probably won't start now. Now stop distracting me. I got you a present."

I lift up my elbow and open the armrest compartment, and his face shifts from silliness to sincerity almost instantly.

"What? Why? It's not the anniversary of the first time I made you sit and watch eighteen hours of *Mythbusters* with me, is it? 'Cause if it were, I would have been obligated to bring flowers—which I didn't, and you'd surely never forgive me." He puts his hand over his heart, and even though we're both being silly, the gesture makes my throat close tightly.

"Ha. You'd never forget a day that important." I give him a thumbs up and a big exaggerated nod of my head. "Anyway, not sure if you remember my screaming a few seconds ago, but..." I drop my voice to a loud whisper. "It's your birthday."

He grins. "If you say so."

I hand him the small bit of black-on-black embroidered fabric, and he turns it over in his fingers.

"It's a patch," I say. "Sorry, I didn't wrap it."

"It looks like a Superman thingy! Kinda. Sorta. I mean there's an 'M,' too, which is problematic 'cause Superman is one word, but I forgive you!"

"Oh, shut up, I know that Superman is one word." I laugh with him as he puts it against his forehead and then on his palm and then in the middle of his chest. "It's for Stage Manager, but I was also thinking about how it could be for Science Man, or Silly Muggle or—"

"Or Stud Muffin!" he says with the patch held against his cheek. "Or Sexy Mastermind." He waggles his eyebrows at me, and I laugh as I waggle mine back.

"I thought you could iron it onto your stage blacks," I say.

Some girls like a guy in uniform, but I am a sucker for a techie in his blacks.

"This is awesome, Gen. I love it. So much." He reaches over and puts his hand on my shoulder. In the moment without laughing and joking, the weight of his hand there presses in on me and keeps me from lifting right out of my seat. Like gravity. "Thank you," he says.

I swallow away the warmth of his hand, tucking it deep inside to remember whenever I need it.

"It's nothing major, I know."

He pauses. "Come here, you." He jerks his head, gesturing outside, and gets out of the car, closing his door behind him.

As I stand in the space of my open car door, he walks up to me. The sunlight is breaking through the tree in his front yard and streaming across his face. He squints his hazel eyes—more green than brown, but definitely both. The skin around his mouth folds into familiar creases as he smiles.

"Come on," he says as he opens his arms wide and pulls me against him.

I press my cheek to his chest and listen to his heartbeat.

We stand there, my arms wrapped neatly around his narrow waist and his arms crossing gently over my shoulders. All that exists is the smell of his hair. I could never describe what it is exactly, but the smell of him and his drugstore hair product does me in every single time. I could live in that smell.

"Thank you for my present," he whispers over my head.

When Grant, Brice, Jonathan, and I step out of the Edgehill Community Theatre at half-past ten, the entire sky is bright with stars. I turn around and look up at the beautiful theatre marquees, glowing with colorful neon lights.

"That was so good!" Brice skips to the edge of the sidewalk and starts balancing on the curb. His grin is a mile wide as Jonathan, hands shoved deep in his pockets, comes to his side. Brice's bright voice fills the cool evening air. "When the Jackal was revealed, I was like 'whaaaaat?!' 'cause I did not see that coming. Did you see that coming, babe?"

Brice holds out his hand for Jonathan, who pauses for a moment before taking it.

I recognize insecurity. One might call it my specialty. It only lasts a second, but that hesitation sticks out at me and I make a mental note to pay closer attention and listen for clues the next time Brice is talking about his boy.

"Definitely not." Jonathan gives him a twirl, which causes Brice to giggle adorably.

While Brice skips over to me, I watch as Jonathan shoves his hand back in his pocket before turning to Grant and mouthing, "Yes, I did." They laugh as they walk down the sidewalk in front of Brice and me.

We follow them closely. Brice's face and wide, round eyes are bright as he chatters.

"And did you see those costumes? The ensemble had to wear at least four different looks, maybe five. That is impressive."

"Well, you could do just as well," I say as I look up at the stars.

Brice smiles. "Probably, yeah."

In front of us, Grant suddenly turns around and runs up to me with a grin on his face.

"HA! Gen, you thought I'd forget? You sneak!"

I laugh because I already know what he's going to say. Grant turns toward the boys and explains.

"Gen and I have a standing ice cream bet for every theatre production we see. She thinks it will be lame. I think it will be awesome. Optimism wins again!" He turns back to me. "You lose. You buy the ice cream."

I scoff and cross my arms. "It's your birthday! I would have bought the ice cream anyway."

He bends down so we're at the same eye level.

"I think you're trying to keep me from my ice cream."

I stand up straight and put my hand over my heart. "I'd never, ever keep a person from their ice cream. I thought you knew me so well."

He winks, and I stick out my tongue before we step onto the crosswalk arm-in-arm.

"So," Brice chimes in, "I don't know much about how you and Grant got together."

He raises his eyebrow a little bit, and my rebuttal gets caught in my throat.

"Not *together* together," Grant says with an easy smile that seems to mean nothing. His words echo off the walls of my chest, banging around between each rib before settling in my stomach.

"Yeah, we're not together. But you *know* that," I say to Brice with a slim smile as the warmth of Grant's arm radiates into mine.

Brice stops and puts a hand on his hip. "Oh, excuse me for misinterpreting." He gestures to our intertwined limbs.

"We've been best friends since kindergarten," Grant says.

"Yeah, it's true," I say as I watch Brice snake his hand through the gap between Jonathan's body and where his hand's still shoved to the bottom of his pocket.

"Gen?"

I shake away my curiosity at Jonathan's hidey hand and pick up where Grant left off. "We really got close right after my mom died in fourth grade." I say the words, but with Grant's body close to mine, I barely feel the sting.

"I remember the day Gen and I became inseparable. I'd crawled under the fence to sit in her living room and play video games—"

"And on this random day, I answered the phone instead of my dad. It was a telemarketer who asked if my mom was home, and I totally freaked out. I panicked and almost hyperventilated. I ran upstairs and crawled under my bed to hide."

Grant turns to me and says, "I went upstairs and crawled right under there with her. And I told her that no matter what, no matter how bad things got, I'd stay."

Brice stops dead in his tracks. "That. Is. The. Cutest. Story. Ever." He sniffles and then turns to Jonathan and starts playfully smacking him on the shoulder. "Can we have a romantic story like that? You need to crawl under my bed real freaking quick, you got it?"

Romantic. The heat returns to my cheeks.

And Grant lets go of my arm.

No, Brice, it's not romantic 'cause we were ten. And even if it happened tonight, we're just friends. Period. Been there, ruined that.

Jonathan smiles at Brice and softly says, "Give us time. We'll get a story." His voice is warm and has a gentle twang. Brice turns and stretches onto his tiptoes to wrap his arms all the way around Jonathan's neck. Brice is a whole head shorter, but other than that, they're a matched set. Twin puffs of honey-colored hair, swept up into fashionable pompadours; square jawlines; and bright blue eyes. As Brice pulls back, Jonathan kisses his forehead before we cross the next block.

As I walk past the glow of a green stoplight, envy swells in my belly. Romantic might be their story, but it won't be mine. Not with Grant. It just won't.

And I shouldn't take our relationship for granted by wishing it was something else.

We finally arrive at our favorite ice cream shop, and I make good on my promise and order Grant a double chocolate chip. He doesn't have to tell me his order. I just know.

I usually get a double scoop of butter pecan in a waffle cone, but after Brice orders lemon ice and Jonathan gets frozen yogurt, I come to the table with a kid's scoop of vanilla. In a cup.

"Where's your butter pecan?" Grant asks.

"They were out," I lie. "But that's not important." I clear my throat with a flourish. I hold up my cup and say, "Here's to Grant. Happy Birthday."

We bump our scoops together. As we dive into our first tastes, Grant leans over to whisper in my ear. "You made it great."

I grin as I dig the tiny plastic spoon in my little paper cup. This boring, old vanilla has never tasted so sweet.

My dripping paintbrush creates the sweetest rhythm as it swipes color across the particleboard. I dip the bristles into the stony grey again, and the wet paint reflects miniature versions of the hot stage lights into my eyes. I can almost hear waves crashing with every brush stroke, back and forth, up and down.

I love the sound.

Grant is working on the opposite side of the stage. He's building a giant, colorful bed for the second act, which rolls on casters and towers thirteen fake mattresses high. I look over at him, perched on top of the giant contraption, whacking a hammer with Thor-like precision. He is hunched over the side with his dark hair flopping across his increasingly sweaty brow. As if on cue, his head snaps up. He's too far away and the lighting is too weird, so I can't really see the details of his eyes, but that's okay. I've had them memorized for years. He looks right at me, standing in front of a half-painted castle wall. I'm staring with my lips apart like an idiot, paint from my brush dripping down the back of my hand 'cause, well, that's what paint does.

He lifts his chin and tries to shake his sweaty hair out of his eyes as he gives me a big smile.

"You okay?" he mouths. I nod at him and stifle a laugh. He's dangling off a ten-foot tall platform and haphazardly using power tools, but he's the one checking on me. Grant crosses his eyes and sticks his tongue out just as Jonathan walks up and asks for help lifting a platform.

I laugh as Grant pulls his tongue back in his mouth and tries to act like a self-respecting stage manager, jumping down from his perch and dusting off his hands. Jonathan looks back in my direction with a grin and shakes his head slightly before punching Grant in the shoulder and then guiding him to the large, heavy step that belongs further upstage.

I lower my brush and wipe my paint-smeared hand across the leg of my already color-crusted tech day jeans. Just then, Grant and Jonathan lean over and pick up the giant platform on "three," and I feel my eyeballs pop out of my head.

I can see Grant's arms as he hefts the platform. He's not "buff," but he's strong and looks good in his bright green shirt. It has white block lettering in two rows. The top row says, "NaCl," and under that are the letters "NaOH." Of course, I wouldn't have any idea what this means if he hadn't taken the time to explain to me once that it was actually a guffaw-worthy science joke: "The base is under a salt!" If he weren't so tall and fast, I would have beaten him over the head with the nearest Bunsen burner.

Brice sits on the floor beside me. He's been painting the shadows around each of the castle's stones as I finish them, but it seems he's taken an eye candy break as well. He's also staring across the stage at this public display of brute strength, and without moving his eyes, he reaches up and holds his phone out in my direction.

"Here. Take my phone," Brice says.

"What do you want me to do with this?" I ask.

"Call the ambulance. I've just died and gone to Heaven."

We turn our faces toward each other and lock eyes before bursting into hysterical laughter.

I gasp for air while Brice is now rolling into a ball on the floor. I'm giggling so hard I plop down onto the floor beside him, and I have to wipe my eyes just to see him at all. I'm suddenly aware of the kids in the stage left wing sorting props into neat piles and the girls stacking gels and focusing the spotlights on giant ladders. Drill bits are whirring, and hammers are clanking. Our director is nowhere to be found, and somewhere backstage, someone is listening to the *Wicked* soundtrack. Again.

Only in the theatre. Two people are making complete idiots of themselves, rolling around on the floor deliriously, and no one's even noticed.

In between gasps, Brice is mimicking his phone call with imaginary EMTs. "Yes, please hurry. My boyfriend is doing manual labor in a tank top, and I don't think I'm gonna make it!"

The bang, like a gunshot, when Jonathan drops his end of the heavy platform, drawing our attention back to the boys. Jonathan shakes out his left hand as if it's been injured before shoving it deep into the pocket of his cargo shorts. Grant looks at me, and his eyes open with surprise.

He smiles as he cocks one eyebrow disapprovingly. "What are you two laughing at? Are you okay?" Grant hollers while Jonathan wipes his brow.

"It's nothing! We're fine!" I call as I try to shrink my smile. My cheeks ache, and my deeply buried ab muscles are sore from laughing. This was not listed as a side effect of happiness in my "So You Wanna Kick Depression?" pamphlet.

"We're okay," Brice shouts loudly across the stage. "But we might need mouth to mou–"

"WHOA MYGOD!" I dive on Brice and practically smother him with so much skin and laughter. Grant and Jonathan snicker and head backstage just as someone cranks up the volume on "Defying Gravity." Again.

"Miss Keegan? Mr. Wilson?" The sound of Mrs. Gild's voice stops all giggles in their tracks. I sit up straight and pull my shirt out at the waist. We face the rows and rows of velveteen auditorium seats, and standing in the center of the house is our director with a stern look on her face. I have seen some sad, scary things. I have been hospitalized for panic attacks. I tried on a pair of shorts last year. But nothing–nothing–chills a theatre kid to the bone like the roar of a pissed-off director.

"If you two cannot be productive, you're welcome to take the rest of the afternoon off."

Under his breath, Brice mutters, "Sweet. I could use a break."

I jab at him with my elbow as Mrs. Gild pushes up the sleeves of her charcoal grey cardigan. I can feel the eyes of the rest of the techies, who are all standing at attention because that's what we do whenever our director speaks.

"As a matter of fact," Gild begins, "you can take the entire semester off and just forgo this production altogether, unless you wouldn't mind getting back to work." Her voice is singsong-y, and just as she sets her jaw and stares at us with her steely eyes, the speaker backstage bursts into the loud, ominous, dissonant music of the last thirty seconds of *Wicked*'s first act.

Gild's posture, combined with the music, seems to say, "I'll get you, my pretties, and I'm gonna ship you back to Kansas if you screw up my sets."

It feels like a punchline, and I swear I see Gild's mouth twitch as she resists a smile. She loves a good sound cue almost as much as I do.

"Yes, Mrs. Gild," Brice and I reply in unison.

She gives us a wink, and the corner of her mouth pulls up into a grin. When she turns to her clipboard, the stage jolts back to life with banging and talking in equal measure. Brice and I return to our paintbrushes and half-done walls.

"So, what's your excuse?" Brice asks as he drags the soggy brush over the particleboard and outlines another stone. I look over at him as he works. His sandy blond eyebrows are drawn tight with concentration, and his tongue is just barely sticking out of his thin-lipped mouth.

"What do you mean?"

"Well, Jonathan and I've been going out for about three months now, thank you very much, so I'm entitled to periodic fainting spells when he's being all adorable." He flip-flops his head from side to side as he emphasizes his point. "But you and Grant are just *friends* and you keep telling me you're just *friends*, and while I'm sure you are just *friends*, you still have a little drool right—" He reaches up like he's going to wipe my chin, and I swat his hand away.

"We are, though. Really, I swear."

I swear. I swear. You have no idea how much I swear.

I bite at the edge of my thumb. All I want in the whole world is to look over my shoulder and see if I can spot Grant again. Not to ogle. That was a moment of temporary frivolity. Grant is not the kind of boy you leer at. He's the kind of boy you love. My neck aches to turn around. I just want to be sure he's still there.

I always feel better when I'm sure.

Brice lowers his chin and looks up at me with a sly smile as he gives his thin paintbrush a perfectly timed twirl. "Well, your words say you swear, but your face looks like a fish on a hook. Mouth all gaping open—"

"Briiiiiiiiiiice, no!" I feel my face spreading into another huge open-mouthed smile. I cover my face when I realize I do actually look like a largemouth bass. I lift my heel to gently kick him in the knee, and behind me, I hear Grant's voice. He's shouting something to someone up on the catwalk. His voice cuts straight into my eardrum. I'm like a radio that only picks up one station.

If he could feel the flush on my cheek, if he could see the way I'm biting my bottom lip.

Obvious. Readable. Again.

I reach higher with my paintbrush, and my long-sleeved shirt tugs at my wrist and lifts in the back. These paint fumes. I look to the open stage door—I can just see a sliver of the outside world through the rows and rows of hanging curtains in the wings.

Maybe I should make a dash for the fresh air.

"—tongue all hanging out, I mean, please. You've gotta play it cool like me," Brice says.

I reach down, drop my brush into the drip tray, and then pull at the hem of my shirt and my sleeves. I turn my back to the set and pull my ankles in as far as they'll go—which isn't very far—as I look out over the auditorium chairs.

"Right. Cool like you," I say.

"Right. But seriously, you like him." He lowers his voice. "He likes you, too. What's the problem?"

I should have jumped out of Therapist George's window when I had the chance.

I keep my lips pulled into a smile for Brice's sake, but in my head, I'm seeing an exaggerated version of our little display of school-girl behavior. All giggling and blushing and desperate looks. I imagine myself leaning forward and staring at Grant with a *let me love you* look of desperation smeared across my face.

And it makes me sick.

If Brice saw it, did Grant? He'd never tell me if he did. Grant would never want me to feel embarrassed. But if he saw it, he'd know what it was. He'd know what every look meant. And I'd promised myself those feelings would be buried for good.

Just the way he wants it.

He's made it perfectly clear that whatever lightning I think is buzzing between us is an illusion. A misinterpretation.

"Brice, we're just not like that. We're best friends." I use too much emphasis. I sound like an actor trying to say a line they don't fully understand.

Beside me, Brice shifts around on his knees as he paints on another contour. I watch as Mrs. Gild marches through the rows of seats with three techies behind her, tripping over their attempts to keep up. With all of the houselights up, the auditorium is utterly unextraordinary. I miss the magic.

"So you've *never* been anything else? Not even a kiss? That really surprises me. Something about the way you look at each other. I really thought you had history." When Brice speaks this time, his voice is more tender. He doesn't look away from his work in the same way people don't look at an animal in the wild so it doesn't spook and run off.

"Well, we've got plenty of history. You have no idea."

My head aches with the sight of Grant behind my eyelids. I can see him sitting there, his face in his hands. I remember the way my bed pulled down as he sat by my side. I remember thinking the bandage on my arm was too tight. I remember the icicle lights next door flickering, sending light falling onto my bed like snow. I think my head may actually pop open.

"Ah-ha! You have kissed!" My pause causes Brice to jump to the wrong conclusion. His pale face lights up like an excited puppy as he turns toward me and waits for the details. Details he's definitely not going to get.

"No," I interrupt him. "We almost, maybe, kinda had something almost happen last year, but it was *not* a kiss and it was *not* a good idea. It was a mistake."

"A mistake, how?" Brice asks with trepidation, his eyes lifting into a concerned shape. His head tilts to the side as if it were so easy to convey compassion.

"'Cause he pulled away from me. I thought there was something more, but I was wrong. He doesn't like me like that. So can we drop it, please?"

Boom.

Grant and I have been best friends since writing our names required twenty-five minutes and an entire sheet of paper. He has been the most constant part of my life.

Grant is my gravity. He doesn't force anything, but he is a force. Something I never even notice until I realize I haven't drifted away.

He loves me and has shown me that love over and over.

But it's not every kind of love.

It's just one kind.

And it's a really good kind.

But it's not the only kind.

It's not the kind of love that grew in me.

It's not like the love that snuck into my heart and set up shop, slowly taking up more and more space until there wasn't a single cell not filled with it.

Just like that, I feel the pressure of invisible clouds hovering over me. Fat and aching with rain they're desperate to spill.

Brice has shut up. And the look on his face as he wipes off a drip of grey tells me he realizes he's just stuck a red-hot poker deep into an unhealed wound.

"I'm sorry, honey. I didn't know," he says without looking at me.

"Let's just keep painting, okay?" I force myself to take a deep breath and blow it out slowly as one of the freshman techies drops a giant ladder he was carrying back to the scene shop. The clatter gives me an excuse to turn my head toward the rest of the stage.

I dip my brush again into the grey and look over toward Grant. His back is to me, but I imagine he can feel my eyes on him. I imagine he turns around and looks at me from under his dark hair. And then he crosses the space between us and puts his face near mine and whispers in my ear that he loves the way I laugh.

But he doesn't turn. He's running to help the kid who lost his ladder. I shake off the ridiculousness of my daydream and get back to work as I reach down to resume the act of turning plywood into stone.

We, the techies of Crestwood High, work until after dark on the sets for *Once Upon a Mattress*. We are completely exhausted by the end of the evening when Gild sits us down and tells us that tomorrow we'll finally be meeting the cast and joining rehearsals after school. By the time Grant and I pile into my car, I feel like I've run some kind of marathon or something. Everything hurts. I am so freaking sore and tired by the time I drop off Grant at his house around the corner that I don't even notice the moving truck parked along the curb until I almost smash into it.

But it's worth it to have been gone the entire time she moved in.

I pull out my phone as I sit in my car and stall. The last thing I want to do is go into that newly sisterified house.

Evelyn has texted me three times. First, to tell me Carmella arrived safe and sound this morning. The second was to ask if I'd be home in time for dinner. "There'll be pizza!" Which apparently means I am some kind of rabid, fat animal who will rush home at the first mention of pepperoni. Which isn't exactly false, but whatever. *Suck it, Evelyn.* And the last says, "Didn't know rehearsal would last so long. Carmella and I are going to bed."

So now, in addition to my significant body odor, muscle fatigue, and emotional rawness, I also get to be moments from a panic attack.

Because she's in there. Right now.

Our parents got married last December. I "met" her right after Christmas, and then she went back to her dad's. And now, in October, halfway through the fall semester, she shows up at our doorstep. She moves into my mom's old craft room. She inserts herself into the life that I'm barely living in the first place. And nobody will even explain what happened that warranted upending her whole life and mine.

I park behind the moving truck in my normal place along the curb, but nothing about sitting here feels the same. I lean over to look out the passenger window and up at the second floor windows sitting side by side. Mine on the right is wide and squatty, while hers is narrow and tall.

I see you, window-related irony.

It embarrasses me to the point of nausea when I realize I am muttering to myself. My behavioral conditioning has kicked in, and I'm droning, "I am whole. I am more than just the pieces that I see. I am stronger than I seem."

I close my eyes and put my head on my steering wheel.

"You have to go inside, Imogen," I whisper.

I wipe my sweaty hands on my jeans before I finally get out of the car.

I step inside the house, locking the door behind me as quietly as I can. I head straight to the kitchen. The lights are off, except for the long fluorescent bulbs under the top cabinets, shining down on the countertops.

I set down my bag and pick up the note.

So sorry we missed you, Imogen, honey. There's plenty of leftover pizza in the fridge. And salad too! Get some rest. See you in the morning!

I open the fridge and toss the box of salad straight to the trash bin, burying it under some plastic wrap and waxed paper.

"No salad tonight, Evelyn. 'Cause you're not the boss of me," I whisper to the empty kitchen. I should give classes on maturity.

As sneakily as I can, I take the cold leftover pizza and my bag and creep up the stairs. It never seems to matter if I take the stairs slowly or quickly because they always creak. As a kid, when I snuck down to the kitchen at night, I tried all sorts of tricks to try and keep the steps from making noise. I walked on the edges, right along the railing. I tried crawling up on all fours. They always creak. These stairs are a miserable accomplice.

My legs hurt so bad. I lug them up, step by step, until I'm outside my room—right next to Carmella's. I sneak past her door like she's waiting to pop out or something.

Inside my room, I lock the door handle. The last bite of my pizza crust is a little burned, which leaves the flavor of char on my tongue. I want to take a shower, I really do, but I'm too exhausted. I tighten my ponytail, throw on some pajamas, and collapse onto my bed, which groans under my weight. I catch my breath and hope the sound of the springs won't wake her next door.

My stomach presses against my quilt, and I breathe in the sweet, freshly washed smell. One point for Evelyn. Just one.

As soon as my body starts to relax, I feel cold wetness seeping into my clothes. The front of my hoodie, shirt, and pants are wet, and it feels like I am lying face down in a puddle.

I roll off the bed and pull back the cover to see one of my robin's egg blue bath towels. Soaking wet, laid out, and hidden underneath my quilt.

I rip the wet towel and sheets off my bed; my mattress is soggy and cold.

As I walk, the water from the dripping towel pools on the floor in the hallway, and I feel tiny puddles under every heavy footfall.

I toss the wet towel into the bathtub. It will probably be mildewed and gross by morning, but I don't care.

When I turn, a neon green Post-it stuck on the mirror catches my attention. Written in black permanent marker:

This isn't just your bathroom anymore. I found your disgusting wet towel on the floor when I tried to shower this afternoon, so I put it away for you. Sleep tight.

I didn't expect this.

I thought I expected this, but I didn't really.

I wanted to believe it was all in my head and somehow she'd come here and everything would be fine.

I wanted to believe the hate in her eyes when she saw me bleeding and crying was imaginary.

I crumple the Post-it into a ball before shoving it in my hoodie pocket. I turn away as fast as I can so I don't make eye contact with my reflection. Right now, nothing sounds worse than looking in a mirror. So I don't.

In the dark hallway I pause, listening for the sound of her cackling like an evil witch or something, but the house is quiet. She's fast asleep. Of course she is.

I peel off my wet clothes and change into some dry sweats, but the chill on my damp skin makes me shiver with anger more than cold. Everything hurts. My legs and arms, my jaw, my feet. My stomach.

At least I can do something about that one. I grab a spare blanket and head to my desk drawer. Under the folders and stapler in the very back is a bag of emergency potato chips. I find that they're often every bit as effective as a Xanax.

I plop down on the overstuffed armchair in the corner of my room. It's not my bed, but it's dry. The bag of chips is half-empty by the time I flip off my lamp and continue crunching in the dark.

If I prayed, I'd pray for sleep.

Sleep is easy. Sleep means no Evelyn. No Carmella. No wet towels and unwanted salads. Sleep means not thinking about my mom or feeling the hollow cavity that's always just behind my ribs. Sleep means a break from being frustrated at my dad. I hate being mad at him.

It's quiet in my sleep.

No dreams.

My nightmares only happen when I'm awake.

So I crave sleep. Too much of it. Enough to make me sick and aching and numb. It's the one vice nobody expects me to say no to.

I take a deep breath and try to clear my mind.

The speckled colors swirling inside my eyelids distract me.

This is good.

Watch the swirly speckled things.

The swirling slowly becomes turning, and the turning slowly becomes dancing.

The dancing slowly becomes my mother.

Whatever she was doing, she exuded this brilliance she always kept just beneath her skin. She glowed. Everyone thought so. My poor dad was drawn to her like a moth to a flame.

He always tells me he felt her before he saw her. As he sat in the audience and waited for the show to start, the actors took the stage in the dim light. The mumbling hushed, and he felt her. His heart jumped, and his eyes, almost desperately, scoured the small off-off-off-Broadway stage for the unseen, unknown thing that he somehow knew was waiting for him. As the stage lights rose, hues of violet and blue fell over the ensemble, including my mother.

Mom and I loved recreating this moment with Dad when I was younger. After my expert rendition of "I'm a Little Teapot," we'd perform the choreography from the rainy New York night when they met. She and I would hold our arms above our heads, and Mom would guide me so that my feet were in just the right position for a quick chassé across the living room toward his easy chair. As I got to the other side of the room, I'd jump in his lap while we watched her finish the performance on her own. Just as she did on that night in their past, she would lower her chin, her eyes blazing and shimmering as they connected with my dad's gaze. I would look at her face and then to his and grin and giggle before making kissy-face noises. She'd reach for my hand, we'd curtsey for him, and he'd say the thing he always said: "Princesses. You shine like stars."

And *she* did. I could only ever hope to be her moon. A satellite that floated around her and was lucky to reflect the light she gave.

Their story was better than all of the other fairy tales I loved.

Except for one thing.

They didn't get a "happily ever after."

My phone beeps on my bedside table, startling me awake. Chip crumbs go flying, like little salty snowflakes, as I sit up in my chair.

"Are you up?"

Grant's text messages are usually my first human correspondence of the day.

"GAH, I'm up! What are you, my mother?!"

I ignore the tiny pang of sadness that follows my word choice, and before I can even set my phone back on the table, he's texted again.

"Heh. More like who's your daddy?"

Just like that, his little joke sweeps away the last scraps of angst from the night before.

I grin and type back. *"Pshhh. I just barfed. Give me 10 mins."*

I step over the pile of damp clothes without another thought.

My jeans leer at me from the back of my desk chair, and I prepare myself for the showdown.

I'd rather skip straight to the inevitable muumuu phase of my life than continue to pretend that my size twenty-two ass is gonna fit in this pair of twenties ever again.

But these are the biggest pair I have.

So I thread my thumbs through the belt loops, give a giant tug, and then I jump again for good measure.

Oh, thank God. Houston, we have closure.

I open my door slowly and poke my head out like the fat gopher who decides when spring's gonna start. The shower is running in the bathroom across the hall, and I realize this is my one chance to escape.

I almost trip over nothing on my way to the staircase, and I take the steps as fast as I can. I am so eager to avoid Carmella I totally forget about avoiding Evelyn. I skid to a stop, but it's too late. I've been spotted by a Real Housewife of Collin County.

As I try to backpedal out of the kitchen, Evelyn is pulling a muffin tin out of the oven. She sets the pan down and pulls her hand out of the oven mitt, wiping it on her black lace apron.

It occurs to me this apron might have been part of some sexy, bad-girl baker Halloween costume or something. It looks particularly ridiculous with her 7:00 AM outfit of a super-short running skirt and a hearty helping of cleavage.

All part of a complete breakfast.

"Good morning, Imogen, darling!" Evelyn's voice is so clear and loud I'm still—months after living with her—surprised every time she speaks.

I almost pitch myself face-first into the tile trying to keep my eyes from rolling out of the top of my head. "Hey, Evelyn. I'm late. I gotta run." I try to say it fast so she'll believe me and I can get the heck out of this kitchen. The last thing I need is to be standing here when Carmella comes down.

"Oh, but I just took these rice flour, golden raisin, and sweet potato muffins out!" I look up as Evelyn runs a finger through her golden, side-swept bangs. "Won't you take one for breakfast?"

I try not to gag. "Yeah, no. I've really gotta go." Far, far away from you, crazy morning lady.

"Well, okay then, honey. Now Dr. Rodriguez called last week and said that since we changed your dosage, we need to keep an eye on any additional weight gain."

Additional. I'm going to hit her.

"He's worried about the change from June to now, so he says if it goes up again during your November check-up, they're going to reevaluate your scripts."

Oh, man, this woman is the worst. How dare she stand there all skinny and talk to me about being fat? Insensitive witch.

"Have you taken your meds this morning? By my notes, you should have five Prozacs left, but I think your Risperdal needs to be refilled today. I'll pick it up for you after yoga."

I hate that she's tracking my meds, and I hate that her calculations are correct.

"Um, yeah. I took my meds," I lie. God, she wears me out.

"Well, have a great day at school, honey! And it'd mean so much to me if you'd keep an eye out for Carmella. It's her first day at a new school, so I'm worried she'll get lost looking for her locker." She smiles like she didn't just say the most ludicrous sentence ever spoken. "Oh, and call your dad later if you can. He misses you."

Does he? I choke back the question.

"Um, okay. Yeah, I'm gonna leave now, Evelyn. See you later."

The sound of her voice saying "dad" brings a sting of bile up in the back of my throat.

If he misses me, it's his fault.

He sold his book. He got married, and then over the past couple of months, he got gone.

So I really don't want to hear about him missing me. And I especially don't want to hear it from her.

Outside, Carmella's little yellow Mustang is parked in the driveway. Cars like that are for girls who never leave without makeup perfectly applied and who wear pants that say things like "Pink" or "Aerie" across their negligible asses.

I look to the curb and take in the profile view of my old boat of a Chrysler—the Grannymobile. Dad offered to buy me something newer when I got my license, but I was so worried I'd smash it into a telephone pole I gladly accepted my giant steel tank instead. It's not pretty, but I like it.

I buckle up, but before I can count to ten, I'm through the curve and pulling up to the fourth house on the left, the one directly behind mine—where Grant lives. His blinds snap back together when I pull up, and in a few short moments, he is bounding down the walkway, arms full of untold miscellany, toward my idling car. His voice sounds muffled through the closed car window.

"Come on, Gen! Open up! This crap is heavy!"

I press the button that lifts the latch.

He throws open the back door and tosses a mountain of gears and pulleys and things I can't begin to understand onto the seat. Then he dives into the front with unnecessary enthusiasm and immediately connects his ancient iPod to my amazing cassette-deck adapter and starts clicking around on its screen.

"Was there a problem at the factory, Mr. Wonka?" I ask as I gesture to the hardware store in my backseat.

"Oh my God, Gen, machines are so dumb," he says as he finally picks a song and sits still. He exhales loudly and then closes his eyes for a second, collecting his thoughts. "Hey," Grant says as he turns to face me. He's frenzy-free for the first moment since he stepped out of his house.

"Hi," I smile.

Today he's wearing a T-shirt that has lots of little boxes from the periodic table, each one with the letters "Fe" inside, and below them the word "IRONY." He is so proud of his shirt collection. For a while, I was convinced he saved his funniest shirts for my worst days. Like he could always tell exactly which pun would be most likely to make me roll my eyes until I smiled again.

He thinks it's the shirts, but I think it's the way he rubs his hand through his hair when he's thinking too fast. Nothing makes me smile faster than that.

"I guess you have a meeting about the science thing today?" I ask.

"Yep." His grin falters. "Did I tell you the regional physics competition is the morning of the rally? Ugh, and the meeting starts in ten minutes. I totally forgot it was today."

I pull away and begin our twelve-minute commute to school.

"The morning of the Rally? Really? Are you going to get to go to both?"

"Well," he starts as he fumbles with his iPod, "if I get to compete, then we should be through in plenty of time to get to the Rally. So you're not getting out of it, okay?" He finally settles on the best song for our ride. Something so cool, I've never heard of it.

The Fine Arts Rally is this giant school dance at Crestwood every year. All of the kids from orchestra, band, choir, art III and IV, dance, and theatre have this huge event in the courtyard the last weekend in October. Everyone usually takes the opportunity to wear formal dresses and clip-on bowties since the school-wide dances—like Prom and Homecoming—are too cram-packed with millions of kids to be any fun. Grant and I have gone once dressed as Target employees and another time in orange prison jumpsuits. Unsurprisingly, only our theatre friends thought it was funny.

"I'm not trying to get out of it! I like going with you. I just don't dance, and I hate people. So it's obviously the perfect place for me."

We laugh as we wait for a red light to change.

"So you said 'if' you get to compete. Why wouldn't you? You guys have been working on those machines since school started, and you're obviously the greatest nerdlete the school has ever known. Or do you prefer the term 'athlete-geek'?"

He turns and lifts his head so he can look down his nose at me. "The preferred term is 'Neurologically and Cognitively Equipped Gladiator of the Mind,' thank you." I reach up and rub at my arm through the sleeve of my hoodie, and Grant instinctively reaches over and adjusts the vent that's blowing on me. "And it will be fine, but it'd be great to win a scholarship for the regionals when we compete at the prelims."

"Well, I'm positive you'll win."

I slow down as we enter the last school zone on our way. Watching other cars pass into the blinking-light section always makes me imagine that we've all just pulled through an invisible cloud made of something sticky that keeps us from maintaining speed.

"Well, I should hope so," Grant says. "I'm the science-iest guy in the world. Have you seen the shirt I'm wearing? It says 'IRONY'–"

"I get it," I say with a laugh.

"'Cause it's covered with iron!"

"I get it, you weirdo!"

"See what I did there? The symbol for iron and then the word irony! Get it?"

We pull into the parking lot as the pretend T-shirt argument continues to escalate. We walk past classmates, putting on a full display of shouting for our own amusement.

"But it says IRONY! Maybe you don't understand it...the shirt—"

"I GET IT!"

We almost fall over from laughing so hard.

"Oh crap, I have to get to my meeting! I'm late!" He pulls away from me before I can blink, and he's rocketing toward the school. Over his shoulder, he shouts, "I'll see you at lunch!"

The mild October wind blows and steals away the last wisps of the smell of him, and I miss it before the leaves can settle again on the concrete.

Crestwood High is a mega-school that sits on the most affluent side of our city just outside of Dallas. Having tons of funding means we've got amazing arts programs right alongside our state champion football team and handful of National Merit Scholars. Sure, the campus looks more like a small university than a typical high school, with its separate buildings and open campus, but it's the walking past three thousand kids each day that I never get used to.

I watch the crowd seem to part when certain people pass. Their beauty or popularity just clears the way. I'd love to walk to class and not have people pressing on me from all sides. I'd settle for being able to take my seat without anyone watching me wedge myself into my chair.

During the mandatory health screening this year, the rec-center girl who took my statistics was all too eager to flip her ponytail and blurt out at me, "Okay! And you're coming in today at 203 pounds! Let me grab some diet and exercise information pamphlets for you!" Hair flip. Grin. Hair flip. Grin.

After avoiding my actual, numerical weight for at least four years, there it was. Bam. You, Imogen Keegan, weigh over two hundred pounds.

I know it's not the same as five hundred pounds or three hundred pounds, but at barely over five feet tall, I can't kid myself. According to Hair-Flip Girl and those god-awful calipers, I'm almost half made of fat.

I'm not surprised I finally joined the deuce club.

Not surprised at all.

I enter Mr. Reed's junior English class and glance up at the clock. Empty desks are scattered around the room in unkempt rows. Mr. Reed is fumbling around his desk, pulling papers from a filing cabinet that is easily a foot taller than he is. He mutters to himself while he digs through the stacks of books and ungraded essays.

Classrooms are so much more enjoyable before all the kids are in them. I'm pretty sure my teachers would agree. The sounds in the hallway creep under the closed door. Shouts and squeals from friends who haven't seen each other since, "Ohmygod, like, Friday!" We're all supposed to wait for the first bell before going to class, but I'm an exception.

There aren't many good things that come with having an "emotional disturbance," but if I'm going to be labeled anyway, I might as well use it to my advantage if I can. If I ever need to get away, I just toss out the words "panic attack" or "depression" and every teacher gives in because most of them are afraid of what might happen if they say no. Nobody wants to be responsible for a nervous breakdown.

I take my regular seat, near the back window, overlooking the courtyard. The heart of the Crestwood grounds is a massive open space sitting at the center of the main building. It's walled on three sides, and the fourth is open to the upperclassmen parking lot. Years ago, before my mom set off to give New York a whirl, this was her school, and the main building was the *only* building. Before they graduated—and before they broke ground on the second of Crestwood's buildings—her class got together to paint an incredible, two-story, freestyle mural on the south wall. From Mr. Reed's second-floor classroom, the mural looks like it could just be a small canvas. Colors and shapes swarm the surface of the bricks. Blocks of words and pictures, abstract and realistic, mix together in a swirl of pattern and color. The individual works of each student are lost at this distance.

The dozens of autographed designs are sometimes hidden in shadows or too small to see from the ground, but I feel her colorful scribbles tugging at me from their hiding place. I just can't shake the feeling I'm staring right at the little piece on this wall that is hers. I've spent hours and hours scouring it, trying to imagine what her part might look like. Maybe she painted something about theatre, or maybe she worked on her part with someone else and I'll never know exactly which parts were her design. But it kills me that there's something right in front of me that is hers but not mine. It's like if she had a piece of jewelry or a sweater sitting in someone else's closet. I don't even care that this mural isn't something I can hold—I want to find her piece to carry in my heart.

The sound of the first period bell startles my attention away from the mural. Little clumps of students enter Mr. Reed's class. They're laughing and joking and continuing conversations from the hallway as they stand by their desks. Books and bags are tossed on the floor and hung on the backs of chairs. Pens are passed from the well-stocked to the unprepared as if it's surprising that they'll need something to write with in English class. Jonathan enters and heads to his seat in the other back corner of the room. I catch his eye and give him a little wave, but he doesn't wave back.

He just smiles and does that annoying thing where boys lift their chin in greeting.

I watch as he reaches down with his right hand and pulls out his notebook and a small square of paper. He withdraws his other hand from his pocket and begins to fold the paper back and forth onto itself.

Mr. Reed's desk is so packed with papers and binders he can scarcely be seen at all, but he's there, tiny and mostly bald—except for his impressive comb-over. He's a little paper boat floating on a sea of academic clutter.

The bell rings, and the other twenty-seven kids sit and chat. Jonathan sits and folds. Just like always. When Grant is beside me, I'll clown and squawk and jump around like an idiot, but on my own, I'd rather they pretend I'm not here than make fun of or misunderstand me. Being ignored means nobody's making fun. It means nobody's making comments under their breath about me being overweight. It means less anxiety. It means they're not thinking about the rumors. *"Didn't she have a nervous breakdown last year?"* *"I thought she tried to kill herself."* *"She's gained a lot of weight since junior high."*

To be ignored is way better than the alternative.

"Good Monday, juniors," Mr. Reed snivels.

I prop my head on my hand to give, I hope, an air of acceptably minute interest.

"Let's get to it, shall we?"

He scans his clipboard and mumbles names as he glances at his seating chart.

"Stephen? And Marnie? And—"

He points to a few more names.

"Andrew?"

"Here." Andrew leans so far back in his chair his head is resting on the desk behind him. The kid thumps him in the forehead with an ink pen.

"Oh, and I have a note that we're expecting a new student!"

The room falls away as if I've just rocketed off the face of the Earth. The twist of my stomach feels like I'm falling, on my way back down. Oh God, no. Oh, no. Ohnononono. I scan the room; she isn't here. Is it her? Maybe it's someone else. I close my eyes. Please don't let her be in my class.

"Miss Cinder? Ella Cinder?" He scans the room and chuckles to himself as the kids start mumbling about Cinderella and asking if they heard him right.

I feel every trace of color slip out of my face.

The door opens in a rush, and there stands my stepsister. Everything seems like slow motion, like she's being revealed to the audience of a teen party movie as "the knockout." She is taller than average, thinner than average, and definitely more beautiful than average. She's perfectly poised, with glowing skin and flawless makeup. Her golden blonde hair hangs around her face and cascades in magazine-cover-perfect ribbons of beachy, effortless waves. Her rose-colored skinny jeans meet her thin ankles at four-inch nude pumps, while her floral blouse hugs her figure in all the right places. I hear an audible intake of breath from the entire population of Mr. Reed's English III class. Her eyes scan the room, and when she sees me, I instantly drop my head. I bring my hands to my lap and begin to rub them back and forth on the legs of my jeans.

I exhale and try to fill my lungs again.

Mr. Reed gestures for her to step further into the room. "Hello, dear. Are you—" He glances back to his list. "—Cinder, Ella?"

"Yes," she beams. "Yes, I am."

Whispered catcalls and chauvinistic comments drift from the male students, while the girls are dumbfounded. In typical fashion, the class bursts into a dozen different conversations.

"Where did you move from?"

She hails from Shallowville.

"Is that your real name?"

Of course it's not her real name. Ugh.

"Do you have a boyfriend?"

I'll bet there's a sign-up sheet on her locker.

As the volume rises, the boys leer and bite their bottom lips or just let their eyes bug out. Some of the girls run their fingers through their hair. They press their mouths closed and re-cross their legs. Some fold their arms over their chests and raise one eyebrow while others look like they're sending up a silent prayer that maybe she'll want to be a part of their group.

Cinder-effing-Ella stands with flawless posture at the front of the class, basking in her admiration for another few seconds before Mr. Reed says, "Settle down class. A brief introduction, I think, Cinderella, is it?" He giggles like he just thought of that punchline all on his own. "Well, you could certainly pass for a princess, my dear."

Gross.

"Won't you please tell us a little bit about yourself?" he says as he perches himself, front and center, on the edge of his desk.

Carmella reaches up and brushes back a strand of her hair, as if it's actually out of place. She smiles and says, "Oh, well, I'm Ella. I just moved from Austin where I attended Conteé Academy."

A.K.A. Stuck-Up High.

"I studied colloquial French, modern dance and ballet, and Renaissance literature."

Obviously. Who doesn't?

"Of course, Crestwood doesn't have any of those courses, so my schedule has been simplified to include

French IV, drill team, and of course, Mr. Reed's junior English class among others."

Poor darling, forced to take normal classes with the peasants.

These words drip from her perfect mouth with so much grinning and saccharin that I want to reach up and slap her for being so fake. The rest of the room eats it up. No one seems to realize she's practically insulting our whole school by saying it's not up to her standards.

Carmella continues. "I'm sure I'll need help figuring things out around here, as I really don't know anyone, except, of course, for my stepsister—Imogen—who tells me she's very popular."

She raises her eyebrows in a smirk and gestures to the back of the room where I sit, my mouth slightly agape as heads turn toward me. Some boys snicker, and I turn toward the sound in time to hear one say, "She must be Cinderella 'cause she's sure got an ugly stepsister." Andrew Bates turns his head away from me quickly so I won't see him laugh at the other kid's joke. How nice of him.

The chuckles spread across the aisles. I can't think of anything else to do but force myself to breathe as I look down at my desktop.

Mr. Reed obliviously continues, "Well, Miss Cinder, that's wonderful. I'm sure there'll be no shortage of volunteer tour guides. You may take the seat in the second row. I'll just finish taking the attendance."

Ella turns back to her audience and flashes a coy smile to the boys before setting her bag down and taking her seat. She lithely crosses her legs and subtly turns her body so that, with just the right movement, she can glance back at her new fans.

Once Mr. Reed has regained most of the attention again, he starts walking up and down the rows, distributing a handout.

Whatever it is, I have no intention of working today. I'll take the zero. I don't care. I'm just about to push up and get out of my seat. All I'd have to do is slide him a note as I leave that says, "Going to see the school counselor. Emergency." By special ed law, he'd have to let me go. But just as I start to grab my bag, Mr. Reed starts to speak.

"Ladies and gentlemen, we're starting a partner research project today. You'll be pairing up and performing extensive research about a specific literary archetype."

Perfect. Interacting with another human. Just what I need today.

"Together, you and your partner will identify the usage of your given archetype in all of the assigned readings we'll be discussing this year, as well as in other works you may uncover in your studies."

As soon as the word "partner" is uttered, the class begins to fidget and twitch toward each other as everyone begins to mentally pair off in an attempt to avoid that last-one-picked feeling.

This is my chance. I'll grab my bag and get out before I have the chance to *not* be picked as a partner.

The sound of chairs scraping against the floor as students rush to stand causes Mr. Reed's delicate voice to fade into near nothingness.

"Hold on, class!" Mr. Reed shouts, his loudest tone recapturing their attention. "I'd like you to tell me your partners first." He gestures to Carmella. "Miss Cinder, perhaps you'd be most comfortable partnering with your sister?"

Without missing a beat, Carmella bats her lashes and then stares straight at me.

"Oh, that's okay, Mr. Reed. I know she was really hoping for a chance to work with a certain guy in class." She ends with a faux-whisper that the whole class can hear.

She gives me a smile, as if this is innocent sister-to-sister gossip, but the class slams to a standstill for a single second before breaking out into a chorus of *ooooohs* and whistles as the guys in class begin taunting each other and praying they're not the boy I'm looking for.

I feel my palms begin to sweat as my heart picks up speed.

"Oh, no, I—" I try to find my voice to tell Mr. Reed and everyone she made it up just so people would laugh, but I can't speak with the power I need. And the class has decided the prospect of me pining for someone is far too delicious to let pass.

Carmella's smile threatens to wrap all the way around her head as I stand there like an idiot, tongue-tied and near tears, unable to find something to say.

Just then, something brushes against me, and Jonathan is standing by my side. He reaches up and puts his arm around my shoulder without a breath of hesitation.

"Sorry, Mr. Reed. Imogen and I were planning to work together." He looks at me but says loud enough for the whole class to hear, "Guess she misunderstood you. But if you want to talk about the cutest boys in class, I'm happy to give my opinion."

Jonathan looks like a stranger. His chin is high, and he towers over me with his shoulders back. He doesn't look at the kids who are staring with wide eyes. He just keeps pressing his right hand against my arm, tucking me safely under his wing.

In a rare moment of awareness, Mr. Reed frowns a little and clears his throat. "Fine, fine, everyone. Grab your things please. We'll be reporting to the library for the next few weeks. Imogen and Jonathan, you're good to go. The rest of you, tell me your partners before you leave." Carmella's posture melts from vixen back to schoolgirl as she walks through the room with everyone else.

"Thanks," I mutter to Jonathan as we shuffle out the door. He gives me a tiny grin, but doesn't respond. He also doesn't remove his arm from its protective position over my shoulder. Even so, I can't help but feel weak. Victimized.

Twenty-five minutes ago, I was blissfully invisible. No laughing. No evil grins. No drama. And now? It couldn't be more dramatic. I've got a stepsister masquerading as Cinderella, the chauvinistic villagers think I'm the ugly stepsister, and the boy coming to my side is more likely to snag a prince than I am.

After an afternoon of ducking into bathroom stalls and taking extra-long sips from the water fountain to avoid Carmella, I practically explode with joy as the last bell rings. As every period started, I waited for her to walk into my class. Jaw clenched, I set my eyes on the door and held my breath, but thankfully, I dodged every single spray-tanned bullet. I didn't see her again all day.

I walk as quickly as my stubby legs will carry me and throw myself through a set of double doors into the auditorium. In the back, between the aisles on the left and right sides of the house, I find my little home away from home: the sound booth.

As the door latches behind me, I'm enveloped in a room with foam padding and dark paint on every wall. Not much bigger than a walk-in closet, sound equipment sits on every flat surface, and cables sit coiled in neat stacks on the floor.

My throne awaits me.

I reach up and slide the large glass window all the way open and then sit in my ergonomically-correct rolling chair and watch other members of the cast and crew trickle in.

"Hey, kitten!" Brice and Jonathan's heads pop up in front of me, their faces pushing through the large open window between the auditorium and me.

"Hey," I say with a smile. "Did you guys have a good afternoon?"

"Sure," Brice answers. "You?"

"It was all downhill after your mister swooped in to save me."

Brice looks at me quizzically and then turns to Jonathan and says, "Awww, you swooped?"

"You didn't tell him?" I ask Jonathan who looks back at me with the tiniest grin on his face.

"Well, I don't swoop and tell," Jonathan says with a glint in his eye. "Come on, I've gotta finish spiking the stage before we start."

"Bye, love," Brice says.

"Bye, guys," I answer.

Brice's arm is looped through Jonathan's as they walk down the aisle. They're completely adorable together. Like, make-me-want-to-barf adorable.

I'm a little surprised that Jonathan didn't tell Brice about what happened in English. Maybe it wasn't a big deal to him, but it really mattered to me.

I make a mental note to thank him again.

My phone buzzes against my palm. Grant's text says, "*If you're in the booth, stay put, okay? Gild is sending the fish your way.*"

"Got it," I reply.

The sound of someone beating an alley cat catches my attention. It is, in fact, the insufferable laughter of Charity Wells as she enters the theatre. She's brazen and obnoxious in the worst way. Not only is she popular for being super-pretty, but she's also an honorary "bro" according to most of the football team. I saw a photo of an altogether impressive keg stand from her sophomore summer—apparently, she's stronger than she looks. Currently she's barreling across the stage saying something I can't understand while snapping up every drop of attention possible. She's been perfectly cast as Princess Winnifred.

I shudder and pull the glass window closed again.

I recognize a few other faces, mostly sneaking through the shadows and skulking in the wings. Other than my crewmates, there aren't too many people I recognize.

There's Andrew. The guy who laughed when someone called me the ugly stepsister. The guy who spent the rest of the class in the back of the library with Carmella practically in his lap. The guy who calls Charity one of his "bros." Three strikes. He's out. I wish I could have shoved his English book right up his smug, snickering nose. I'm sure he and Charity will have a lovely time being total asshats on stage together.

At lunch, when Grant and I analyzed the cast list and discovered Andrew was Prince Dauntless—Winnifred's love interest—I asked Grant to stab me with a fork. He declined.

The twist of the door handle startles me, and as I turn, my chair rotates to face the sound. I actually have to lift my head to find her face.

"Hi. Are you Imogen? I'm Antonique. Your side-fish. I mean, sidekick. Oh, God. Fish-kick. I'm sorry." She reaches up to tuck a thin braid behind her ear. Her fingers are long, as are her arms. Seriously, she's about six feet tall. She stands in the doorway as if she's unable to come in without an official invitation.

I smile at her reassuringly. "Hey, no worries. It's a stupid nickname for you guys anyway. But yeah, I'm Imogen. It's nice to meet you. Come on in, you don't have to stand at the door."

Having a "fish-kick," or freshman sidekick, for this production means I have a fifteen-year-old shadowing my every action in the sound booth. Not the best news I've ever gotten, but she seems polite. Her limbs are long, and she looks like she's been stretched in every direction. But she has kind eyes.

Her grin almost knocks me back into my chair as she enthusiastically says, "Awesome, so what can I do?"

"Knock, knock, ladies! Never fear, your stage manager is here!" Grant tips his head into the doorway without entering. "Gen, I see you met your fish-kick?"

"Yep, I just did, actually. Antonique, right? This is Grant. He's the stage manager for the show."

It looks like every single finger is shaking with nerves as she tangles them into a knot behind her back so Grant can't see.

"Hey, good to meet you," Grant says as he reaches out his hand, and she takes a tiny step to grab it. Her jaw is locked tight, and I smile as I imagine all the effort she's using to keep her hands steady. "Allow me to impress you with my stage manager prowess and give you a tip." Grant walks over to my chair and puts his hand on my shoulder. "Stick with my Gen. She's the Sound Goddess. She was the youngest solo sound designer in the school's history when she worked on *West Side* as a sophomore last year. I'll hold for your applause."

Antonique smiles, and her eyes sparkle as she claps for me.

"But in all seriousness," he adds, "she'll take good care of you." He nods his head toward her in an assuring way, and my face warms at the cheeks when he turns around and gives me a wink.

"Sound Goddess? I could get used to that nickname," I say.

"I know. It's awesome. That's why I made it up." He smiles as he spins my chair to face him. "I gotta run. I'll see you ladies around." He marches back through the doorway, and I watch him bound back down the aisle to the stage.

I laugh a little as I spin my chair to face her better. Her eyes are so brown they're almost black, and she has the longest eyelashes I've ever seen.

"So," she asks, as we look out the glass at the beautiful set that almost looks like a real castle. "What do you think of the show?"

This is the sweetest, most vague question ever, and I think she is adorable. She has no idea how deep my musical theatre knowledge goes, but I don't have even the slightest desire to snark about it. There's nothing about her that makes me feel defensive. Her trusting eyes and generous smile have warmed the sterile, dark room in under ten minutes.

"*Once Upon a Mattress* in general or our production?" I ask.

"In general. I haven't been able to spend much time with the script yet so I don't know much about it."

"Oh, it's awesome. I spent most of the summer watching videos of other productions and memorizing cue lines. It makes running sound *so* much easier." I decide to give her the single-sentence recap instead of launching into a one-woman monologue of the *Once Upon a Mattress* Wiki page.

"It's a totally campy, late-fifties retelling of the *Princess and the Pea*. Except, you know, the Princess isn't very delicate or princessey at all. I've read the script about four thousand times, and I've listened to the cast recording at least twice that much. It's one of my favorites. I think princesses are pretty much the worst. Having a musical about an anti-princess is kinda perfect."

"It sounds funny." She smiles as she brings her tangled hands in front of her and continues to fidget. "If you like it so much, why didn't you audition?"

I almost choke as I blurt out, "Oh, God, no!" I laugh louder than is necessary considering the size of the room. "Oh, no. I don't do that." I gesture through the glass to the stage where various actors are stumbling through choreography and looking like synchronized toddlers learning to walk. "Don't get me wrong, I love music and musicals and I'm pretty much obsessed with everything theatre, but I'm most comfortable way back here. In the dark. Wearing black. Where no will see me or bother me or talk to me."

"Oh. okay. I'm sorry if I was talking too much," she says as she looks down at the board.

"No, oh, no! Not you. Techies stick together. You're one of us now."

On the stage, Grant is walking behind Gild with a clipboard, following her finger as she points at things and gestures all around.

Antonique laughs. "I am? Well, I know you have tons to teach me. I'm really excited to be working with you."

"I'm excited, too." And I really am. She has a gentle face that soothes me somehow. I've known her for minutes, but I feel like everything is exactly what it seems. It doesn't feel like drama. It doesn't feel like defensiveness. It feels new...and nice.

"So when do I get to sit in the big spinning throne?" Antonique grins widely from her rock-hard folding chair beside me.

I shake my finger at her with a smile on my face. "Not so fast, fish-kick. We've got a lot of learning to do if you want a turn in the fancy chair. Let's start with the most basic, most important button on the entire console."

I turn to face the soundboard, and Antonique lowers her face so it's unnecessarily close to the contraption. She looks as if she's ready to memorize my every word so she'll impress me with her dedication. I gesture to a little button beside the main volume fader.

"This button will preserve your sanity. It will also save you from a multitude of uncomfortable and awkward situations. It is the most critical, most important, most powerful button on the entire board."

I lower my eyes, building her anticipation. She's leaning forward like a kid waiting for the ending of a ghost story at a campfire.

"What button is it?" she asks, her eyes wide.

I look from side to side, as if I'm making sure we're alone before revealing my greatest secret. I pull closer to her, and right on cue, the sound of Charity Wells screlting out a note just out of her range comes through the hanging house mics and echoes through the tiny sound booth.

"Mute," I whisper.

I depress the button, and the tiny monitor speakers click off, silencing Charity's screeching. The sound is replaced with laughter as Antonique and I break into cackles and rattle the walls with squeals of our own.

8

*M*ondays are always long, hard days. Mondays with a five-hour rehearsal tacked on to the end of the school day are even worse. It's just after nine when Grant and I climb the stairs to my room for a quick bite before he goes home. Grant always goes up the stairs in front of me. He tried for years to convince me I should go up first in case I trip over nothing—which, frankly, could happen.

He proposed that he'd "catch me."

Even before I was plus-sized, I felt like a big, clumsy thing. I scoffed and told him that my ass being at the level of his face while climbing stairs was simply not going to happen, and he eventually dropped the subject.

So, he's in front of me, taking the stairs two at a time, holding a tray at shoulder level, like a waiter.

As we get to the landing, he pauses by the bannister so I can pass him and enter my room first, but before I can cross the hallway, the bathroom door flies open and steam billows out in a gush that makes me feel like I've stepped into a sauna.

Right on cue. God, it's like she's been waiting in there with a steam machine for this exact moment.

"Oh, hi, Grant." Carmella steps through the doorway wearing the *actual* smallest shorts that I have ever seen in my life and an oversized T-shirt that has been artfully hacked so that it falls off one shoulder and only covers down to her ribcage. Her hair is twisted in a white fluffy towel and her skin glows. She doesn't have a drop of makeup on, but she is absolutely gorgeous. And she's ninety percent legs and ten percent clothes and she's standing a foot away from Grant. My Grant.

I'm so distracted by the fact that my upper arm and her thigh are approximately the same size I don't realize she spoke to Grant by name until he responds to her.

"Hey, Carmella—"

"It's 'Ella.'"

"Ella. Sorry." Grant swallows and turns toward my door and then sort of scampers toward it, abandoning me in the hallway still unable to move properly.

"Hey, Imogen." She reaches up and fans the bottom edge of her shirt, flashing her flat stomach at me and then looks over my head into my room.

Don't look at him.

Don't look in my room.

Don't look at what's mine.

Please don't take what's mine.

"Grant—don't forget to send me those notes from third period over the Constitutional Democracy ideals and practices, okay?"

Apparently, Grant is in my room, hiding in the dark. I glance to my door, and the lights are still off. His voice comes eventually, and he mumbles, "Sure, okay."

Carmella pauses at her door and calls back over her shoulder to Grant. "And think about what I said about the Rally. I'm sure we'd have a really good time."

The Rally?

She was talking to Grant about the Rally?

"Well, that was awkward," Grant says as I enter my room and turn on the light. He's sitting on the ottoman in front of the squashy chair in the corner by the window, and he's set the cardboard tray in front of him.

"Yeah. Awkward."

I think I somehow expected I'd be able to keep her out of my life, even if she lived right beside me. But clearly I was wrong. Grant isn't an object to own, and they've got a class together, and she knows his name.

It killed me when she said his name.

I feel totally deflated. No wind in these sails.

Grant gestures to the tray and pulls off the tea towel that was lying across it. I see a sad little pizza with hastily placed pepperonis and questionable cheese distribution. "Okay, it's not delivery...but it's DiGior—forget it. I'm starving." He laughs way more than he should at his own joke.

I perch myself on the foot of my bed, the ottoman and the pizza between us. He grabs a slice. "Chow down, Gen."

Chow.

I'll bet Carmella doesn't "chow." Ever.

Silence.

"Aren't you hungry?"

"No, if you can believe it. I mean, I know this is breaking news, but I'm actually not perpetually hungry, so..."

I lie back on my bed and pull myself around so I can see out the window.

"Whoa," he says as he sets down his crust, which he usually saves for me. "What's the matter, Gen? I'm a little confused here because everything was okay in the car, and then we came upstairs and now you're all weird."

"Right, and nothing else happened when we got upstairs? Like, you didn't see Carmella, fresh from the shower, water dripping down her ten-foot-long legs? Right. That didn't happen."

"Hey." He scoots around and kneels on the floor beside the bed. He reaches up and puts his hand on my back and rubs in large, gentle circles. Instantly my eyes fill with tears.

It's like magic.

Sadness (mine) plus kindness (his) equals tears. Always.

The light through my window has faded to the color of a bruise. Deep and purple, with tinges of yellow still lingering at the horizon.

"Grant, trust me. I am being ridiculous. I am being immature and weird and petty and gross, and you won't understand, okay? You won't like me if I say it out loud."

"Dude, just tell me," he says.

At his "dude," my spirit sinks another notch.

I watch as the silhouette of a bird flies past my window and settles on the roof next door. I wait for her song, but she never sings.

"Is there any chance of you *not* making me talk about all the crap that happened today?"

"No," he says. "There's not."

"Fine. But you're going to think I'm a drama queen."

"I *know* you're a drama queen." He brushes a hair off my face as he repositions himself on the floor. He puts his back to the window and faces me where I lie sideways across the foot of my bed.

"She was in my English class."

I pause.

For effect.

I roll onto my back and let out an exasperated, "See? You don't get it."

"Gen, I know you think there's some real drama between you and her, but if you don't tell me, how am I supposed to understand? All I know is you say she decided she hated you last Christmas. Other than that, you've shut the Carmella door and locked it."

"Only because I don't want her getting to you. I don't want her to ruin you."

He laughs. "Ruin me? How?"

"What if she uses her feminine wiles to make you hate me, too?"

"Did you just say 'feminine wiles'? Please tell me you did not just use the phrase 'feminine wiles.'"

I reach up and pull my hoodie out from under my neck and bring it over my head and face.

He reaches up and pulls the hood open and brings his face horribly, soul-crushingly close to mine. "Gen, I could never hate you. Never."

I close my eyes because staring at him that close is making my heart break, and I can't handle more cracks in there.

"Now tell me what really happened today."

I speak slowly and force myself to look at the ceiling so gravity won't pull my tears out and so I won't be tempted to look at his hair when I'm trying to focus.

"She was in my class. And she came in all gorgeous and perfect. And I don't care that she's gorgeous, but it was like she was doing this super-sexualized flirting thing or something. And all of the boys were making gross comments, and she seemed to *like* that."

"Well, maybe she enjoys attention," he says reasonably, as if that somehow is supposed to make me feel less like a Judgy-McJudgerson.

"That's not really even the bad part. I mean, if she wants attention, more power to her. I don't care about that. The bad part is that she came in while Mr. Reed was taking roll, and he called her last name first..."

Grant is sitting, watching and listening with his most attentive face, but he has no idea why that is a problem. I'm going to have to say it.

"He called her Cinder-Ella, Grant. In class, he called her Cinderella."

In a burst, I recount the wet towel-under-my-sheets incident and what she'd said in class today and how Jonathan had come to my rescue. When I finish, I take a giant breath and try to regain my composure.

"But, wait," he says. "Her name is Carmella."

I roll over to face him and ask, "How is that the only thing you took away from what I just said?" He pushes back with his feet and props himself up against the wall below the window. The increased distance between us makes it so I can finally breathe properly again. "Of course her freaking name is Carmella, but I guess Evelyn let her register as Ella. There's no other explanation 'cause Reed's official roll sheet said Cinder-comma-Ella." I pause. "If she's Cinderella, just who does that make me? Ugh! I wanna hit her."

Grant holds up his hands and cowers against the wall. "Easy tiger, no need for violence."

"Stop making fun of me, I'm serious."

"I'm not making fun of you!" He crawls to the foot of the bed again. "Okay, I am making fun of you, but just *barely*, so it doesn't count."

He's close again, and I can smell his hair and I just cannot.

"You know what we need?" he says as he stands up and grabs my hands, pulling me up into a sitting position. "We need some *Mythbusters*."

"I hate *Mythbusters*."

"Blasphemy! How could you say that? It's our show!"

"It's *your* show, but I endure it because I love hearing you say, 'Myth: BUSTED!'"

"Well." He crosses his arms and raises his chin. "That makes it our show."

He grabs the pizza box while I scoot back to the headboard and turn on the TV. He sits next to me on my bed, his legs over the covers, but right next to mine.

"Grant, *Mythbusters* is not the answer to all the world's problems."

"Isn't it, Gen? Isn't it?"

We eat some more pizza. I keep it to a preposterous two slices, even though I'd slap a baby for a couple more. We watch as myth after myth is unceremoniously busted, and as the team is building some sort of catapult contraption, their gear reminds me of all the crap Grant carried into school today.

"So how was your meeting this morning? Was there any news about the competition?"

"Well, Mr. Simmons keeps hounding us for our sign-up money, but I'm not worried about it. If I do okay at the preliminary meet this week, I'll earn my way in."

"That's a good point." I lean over and bump his shoulder.

"Plus it's the same day as the Rally, so even if I don't get to compete, I'll have something to distract me from the misery of defeat later that night."

As soon as he mentions the Rally, the sound of Carmella's voice in the hallway earlier rattles around my head like a penny in a jar.

She said she'd spoken to him about the Rally.

That's the dance.

Our dance.

I mean, we don't actually dance, but it's still ours. Like *Mythbusters*.

"So, um..." I swallow. "In the hallway before, she mentioned the Rally. I mean, I don't want to intrude on your conversation or anything, but—"

Grant's face flushes red.

My heart falls to the pit of my stomach.

"Um, well, we're in the same AP History class, so, you know...third period. I mean, she was just asking me about the school and, you know, the clubs and groups, and, like, the Fine Arts Rally came up," he says without looking at me.

I think he hears me gulp because he looks at me so intensely. The familiarity of his perfect eyes surrounds me, and I'm asking him—with my dull ones. I'm begging him to tell me I'm wrong about the answer he must have—that almost any boy would have—given to a girl who looks like her.

My voice sounds flimsy as I speak. "So did she, like, ask you to go to the dance with her?"

"She just...yeah. Like, if I wanted to go with her and show her around or whatever."

My mouth dries out, and my tongue feels like it's choking me. I look down at the bed and see Grant's skinny ankles next to my giant clubbed feet. I follow our legs up the bed toward our hips and I see that my side of the bed is sagging lower than his and I can't be next to him anymore. I sit up quickly and then scoot off the bed.

"Right." I knew it before I'd asked it. My sadness at the news quickly boils into anger. I want to be angry at her, but I can't. She'd be stupid not to ask him. He's beautiful and kind and funny. I can't be mad at her because it's the one reasonable thing I've ever known her to do. But in my chest, the ache turns to fire and I connect all of the dots that I see in my mind, and when I've drawn the last line, I'm left with him. He's like any other average, seventeen-year-old, straight guy being asked by a beautiful girl to stand inches apart and sway together for three sweaty hours. Who could blame him for saying yes?

"Well, you'll have an incredible time with her." I begin rationally, but quickly derail. "I'm sure if you ask really nicely, she'll let you carry her purse and might even let you see a boob!"

His face scrunches up, and his brows come together as his mouth purses into a tiny circle before opening wide. "Yes, Gen, yes! I'm going to go with *her* to the Rally and ask to see *her* boob! Dear, Cinderella, even though my *best friend* is your sister and you make her have all of these horrible feelings, I'd like to spend more time with you! And also, please let me see your boob!"

He's waving his hands around and saying every word with such ridiculous emphasis that I know in a second I was wrong. The words could never have come out of his mouth any other way. He stands and holds one palm up to the ceiling.

"Oh, Cinderella, wherefore art thy boobs?"

"Grant, that doesn't even make sense! And stop saying boob!" I'm laughing and also trying not to cry, but I can't figure out why. I've managed to confuse myself, so I walk toward my window.

"You said it first! How do you expect me, a mere male mortal of seventeen, to let it go when someone just starts screeching about boobs?"

"Stop saying boobs!"

Our laughter dies down, and we're both just standing there. He's at the foot of the bed, and I'm to the side. The air between us thickens, and the silence swells and pushes against my skin. We're standing there, and I know I have to turn away from him or move or jump out the window or something. He scares me when he speaks into the quiet.

"You could show me *your* boob."

The spell is broken, and I lurch forward and smack him on his chest. "Grant, you're such an ass."

"I know. That's why you love me."

"Yeah, sure, that's one reason."

Out of a million.

We sit again on the edge of the bed, but the weight of the unanswered question is still on my shoulders. I bump his knee with mine and hate myself as I open my mouth to speak.

"Did you really tell her no?"

"Gen, of course I told her no. I told her—and I quote—I wasn't interested in going with her. And I told her I'd be going, as I do to every school function, with my best girl, my best friend, Imogen."

Oh, my heart.

"Case closed. No lasers in her eyes or talons or animal sacrifices or anything. Honestly, Gen, she didn't really seem to care."

"You told her I was your best girl?"

His best girl. Not an ugly stepsister.

He nods. "How could you doubt me? Do I need to remind you that I just asked to see your boob?"

I reach over and punch him just above the knee. "Thanks. For, you know, not falling for her siren song."

"You shouldn't have had to ask."

"But, I did, Grant. I did have to. I know it's hard for you to get it because you're not a girl, but there's something about the way she treats me that I can't figure out. Like with the towel thing. That's not just nothing. That was mean. Like, really, really mean."

"I can't figure out what would have made her do that. And you're right, that wasn't cool." He uses his most assuring tone, but I'm not soothed.

"I would have been so sad if you'd decided to go to the dance with her, but I think more than that I would have been scared."

"Of what? What do you have to be scared of?"

"I don't know how to say it, but it's, like, I'm afraid that somehow having her here, in the house I grew up in, asking my best friend on a date, being all of these things that everyone sees as wonderful...I'm worried I'll just fade away. Like she'll scoop up all the good things that might have been mine if I'd been her."

"Gen..." He smirks my favorite special-occasion smirk, the one that reveals the secret dimple on his left cheek. "You are not her, and you would never have been her."

"I know that. But, without all of this..." I make a vague gesture to my belly and my legs and my scarred-up arm and my head. "Without all of the messed-up parts, maybe I could have been."

There is a giant pendulum. And every person who lives with it looming above them knows how it feels when the weight is suspended in mid-air, waiting for the next opportunity to drop and change everything again in the blink of an eye.

The bird finally sings outside my window, drawing my attention. Her song is too sad. I see the sky has blackened, leaving only the faintest traces of indigo around the edges of the world.

The weight drops.

The pendulum swings.

As it moves through my insides, it sweeps heavily through every small pile of joy that I'd gathered and saved up tonight. Every joke, every moment. Every smell of his hair. Every quip that left me feeling smart. Every smile that made me feel like something beautiful might have shined from behind my eyes. Every joy is knocked down.

And I know in my gut that Carmella is the one that let it loose.

If I were stronger, maybe others wouldn't have that control, but I'm not.

And she is.

"I'm super-exhausted," I tell him numbly.

I know he can see the old, familiar sadness that has reclaimed its usual spot behind my eyes.

His whole face is different as he reads mine.

He knows this face, this tone of voice.

He gets up from my bed, walks to the bedroom door, and swings it open wide. In two short strides, he's back at my bedside, taking the tray and pizza scraps and moving them to the floor. He pulls off his shoes and flops himself into my overstuffed chair, props his feet on the ottoman, and lays my red fleece throw over his legs.

Over the years, when things were bad, Grant would sleep in my chair to keep me company. More than once, he came to the floor by my nightstand and held my hand as I cried in my sleep after Mom was gone. As the medicine got stronger and therapy went better, eventually I stopped dreaming at all. The last time he parked in that chair was last Christmas. And the time before that, I can't even recall.

"Well, it's been a while, but you know the drill, Gen. I'm not going anywhere."

I look at him again before pulling my legs under the covers and rolling over onto my side. I'm still wearing jeans, and I don't care enough to change. Frankly, I don't feel like doing much at all. As the creeping pang of sadness that I fight off with sticks and snacks and a spiral notebook claws at the back of my brain, I look up to the top shelf of my bookcase and feel a tickle whisper across the top of my left arm. I reach over and rub it away.

The sound of the TV stops completely, but the colors from the muted screen still dance across my wall. I let my lids close. I hear Grant reach up and flip off the lights before muttering his regular words of assurance. My lips almost move along with his as he whispers to the darkness—both the room's and mine.

"I'll stay, Gen. I'll stay."

*C*langing and laughter waft up from the kitchen. It's 6:13 AM. What is *wrong* with these people? I throw back the covers and notice Grant's Vans on the floor. He's still here. I'm glad.

I shower, throw on my clothes, and head downstairs only to find the whole happy crew chatting over their organic, freshly squeezed, non-pasteurized orange juice. The sight of Evelyn, Carmella, and Grant all in one room, smiling and being pleasant makes me feel like an *actual* grumpy, old troll.

"Hey, sunshine!" Grant is positively shouting at this ungodly hour.

"Good morning, darling!" Evelyn coos. "We're frying up some veggie bacon and I made some millet waffles for you!"

I've never been hungover, but I think it's probably a lot like this. Tired and groggy. Hungry, but not in the mood to eat. Plus everyone's too cheery, and I kinda want to punch them all in the face.

"It's fake bacon! It's facon! And it's actually pretty good. Here!" Grant is already in front of me with a handful of something that smells vaguely like bacon and dirt. He reaches up and puts his hand under my chin, causing me to open up as he feeds me this faux-meat with an impossibly peppy grin. "What do you think?"

"Oh, um. It's good, I guess."

Evelyn chimes, "I picked up that Risperdal prescription, so you're all stocked, sweetie! Want some juice?"

Brilliant. Let's talk about my crazy pills in front of every-damn-body. I look to Grant, but he is stuffing himself with food straight out of the pan. I spin around slowly to look at Carmella. Maybe she didn't even hear.

"Morning, sis. Good thing you got that refill, huh?" Carmella, perched on a stool at the breakfast bar, manages these words with a smile, though it doesn't reach her eyes. As Grant and Evelyn chatter over the stove with their back to the rest of the kitchen, Carmella reaches up and puts her finger beside her ear and makes little circles. When Evelyn picks up the pan and spins around to set it in the sink in the kitchen island, Carmella picks up a curl and continues as if she'd just been twirling her hair.

Crazy. Me.

"Carmella, sweetie, what were you about to ask me a minute ago?"

My stepsister's voice goes cold. "Mom, you said you'd call me Ella."

Evelyn turns with an apologetic look in her eye and puts her hand near her forehead. "Oh, I'm sorry, hon. I'll get the hang of it eventually." Evelyn smiles at her little girl with dreamy eyes.

"I was gonna ask if I can have some money? I'm going shopping after dance practice. I need to buy some new bras."

"Ella!" Evelyn sounds scandalized, and she glances to Grant and back to her daughter. Like at the sound of the word "bra," Grant might just jump on top of her kid right then and there. Evelyn nods to Carmella and then traipses from the room to fetch her precious daughter's latest whim. Grant turns to watch Evelyn leave with a sad sort of look on his face. How nice it must be to ask for cash and have it delivered in sixty seconds flat.

"Grant, are you ready? I'd like to go." I try not to fidget in front of Carmella, but she's just sitting there and staring at me. It pisses me off that she doesn't even have to do anything to intimidate me into total insecurity and silence.

"Sure, let me go grab my shoes."

As he flies up the stairs, I'm left in the kitchen. Alone. With her.

"So, Imogen, good thing Mom refilled your antipsychotics. If this is you pulled together, I'd hate to see what a hot mess you are when you're unmedicated."

I know, logically, that I have no reason to be ashamed of my therapy, but that knowledge makes absolutely no difference.

She stares at me for a second, relishing my discomfort. It looks like she's planning what to say, how to make sure it's really going to hurt. I brace myself.

"I hear you miss a lot of classes to see your shrink. Crestwood lets you miss all the school you want just because you're crazy? That doesn't seem fair." She bounces her crossed leg and points her finger while she talks. She has me in the palm of her hand. "Seems weird to me, but I don't make the rules for special ed kids. You are, right? Special ed? You know, I had no idea you could be special ed just for being a basketcase, but that's what my mom said."

Bam. The force of her words slices through the kitchen, and I stagger back as if I've been hit. "I...I..." I drop my gaze to the floor and press my open palms to the sides of my jeans, hoping to push the sweat back into my pores.

She smiles as she watches me squirm.

"I noticed your buddy Grant spent the night. Seems pretty bold, but I guess it's never too early for society to start making certain concessions for people like you. Better to keep you happy than risk making you snap."

Her "p" pops out of her lips, and she just stares at me. Is she waiting for a response?

"You know, it's really none of your business." The words are out before I can measure their weight.

She stands up slowly and crosses the room. I back up against the counter until I feel the cold stone pushing against me.

"Let me be sure you understand how this works. *Some* people have power and some people don't." Her fake smile is gone, and her eyes are dark. The muscles in her face are tight, and she's towering over me in her heels. She looks like a monster. "When people who don't have power pretend that they do, they lose. Sometimes they lose what they have. Sometimes they lose what they want. But they lose."

My heart is pounding so hard I feel like I might pass out. I can't decide if I should scream or sit down or push her away or what.

Her eyes are locked on mine, and the echo of her threat is still ringing in my ears when she pops the smile back on her lips and her eyes soften.

"Gen! Let's go!" Grant calls from the front door, and without another word, I pick up my bag and almost run out of the kitchen. I smash into Evelyn as she rounds the corner with her wallet in hand.

"Oh!" Evelyn stumbles back a step and bumps her head on the side of the wall.

"Evelyn, I'm sorry."

"Imogen, please be careful! You're not a little thing anymore, you could hurt someone!"

I am about three seconds from going back upstairs and crawling into bed.

"Gen!" Grant calls to me a second time.

"Yeah! Gimme five minutes!" I yell toward the door.

When I turn back to Evelyn, she's handing Carmella her money and sending her on her way. "Bye, sis," Carmella says as she strides out of the kitchen.

As soon as Carmella walks out of the room, I burst into tears. I can't stop it. I can't even pretend I've got something in my eye. I am straight-up crying.

"Imogen, honey, what's the matter? Did you hurt yourself when we bumped?"

"When we 'bumped,' seriously?" I walk to the little bakers rack standing by the sliding glass door and pull out a tissue. "We didn't bump, Evelyn. I'm a freaking rhinoceros." I sniffle and wipe at my eyes while I gesture all around myself. "I can't breathe."

"Here, honey, sit down." She pulls me over to the chair at the kitchen table, and I try to keep breathing. My lips are swollen and tingling, and my vision is clouded with bright spots. "Imogen, honey, I hope you know that when I said you weren't little, I meant you're a grown up. You're not a baby. I didn't mean anything... else, okay?" She looks at me awkwardly and pats my knee like a robot. "Can I get you any medicine?"

I like to keep my medicine separate from the people around me. I don't like to think of others knowing what I take, when I take it, and why. But even though she's awkwardly patting my knee, she's doing this shooshing sound, and it's making my pulse slow to normal.

"Yes," I say. "Could I have a half of the little pink one, please?"

"Of course, honey." She springs to the medicine cabinet and comes back with half of a pill and a glass of cold water.

"Thank you, Evelyn. I really appreciate it. This was not a good morning. And it was not a good night last night either. I really don't know if I can go to school today." Just saying the word "school" starts my heart beating faster again as I blow my nose and wipe away the last of my tears.

"Honey, I don't think you should stay home. But it might be a good idea for you to call George and see if he can fit you in this morning. What do you say?"

I take a deep breath and blow it out in a narrow stream.

"Yeah. I should call TG. Thank you. Again. I'm sorry I ran into you."

She smiles at me gently. "It's nothing. Anything you need, you can come to me, okay?" Every part of her face is soothing except for her eyes. She is looking at me so intensely it makes me want to look away.

"Actually, there is something else I need." I pick at the skin on my left thumb. "I was hoping you could call the school for me? I need to...I need to change my first period class."

"Is something wrong? Are you not getting along with the teacher?" Her face is contorted with concern, and the longer I look at her the more I see Carmella's features lingering on her skin. Their eyes are the same color. Carmella has her mother's nose, too. It makes me want to shut down completely.

"I'm having some weird anxiety flare-ups in there. I don't do well with change, and there are some changes in there and some kids have been saying some things that have made me uncomfortable. Triggering things." I throw out the buzzword and hope it works.

"Avoidance is an easy way to block off healing. Have you thought about what you might be avoiding by changing that class?"

Uh, yeah. Your daughter.

She's reaching out and holding my shoulders while I try with all of my willpower to keep looking in her eyes. A moment ago, she seemed so sincere, but now all I see is the mother of the villain in my story. And I just feel so crazy. Things have gotten so bad so fast. And it's all because of Carmella. And by extension, Evelyn, too.

"Gen! I can't be late to this meeting!"

"Coming!" I scream at him, causing Evelyn to jump back as if she'd been slapped.

"Sorry, I have to go. Grant's got a meeting before first period, so I'm dropping him off, and then I'm going to swing by George's office. I need to see him. If I go, he'll see me. Please call the school about my schedule. Please."

I push out of the chair and take note of my heartbeat. It feels steadier already. She pulls her lips together in a tight line. I can smell her disapproval at my "avoidant" behavior, but she offers me a tiny nod.

She doesn't understand me. And I know that. And the way she looks at me as I gather my things makes me feel confident she never will.

At 8:56, after dropping Grant off at school, I walk into the waiting area of Therapist George's office. I sit on the stupid chair covered in stupid fabric and stare up at his stupid painting of a stupid dog, and my left leg bounces uncontrollably. When I met Grant in the car, he asked what was wrong. If anyone can tell when I've been crying, it's him. I told him I'd hurt myself when I ran into Evelyn and bumped my head. I don't think he bought it, but he had the decency to let it go.

The entire ride to school I asked myself why in the world I wouldn't want to tell Grant about the horrible, threatening, unacceptable things Carmella said to me in the kitchen. For the first time in my life, I can say I totally understand that "shamed into silence" mentality I've heard mentioned.

Even though I know she's the one who crossed the line—she's the person who violated human compassion and who lashed out with cruelty—it feels like I'm the problem. It feels like there's a whisper of truth in the idea that things would be better if the weak would just stay out of the way.

When I came in today, Sarah, the girl behind the counter, asked me if it was an emergency, because usually, I don't miss school for appointments. Sometimes I have them during our open lunch block and sometimes I come after school, but it's pretty rare to just blow off a class for therapy—contrary to Carmella's belief. But every time I tried to answer Sarah's question, I got so blinky that, eventually, I just turned away from her and went to sit down. Right now, I can't stop blinking. I'm blinking so fast and so often that Sarah looks like a stop-motion cartoon version of herself.

Exactly four minutes after I arrive, his office door swings open, and TG gestures me in.

"Imogen, it's nice to see you. Come on in."

George looks exactly like he always does. His sleeves are rolled up to his elbows, giving me the impression he's been working hard all day, even though it's only 9:00 in the morning. On his desk, I notice his cufflinks—today's are in the shape of beer mugs.

As I walk to my seat on his tufted leather sofa, he closes the door behind me and asks, "So what's going on, Imogen? I wasn't expecting to see you so soon after our visit on Saturday. Are you okay?"

"I guess so." I feel my bottom lip begin to quiver. Just being in the room with one of my "trusted adults" gives me the same sort of feeling I have when Grant is nice to me and I'm trying not to cry. It just makes it harder to hold it all together.

I reach into my bag for my journal, and a sigh escapes my lips. I can't bring myself to look at him. I can't shake the shame that is sticky, all over me.

Blink. Blink.

"Imogen, are you sure you're all right?"

"I'm—no, TG. I'm not."

"You're here now. I'm here. Would you like to tell me what's the matter?"

Blink. Blink.

Maybe coming here was a bad idea. All he wants to do is pull this out of me, and all I want to do is leave.

"I...it's time for writing. I should write. I'm fine." I say it over and over in my head. I'm fine. I'm fine. I don't believe a word. "Can I start?"

George has his hand on his chin like he's scrutinizing a painting hanging on a museum wall. What is Imogen thinking? What is Imogen doing? Why does she keep blinking?

"Sure. Go ahead. I'll stop you in ten minutes."

I scribble my pen across the page, making small, meaningless circles at the top of my paper in an attempt to convince him I'm journaling. I blink and blink and try to keep tears from falling onto my paper because then I'll have to see them. Those wet spots. Those paper-wrinkling wet spots mean I'm crying. Because of her. Again. My doodles turn into words.

She's in my head. I see her perfect hair and her skinny legs and I can't stop seeing her every time I look in my mirror. I'm basically the old witch who is looking into the glass but instead of asking about who is the fairest, I'm looking at my own reflection and saying, "Oh, you know who the fairest is, cupcake, and it's not you." And she hates me. But she doesn't need to hate me. It's entirely unnecessary. Girls like her don't have to spend time hating girls like me. They're perfectly fine to just go about their business and look down their noses at us. Hating is a complete waste of energy.

I am made of glass.

And I've been broken before.

I've been in a million little razor-cut pieces and I've been totally lost and alone.

I've screamed for a mother I remember more as a dead woman than I remember as alive.

I was swept up by loving hands and painstakingly glued back into a shape that looks mostly like me. I'm mostly myself, but there are still cracks.

Glue is fine and useful and I'm glad I've mended well, but don't be fooled: I'm just barely holding it together. And she is this tiny, little, hi-ho-bag pickaxe and she's tapping on me. And I'm breaking.

"I'm breaking."

The sound of my voice cuts through the silent room like a solo microphone that's up too hot in an empty theatre.

"Imogen?"

My chin lifts, and I look at George through a blur of tears. His face is hard to see, but his voice is tender and full of worry. I can't make out much through the tears, but his shoulders are wide like my dad's. And I can't stand it. Any of it. The sadness, the disappointment, the fear. It weighs me down, causing my chin to lower again, and when it does, the tears finally fall.

"I can't," I whisper into my hands. I watch as fat circles drip onto my palms. I catch my tears like precious objects. Symbols of what I have to lose.

What Carmella says weak people never manage to hold onto.

"Tell me what's happening. I'm here. I am right here, Imogen. Look at me. You are not alone." George pulls his chair forward across the floor—something he's never done before. He is almost knee to knee with me, but never touching. As much as he cares for me, I know there is a professional limit he'd never cross. And the fact that all I want is a hug just makes me miss my actual dad even more.

"George, I'm worried. I'm really worried. Things haven't been this bad in months and months, and now I feel like I'm back to square one. I can't hold it together. Not with her around. I can't. She's killing me."

"Who, Imogen? What's changed since we talked on Saturday morning?"

I ignore his question and just let the words flow. It feels more important that I get the words out than I answer his questions. George is holding his luxury pen and twirling it between his fingers. A rare gesture of stress. He's worried.

"I know she's my stepsister, and we're supposed to be family now or whatever, but I can't look at her without seeing every single thing I'm not. I hate myself when I see her. I hate how I feel when I'm anywhere near her because I will never be what she is."

"So you want to be what she is?"

"I should have been! I should have been, George! And I hate that I want to be. Or that I might want to be. Because she's mean. It was not just a misunderstanding at Christmas. I wasn't confused. She hates everything about me, and maybe she's right! If I weren't trapped in this skin, I'd probably hate me, too!"

I wipe my eyes on my sleeves and feel the rush of adrenaline recede. George is looking at me with patient eyes. I want to look away, but I force myself to keep my eyes locked on him. I try to remember all the things I'm not doing right now that I should be.

I count as I inhale and exhale, keeping my breaths slow and steady. I visualize my little heart pumping gently. I try and make myself still, even though my skin still feels the tingle of oxygen deprivation.

"George, I would have been her. If my mom hadn't—if I hadn't fallen apart, that girl who is pretty and smart and driven—that girl would have been me. And now I'm living next door to the person I might have been and I don't know what to do. And she hates me, George. And that makes me feel like I'm somehow hating myself."

I purse my lips together while I close my journal and re-cap my pen.

"What am I supposed to do, George? I was doing okay, right? After Christmas, we worked so hard. You and my family and me. By May, I was going to school more, and I stopped flushing my meds, and I remember the day I gave you and my dad my blades and I really believed that maybe this disease wasn't permanent. The thought of waking up one day and leaving sadness and worry in the bed behind me was incredible. I had hope for the first time in my life."

But the only me I really remember being is this.

My lips shiver as tears fall into my lap.

"I had hope. I felt like I had climbed out of this giant cave I never, ever thought I'd get out of. I didn't even know people *could* get out. But now I'm there again, right at the edge, and if I make one wrong step, I'm going to fall back to the bottom."

George's hands are folded carefully on his notepad. "You are doing all the things you're supposed to be doing. You are coming to talk with me, and you are working with your school case manager, you are journaling, and you are taking your prescribed medication. You have tools, Imogen. You are not alone in this."

"But I feel alone. I feel it. And it doesn't matter what you say or what should be, George."

I'm fighting in this horrible war alone. All anyone can do is hand me weapons and shields and Band-Aids, but I'm standing here, begging someone to help me fight.

"George, I'm tired. I'm so tired of fighting this, and it seems like the whole world thinks I should be able to snap out of it. And I know there are people who care, but in these moments..." I gesture to the ground and grit my teeth. "In this specific moment, I am in a battle, and I am absolutely by myself. And if you can say I'm not alone, then you don't understand anything at all."

He pauses and looks at me without moving a muscle or saying a word. I expect him to argue or try and soothe me again, but eventually, he just nods.

"You're right. But don't underestimate how strong you are. How much you know. Okay?" He points at me with the end of his pen.

We sit in silence for a moment. I find myself staring out the window and watching the morning clouds pass through the sky. Autumn in Texas is always mild, and the first crisp breezes are finally pulling the leaves off of the giant oak tree outside of George's building. A few fly past and scratch at the glass on their way to someplace new.

"You okay?" he asks after several more minutes of silence.

"Yeah." The only good thing about fighting alone is when I'm done with a bout, I'm fully exhausted and there aren't really any feelings left to feel. The numbness that comes after an emotional breakdown is such a welcome relief. It almost makes the entire thing bearable.

"I know you think it's cheesy, but did you try saying your affirmation? You wrote it to guide your thinking in moments just like this one. Maybe you could say it now, so it will be fresh in your mind before you leave today."

"I really don't feel like—" He sits there with his crisp shirt and his shiny shoes, and he's waiting for me to say his magic words. And I realize that by me saying them, he'll feel like he's done something. Plus, the sooner I say them, the sooner I get to leave.

And there's also the part about when I get through a therapy session, I get to hit up whichever drive-thru I want.

"Yeah, yeah. I'll say the thing." I drone the words I've said over and over through the years. "I am whole. I am more than just the pieces that I see. I am so much stronger than I seem."

"And how do you feel right now?"

I'll never admit that I feel better. I try to break the tension I've brought into the room like a curse.

"I feel like I wanna kick you in the junk for always making me say that stupid mantra."

He laughs as the humor slips back into our conversation. "It isn't stupid, Imogen. And if you ask me, junk-kicking makes it sound like someone is feeling a little more empowered than they were when they walked in." He's beaming and scooping up all the credit for the battle I waged in his office. Figures.

"Thanks. You're not in the fight with me, but you're not a bad strategist." I give him a little grin so that he'll feel proud. I figure at least one of us should walk away from this meeting feeling accomplished. He's so eager to believe me. So eager to check off the "I fixed Imogen today" box. I watch as he smiles and writes something down in my file.

That's just the worst.

I turn from George and his notes and get off the creaky, leather couch to cross behind his chair. Alongside his carved wooden desk, I stand beside the window. I walk right up to the glass and look out into the sky. If I keep my gaze at the horizon line, I don't notice the buildings and trees and concrete things below. If I keep my gaze high, I can only see the sky. I stare into the endless blue and try to imagine what real, unfiltered joy would be like. Rushing excitement, wonder, and the knowledge tinged with fear that it could come to an end at any moment. As I drop my chin, my eyes take in the distance to the ground, and I suppose that, perhaps, joy might be a close match for falling.

The crackle of the speaker startles me as I roll down my window with only two minutes until the end of breakfast service. I'm so happy I almost start crying again.

I reach for the sunglasses in my seat. I always wear my sunglasses in the drive-thru. Daytime, nighttime, it really doesn't make a difference. I don't want the kid running the register to see my eyes.

"Yeah, I'll have a large Dr. Pepper, a Bacon, Egg & Cheese McGriddle, an Egg McMuffin, and a box of the Cinna-Melts."

I say it quickly, out of desperation for those breakfast-only, little bites of dough covered in so much gooey cinnamon and icing that I've seriously considered trying to climb *into* the box.

I turn to look out the passenger window just as a loud, yellow Mustang cuts through the parking lot and screeches out onto Main.

It's not her, but it's just like her. Loud, self-indulgent, and desperate for attention.

I *hate* her.

The scratchy, distorted voice repeats my order back to me.

"Oh, and also, a hash brown," I add.

Yep. That'll teach her.

I pay, keeping my face forward as much as I can, and then pull around through the parking lot to my favorite corner of the shopping center across from the side entrance next to a tiny pond. McGriddle, McMuffin, hash brown, Cinna-Melts, meds, gulp of DP, and I'm already feeling more calm than I did at any point in TG's office.

I visualize my prescription cocktail moving through my veins and pretend I feel it taking away all my crazy urges. Like the urge to drive straight to school, march into our first period class, and tell her off for being such a bitch this morning. Or maybe the urge to drive to the edge of town, find a grassy place to lie down, and never wake up again. Either one.

The greasy, salty smell of the hash brown instantly settles my nerves until my ears pick up on the growing sound of my chewing. I reach down to my phone and turn on my *Once Upon a Mattress* cast recording. It is almost painfully loud, but at least I can't hear myself chew.

I lick the salt from my fingertips as I scour the sky for birds or planes. Anything to keep my eyes off the wrappers and crumbs. That's my other rule. First, don't let the drive-thru kid see me cry, and second, never look at the aftermath.

I roll down my window and drop my trash into the can right at the curb.

When I check my phone, I am ecstatic that my session plus breakfast has effectively eaten up the first part of my day. I should get back just after third period, which is absolutely brilliant. I pull the gearshift to flip the car into reverse as my phone pings on the seat beside me. A message from Grant. I keep my foot planted on the brake.

"*Hey, think you're going to make it back to school in time for lunch? I have news about my physics thing.*"

I take a long, final pull on my Dr. Pepper and hear the straw rattle against the bottom of the empty cup. I toss it out the still-open window into the trash and then type my reply.

"*Sure. I'm starving.*"

"They were closing up the line, so I grabbed a burrito for you." Grant pushes the little paper boat holding a plastic-wrapped fiesta toward my seat at our end of the long lunch table. I drop my bag on the floor under the tiny little circles that are supposed to correspond with actual human butt sizes. I'm convinced it's a conspiracy.

"So, tell me your news," I prod. "It will give me a chance to eat while you talk." I tear open the wrapper and take a big bite. I tell my brain that it is forbidden from processing the still-fresh smell of McGriddle grease lingering on my fingertips.

"Okay, well, I got confirmation about the prelims." He reaches down and pulls a sad stick of celery out of his plastic cup. "If I get into the top three, I'll get to automatically enter the regionals competition."

I swallow a lump of my burrito and cover my mouth with my hand as I talk. "That's great! I'm sure you'll be in the top whatever. That's, like, not even up for debate. You'll make it. I know it."

"Well, I'm confident because I know I'm not bad, but it's also pretty crazy because they don't announce the top spots until the Friday morning before—and

Saturday morning is the contest. It's gonna be a stressful day."

As he says the word "stressful," he tilts his head down and rips open his package of cookies. He holds the open pack out to me, offering one. I hold up my hand and shake my head.

"I don't want you to be stressed," I say.

"Forget it. I don't want you worrying about me. I'm fine."

He makes it look so easy to stare stress in the eye and just brush it off like a crumb.

He pops a cookie in his mouth, and then he reaches over and puts his hand on top of mine. My eyes sweep across the cafeteria. When I look back, and I realize how loud the big, echoey, room really is. When I look back down at his hand, it makes me want to pull away. I'd hate for anyone to see it and misunderstand. I would hate for someone to think he liked me and make fun of him for it.

I pull my hand and pretend I need to adjust my sleeve.

He reaches back over and grabs my hand, pulling it back into the middle, giving it a big squeeze and looking me straight in the eye. He crosses his eyes at me and then makes himself laugh, enough that his hidden dimple appears on his cheek.

Oh, this boy.

I shake my head and try to bring the conversation back to something that doesn't make my mouth get dry and my face get hot.

"Just tell me if you get stressed, okay? I'll teach you the best breathing techniques I know."

Grant reaches up with one hand and rubs his palm all over his hair, crushing and tugging at his pokey strands, and somehow, when he takes his hand away, he looks even better than he did before he attacked his hairdo. As he fusses with it, I can smell his hair product and I can't help it. My eyes flutter closed for just a second as I try to pull myself together.

My God, this boy.

"Okay, you be my expert," he says as he props up his head.

"I won't let you down." I hold up my fingers like a Girl Scout. Or like what I think a Girl Scout salute looks like. I really have no idea.

"Thanks, Gen."

"Don't mention it."

We look down at the table at the same second and realize that our free hands are still intertwined. We're both just looking at our hands as kids all around us stand up and grab their bags and scream to each other across the open space.

The bell rings, and our hands snap apart.

"Gen, I've gotta go, but I'll see you in Tech." He reaches to take the pile of garbage from my hands and dumps it all in the trashcan as he strides out of the cafeteria.

My belly was so full after back-to-back meals that I floated through the next few hours in a gastrointestinal-shock-induced coma. My math teacher woke me up three minutes after the last bell, my face soggy from drool and a giant streak on my cheek from the seam of my hoodie sleeve. Faced with the choices of A) jogging to tech theatre and arriving winded or B) being a couple of minutes late, I opted for tardiness.

So as I open the door to the theatre room, Gild is already in full-on drill sergeant mode.

"...We have much preparation and work to do, so please get started on either the platform assembly in the scene shop or painting the sides of the two main set pieces. The sides only..." She is waving her arms, and people are starting to scatter around the room, looking for ways to stay busy and out of her line of fire. She's still hollering as I try and make my way to Grant and the rest of my group. "...And if you think you don't have anything to do, let me know and I'll find work for you."

She turns, and the room fills with chatter before I can duck out of sight.

"Miss Keegan, you're late." She puts a hand on her hip and tries to make her face look stern, but as I cross toward her, she gives me the tiniest of grins. "Everything all right?"

"I'm fine, Mrs. Gild. I'm sorry I'm late. There was a line at the bathroom."

"There's a line on your face, too, Scar." Grant approaches from our table at the back, and with a giant smile, he reaches up and runs his thumb gently along the red stripe on my face.

This is the third time today he's touched me, and all I can think about is how much I hope he finds a reason for a fourth.

He laughs and sets off toward the scene shop singing "Hakuna Matata."

"Hey!" I chuckle before turning back to Gild. "I'm sorry. It won't happen again."

She reaches up and puts her hands on either side of my shoulders and gives me a warm smile. Gild is tough on us, but we're like family. The feeling of her hands on my arms makes me feel at home.

"Good," she says. And then she sets off. "You can go get started. All of the mic packs need new batteries and labels, and round up all of the mic tape you can find because as soon as class is over, I need you on stage ready to start showing the cast how to wear them. Got it?"

She says all of this while she's writing on her clipboard, sorting papers into piles, and pointing at objects for the prop crew to take out to their tables.

"Yes, ma'am." I give her a thumbs up, and she heads out the side door to the hallway by the wings.

"Missed you in first period today," Jonathan says as he strides over to me, one hand tucked away and the other holding an old, blue, rusted toolbox by the peeling handle.

"Sorry. I had to go see TG—errr. George. He's—" I shake my head and feel myself blink five times in a row. "I had an appointment."

He waits for a moment, pulling his mouth to one side for just a second before repositioning his grip on the toolbox with his visible hand. "We've all got stuff," he says plainly before gesturing to me with the box and stepping backward toward the door. "Here comes my beloved. I better go before I get roped into another rousing round of 'Kristin Chenoweth is More Fierce Than...'" He laughs to himself. "He's cute, but he's *loud*." Jonathan's playful smile lingers even after he turns around.

I grin as he sneaks out the door, and I spin just in time to see Brice drop his bag and apply a fresh coat of lip balm.

"Hey, dollface." Brice approaches and runs a hand through his golden hair. He's wearing a lavender sweater that looks like it probably cost about as much as my Grannymobile.

"Heya, mister," I say as I set down my bag and pull my hair back into a ponytail.

Everyone in the classroom is shedding their personas as students at Crestwood High and stepping into their roles as vital members of the Tech Crew.

The sound of power tools whirring to life makes me feel at home.

Brice pulls off his gorgeous sweater to reveal a plain five-dollar T-shirt underneath.

"Awwww," I say, letting my face droop with disappointment.

"What?" Brice asks as he folds it into a perfect square.

"I liked your sweater. Now you just look like another kid in a T-shirt."

He chuckles and puts his hand on his hip. "Yeah, but have you seen the boots?" He looks down to his feet, and I notice he's got these pretty incredible combat boots that are all folded over and chunky. He steps away from me and then turns on a dime to pose and give me the full picture.

"You're totally right. Those boots make even your T-shirt look like a million bucks."

He throws up his hands with exasperation and says, "You doubted me?" He grins as two freshman girls walk toward him in perfect unison and stand beside him without saying a word.

"Uh, Brice, you have some people," Grant says, as he approaches with arms full of props.

Brice turns and looks at the girl on the left. Her delicate eyes are dark slivers, and her jet black hair hangs in a perfect pixie cut. "Fish-kick 1: You're going to go to the dressing room and start checking the principal character costume list. Make sure they're all hung in the right section." He snaps his head toward the second girl who has wide-set green eyes and long, blonde hair. "Fish-kick 2: You're going to start writing out a list of costumes that might have a tight fit around the waist if we try and fit a mic pack in there. Got it?"

The girls nod at him fiercely, and then he raises his hand and sends them on their way.

"Brice," I say with a stern look on my face. "Why are you torturing your freshman?"

"I'm not! When they came up to me on the first day, they were so freaked out they just sorta started acting like I was a drill sergeant. So I rolled with it. I mean, consider the boots." He gestures again and then raises his hands to me in question. "What was I supposed to do?"

"You're right. You clearly had no choice."

Brice steps to my side and links his arm through mine. We take a few steps through the classroom toward the doorway by the backstage corridor.

"I'm going to start with the boys' microphones right after school and then move onto the girls'. Will that give you plenty of time to check the dresses with Thing 2 back there?" I ask.

"Sure. Fabulous." He pulls his arm from mine and starts scanning the room. "Crap. I've gotta move some giant hanging racks. Thornton!" he calls across to Grant who's been trying to double-check all of the spotlights out in the hallway. "Can you help me move some racks?"

"Sure, bro," Grant says as he comes back in the room and wipes his already sweaty brow.

"Thanks, Mister Stage Manager, sir," Brice says with an uncertain salute. "I'd have Jonathan help me, but he and his toolbox snuck out earlier when he thought I wasn't looking so you'll have to do." He clicks his heels together and shouts, "Sir!"

My head and Grant's snap back at the sound before we start giggling.

"Gee, thanks. And, um, at ease, soldier," Grant says as he glances first at Brice's boots, then to his limp salute, then back to me, and back to Brice again. "It'd be my pleasure. Gen, I'll see you in a bit. Let me know if you need help with anything until Antonique gets here."

"Sure, thanks," I say as Grant starts to walk out into the hall toward the racks without Brice.

"Ahem." Brice gestures to Grant's arm and clears his throat.

Grant laughs and then crosses back to Brice and bows. "Oh, my mistake, soldier." Grant bends his elbow and offers it to Brice before looking over his shoulder and rolling his sparkling eyes.

In the sound booth, I sort through my giant case of wireless mic packs. I love the way they all look the same. Little ducks in a row, the little plastic boxes that make sound fill a room all the way to the corners.

I've already replaced nineteen out of twenty sets of batteries before the little door to my sound booth snaps open.

"Honey, I'm home." Antonique blasts through the door in a flurry of motion. Her skinny braids lift away from her shoulders and fan out as she turns around to set her bag under the desk. Her strong, dark brown shoulders are bare as she pulls off her cardigan, revealing a narrow torso in a tank top. "I'm ready to help. What's happening?"

"Well, I've just replaced all the batteries." I gesture to the box full of microphones and then turn to face the big glass window looking out into the house. The stage is set and the finished castle is one of the best-looking set pieces Crestwood has ever had. "In a few minutes, once everyone gets signed into rehearsal, we've got to start doing pack fittings and showing the cast how to wear and tape them." I lift up the little rolls of mic tape and spin one around on my finger.

She flops down onto her folding chair with a defeated look on her face. "That sounds complicated."

"It will be a piece of cake. I'll walk you through it."

She turns her face from the glass and smiles at me. Her teeth are so perfect. I pull my own lips closed and run my tongue along the uneven row across the bottom.

Antonique sees my facial expression change. I can tell because her smile fades just as mine does. She clears her throat before changing the subject. "So is Ella Cinder really your stepsister?"

Like a roundhouse kick to the gut, the wind is knocked out of me.

I wonder for a second if I'll ever get used to the way it feels when Carmella is forced into my mind unexpectedly. Maybe it will get better over time. Somehow I doubt it.

Antonique is still looking at me expectantly.

"Uh, kinda. I mean, yes," I answer. "Why?"

"Oh." Her expression changes. Her eyes dart back and forth.

"Seems like you didn't expect that to be true," I say.

"Right, well..." She reaches up and tucks her braids behind her ears again. "It's just that some girls in my lunch were talking about her. They were saying she joined the dance team and immediately tried to re-choreograph their entire routine. And one girl said she laughed when the captains were doing their dance solos. They said she wasn't very nice." She looks down and mutters to her hands, "Sorry. No offense."

I look through the glass at the chorus huddled in the center of the stage, mumbling the song "An Opening for a Princess." I can just barely make out the sound of them singing through the soundproofed walls. I look down and see the mute button is still glowing red.

"Seriously, none taken, Antonique. She is horrible. They're not wrong."

"It's just that I was telling my table she couldn't be your sister. 'Cause you're so nice, I guess I thought if you did have a sister, she'd be more like you."

More like me.

I try to picture Carmella and I if we'd grown up together. Would we have more in common? Would I be more stuck up and pretentious? Would she be more insecure and emotional?

I can't see it. I can only see her, and I can only see me. And I can't find a single way that we'd bring out anything but the worst in each other.

"Did you not grow up together?" Antonique reaches up to the box of mic packs and pulls one out, flipping it end over end in her palm.

Blink. Blink. Blink.

"Uh, no. We definitely didn't. Yesterday was her first day at Crestwood, actually. My dad and her mom got married last year."

The sentence repeats over and over in my head.

My dad and her mom got married last year.

My dad got married last year.

My dad got married.

I start to rock in my giant chair, the springs helping me bounce back and forth.

"Oh, that's cool," she says. "Where's your mom?" She continues to stack the mics into neater piles.

Oh. My head feels like it's being twisted around and is about to pop right off my body. The light from the stage and the sound, even muffled, is instantly too much. My head bursts into migraine-level pain. I'm burning up. I push back from the desk and put my arms on my knees so that my head can hang down nearer to my legs. My hoodie has become an oven.

"Imogen?" Antonique squeaks out my name and stands up from her folding chair. "Imogen, are you okay? What's wrong?"

I try to breathe, but I can't make my lungs fill up. It's so hot. It's like I'm stuck in a sauna and the door has locked behind me.

I can feel my face turn green and clammy, and it occurs to me that if I don't crawl out of this chair, I might crack my head on the desk and die. This would not be ideal.

All I keep thinking is that I can't breathe. I'm trying, but I just can't breathe.

I pull myself off the chair and sit on the floor in the tiny little, foam-padded closet. I lean against the sound proofing material, which is soft against the back of my head. I begin to count. I'm not listening to her, but I can see Antonique moving and gesturing and I think she's reaching for her phone.

"I'm okay," I say to her. "I'm sorry, I'm okay."

Blink. Blink.

My blurry vision clears, and my lungs finally open up to the oxygen they need.

Antonique plops down beside me, sitting up on her knees. "Are you sure you're okay? What happened? You went all white, and I'm freaking out." She holds out her hand in front of my face. "Look, I'm shaking."

I smile at her. "Me, too."

I hold out my unsteady hand, and she grins, sitting back on her heels and letting her shoulders drop a bit lower.

I close my eyes for a moment and then jerk suddenly as I feel her hand on my forehead. My eyes shoot open, and she pulls her hand back like she's been burned.

"Startled me," I lie. I didn't expect her touch. I'm glad I didn't instinctively reach out and pop her in the jaw.

"You're burning up, seriously." She reaches toward my chest, and I try to resist her, but my head keeps sagging from one side to the other. I sit up so that together, we can unzip my hoodie and try to get me cool.

"I like your shirt," she says gently as she pulls off both sleeves.

I drop my head and look down at my *Starlight Express* T-shirt.

My breathing slows down to normal, and without my hood, my temperature drops from lava to human levels. I look at this sweet girl who's just helped me through a full-blown panic attack. She looks sick and worried and confused, and I feel horrible.

I can't just go totally crazy and take her help and not tell her why.

"She died," I say. Softer than I mean to. "My mom."

Heat presses against me on all sides. I close my eyes and mumble into my lap while I force my shoulders to move up and down with my breaths.

"She was on her way home from the cast party of a stupid community theatre show and there was a semi-truck... He just didn't see her. I was ten."

The sweat that has beaded on my nose and upper lip starts to dry.

My lungs fill fully, and my skin cools almost instantly. I sit in quiet for a moment, Antonique beside me, her eyes wide.

"I'm usually okay, but sometimes, something can just hit me and take me by surprise."

Antonique's braids have fallen in front of her ears again but she doesn't seem to care. She lets them hang as she stares at me with sad eyes.

"I'm so sorry," she says. "I didn't mean to...I didn't know. I'm so sorry."

"No, Antonique, really. I have had panic attacks and...other problems for years. You didn't know, and I didn't know. It just happened."

She gives me a tiny smile, but she still looks shaken.

"Hey, at least if I had to go crazy, I did it in a padded room, right?" I joke, trying to make her laugh. Trying to make her remember that I'm not just the mortifying display she just saw. I don't want to be crazy in her eyes. Especially not after two days.

I reach across the space between us to pull myself back up and freeze like an animal being hunted.

I feel her eyes and my eyes travel down my exposed arm together.

They're faded for the most part, but when there's focus on my skin for more than a moment, they're definitely visible. The faint lines are whiter than the rest of my notably pale body. I consider pulling my arm back, but then I see her eyes flash away and I know there's no point. There's no little joke I can say. There's no way to make this not what it is.

She smiles gently.

"It must have really hurt." She swallows. I look at her as she looks at me, and she doesn't break eye contact. "Losing her, I mean. *That* must have really hurt."

I open my mouth to speak, but there is nothing I can say. I close my mouth again and give her a tiny nod.

She nods back, and the moment floats away.

She stands up and brushes the melancholy off like crumbs after cookies. "Should we go take a seat?"

"Yeah. I'll grab the box."

Since all of the packs aren't sitting in their little foam cubbies, the metal case is open and awkward, and I have freaking Tyrannosaurus arms, so it's only a few steps down the aisle, being bumped by passing ensemble members, before Antonique recognizes my struggle.

"Here, let me help you." She reaches toward me as kids continue to pass us in the aisle, and her long graceful arms look like they could wrap around the case twice with no trouble.

I try to hang on to it, but I feel my pride turn purple and bruise a bit as this tall and strong freshman takes the weight from my grip and effortlessly begins to walk down the aisle.

Twice in ten minutes, she's carried my burden. She saw me curled into a ball, barely breathing, and now she's saving me again. She doesn't even break a sweat.

The feeling of weakness, inside and out, stings at my confidence.

All at once, my sacred place—this room and this stage—seem out of my league. I'm supposed to feel strong here. I'm supposed to feel like I belong. Like I have something to give. But what does she—what do they all—see when they watch me out of breath, trying to carry this box or just carry myself through my job? The stickiness of my arms at my side and the feeling of my thighs rubbing together through my jeans must be calling them all to watch me.

Antonique walks effortlessly down the aisle toward the front of the auditorium where most of the cast is assembled and waiting for the start of rehearsal notes. Two separate dudes—two dudes who walked straight past me just seconds ago—jump out of their chairs and offer to grab the case from her.

My cheeks redden, and I close my eyes tight. When I open them again, I'm at the row where Antonique has taken a seat and saved one for me.

"Here you go, Sound Goddess." She smiles and doesn't even know that, in my own crazy head, she's spent the last sixty seconds making me feel like a loser. She reaches over to push down the folded-up seat so I can sit. One minute she's my savior. The next minute I hate her for being strong enough to save me. Shame flushes through my skin, and I feel goose bumps sprout up all over my arms.

Wow, I'm messed up in the head.

"Thanks," I say, taking the seat by her side. Maybe if I suck it up and stop being so annoying and whiny and jealous and childish, I'll feel better.

I try to wedge myself against the armrest opposite her so she's less aware of how tight the tiny auditorium chair is on my significant backside. The guys that helped her are still glancing over their shoulders at her while I try to melt into the chair unseen.

Grant's perched on the edge of the stage, and Gild is already spouting notes and objectives for the day.

"–Imogen?" I blink away my daze and see the whole lot staring at me as Gild repeats my name. "You have some instructions for microphone business today?"

It sounds, suddenly, like water is rushing through my head. The last thing in this known universe that I want to do right now is lug myself out of this chair and address fifty people who are looking at me as if I'm the main attraction in a freak show.

Oh my God, shut up, I tell myself. *They're looking at you like you're supposed to be talking. Because you're supposed to be talking. Hold it together!*

And then I see Grant.

My eyes slam into him with a thud I can feel in my lungs, and I take a deep breath as he gives me a wink.

"Yeah. I do. Um. My fish-kick, Antonique, and I are going to be showing you how you'll be wearing mics during the show. How to tape them, where to put the battery packs, and how they work. We're going to start with the guys so the girls can check with Brice about costume changes, and then we'll switch."

I'm sitting again and trying not to audibly gasp for air, and Gild is already barking other orders. Before I can catch my breath, everyone is disbanding, and Antonique sets her hand on my knee.

"You good to go?" she asks.

Her eyes are kind, and I glance to her hand.

"Yeah. Let's do this," I say, strengthened by her small display of solidarity.

I try to get the attention of a dozen teenage boys.

"We're going to have to strap the mic packs around your chest under your costumes, so when you come up, grab a pack and one of the elastic bands and we'll show you how to set the strap so it won't move."

My words seem lost in the crowd of inattentive ears, but I turn around and grab the first pack anyway.

I flick the on switch, untangle the wire, and loop the roll of mic tape around my index finger.

When I turn around, I nearly smash my face straight into the bare-naked chest of Andrew Bates.

"Oh!" I yelp and stumble back, so startled that I catch my left foot against my right. I'm plummeting to my doom in front of this half-naked man-boy, and as I'm imagining what my skin must look like as it's rippling in the wind, he steps forward and grabs my arms, steadying me and standing me upright in one fast motion.

"Dude, I'm so sorry." He says it as if he's the reason I tripped over my own body.

"No, it's fine. I...um...You do not have clothes on. I mean...Where is your shirt? You have lost your shirt."

I try to avert my eyes because somehow, looking at him without his shirt on isn't as fun as I might have thought it would be.

He chuckles for half of a second, and I'm not sure if he thinks I'm funny or if he thinks it's flattery, but then he says, "No, it's cool. You said it had to be strapped to our chests anyway, so I thought it would be easier like this."

"Okay. So, um...I need to show everyone how to do this."

I look over his head at the guys who have no intention of shutting up any time soon. I take a risk and look him in the eyes. I gesture over his shoulder with my head and give him a look that I hope means "please help me" and not "wanna be my topless-man-partner?"

"Guys! *Shut* it!" He grunts his command, and the rest of the monkeys fall silent as their alpha insists that they watch my demonstration.

Well, that was effective.

I clear my throat. "So, well, you need to, um..."

It is at this moment that by brain realizes that I will have to strap this mic pack around his chest. This will require the use of my hands. Which will be touching him. And his naked muscle-boobs, so...that's going to happen.

"Just clip the pack on the elastic here, and then wrap it all the way around you, cross it in the front, back to the back, cross it again, over the pack, and then pin it the rest of the way."

I look at him, but he's just staring up at the techies hanging lights and is utterly uninterested in the fact that my nose, once again, is virtually on his body and my godforsaken T-Rex arms are wrapping all the way around his back, over the front, and around back again.

Antonique grabs one side and pins it while I pin the other.

"Hey, what's your name?" Andrew, who has been only mildly interested for the past five minutes, is now channeling his inner skeezy, overly flirtatious macho man, raising his eyebrow and pointing his still very naked chest at her like a double-barrel Nerf gun.

I watch them for a second, but neither turns to look at me. I roll my eyes and step around them in front of the group of guys who have already started to chatter again.

"Guys!" I scream, and this time every single one of them turns and gives me their attention. "If you line up here, I'll get your pack and band."

I hand the chimps their bananas and watch as Andrew does this thing where he makes his shoulders look even wider, and I hear him say to Antonique, "Thanks for helping me get this thing tied on. I hope you'll be around to help me get it situated next time." He raises both eyebrows in unison and blasts her with a smile.

They're both giggling, and she's saying something about how he's a big boy and can certainly do it himself.

She is beaming with confidence and he's beaming with confidence and they're all confidency, and I realize that as far as he's concerned, she's the only one who pawed at him. I am a non-entity.

"Antonique, can you finish up with the guys and then get the girls squared away? We may have to keep the packs lower on their waist to fit under the bodices of the dresses."

She doesn't really look at me while she responds. She's staring at Andrew, who's cheesing at her. And it doesn't make me mad. I mean, she's a freshman and he's a junior and attention is awesome, I get it.

"Yeah, no problem, Sound Goddess." She smiles and gives me a thumbs-up. "Where are you going?" she asks without turning her head.

"I have some stuff I need to take care of in the booth. Looks like you've got all of this...handled." I can hear my tone. I sound bitter and sarcastic and, well, I sound an awful lot like Carmella.

She turns toward me and then cocks her head to the side like a tiny bird, and as her grin fades slowly, like water draining out of cupped hands, I step backward up the aisle, turn, and head toward the sound cave.

Antonique really needs to think about what kind of reputation she wants. Because if she's content to be a body with no brain, then by all means, she should keep flirting with half-naked guys just because they look at her funny. I mean, she's a sweet girl. She's not just pretty. So why do girls constantly shrink into giggling, eyelash-batting schoolgirls just because a guy gives them attention? Granted it was Andrew and he didn't have his shirt on...but still. Andrew doesn't have much in the way of brains, but apparently he uses the few neurons he does have to flirt with freshmen and laugh at people. 'Cause that's not a waste of oxygen.

"Knock, knock." The door to the sound booth opens quietly. Grant comes in and closes it behind him. Of course he's here. Antonique probably told him I freaked out earlier, and now I'm huffing off during mic duties so here comes Grant to reel me in.

"Hey." I shove my nose in the air and push my shoulders back before I calmly close my journal. Like there is any percent chance he hasn't already used his best friend Jedi powers to zero in on my emotional breakdown. I slide the spiral notebook into a binder and out of sight.

Grant leans back against the closed door and looks at me for a second before he speaks. "Everything okay? Did he—Andrew—I mean, did he say something to you?" At first I think he looks concerned, but then something about the way he clenches his jaw confuses me and I think he looks angry.

"Did Antonique talk to you? Are you mad or disappointed or something? 'Cause I definitely *can't* handle you coming in here and lecturing me right now."

Grant turns his eyes away from me to look down at the stage. "Lecturing? No. I want you to tell me what Andrew said."

"What are you even talking about?" He turns to me and I turn my chair so that we're facing each other dead on. I lock eyes with Grant and stare at his Protective-Boy-Face, and I don't even know what he could be thinking just happened down there.

"Nothing," he says, breaking our stare. He pulls on the neck of his T-shirt. "I just...I saw you working with him, and then he took his shirt off and then you seemed to bolt back up here." He looks to the floor and back to the window and then finally to me. "I just mean that I noticed you left right after that, and I wanted to be sure that he didn't do or say anything to upset you."

The look on Grant's face is unfamiliar. He looks angry and scowly. His brow is heavy, and there's not a single trace of his secret dimple.

I snap at him, "He literally didn't even know I was there. He was talking to Antonique pretty much the whole time, and it's not your job to worry about me—"

He fires back without lifting his head. "'Cause as the stage manager, it *is* my job to handle any conflicts or problems in the cast or crew."

It kills me that I don't know why he stopped looking at me. "Okay, and that's why you stomped up here? It wasn't to take care of fragile, broken Gen, was it? It's just your duty as stage manager!" I can feel the tension between us pushing against me, and I want to scream. I turn away from him because I can't stand the way he manages to look sad and angry without ever making eye contact.

"Oh God, Gen, of course not." He raises his voice and his hand and his head, finally. "If he hurt you, I would break his face. Don't—don't even start okay? I just came in here to check on you, to be sure he wasn't being a creep."

"Oh, he's a creepy, flirty, huge-ego-having assclown...just not to me!" I throw up my hands and paste on a plastic smile. "Isn't that great? No need to worry about that with me! For me to have a problem with a guy harassing me, a guy would have to notice me first, right? Well, don't worry—that doesn't happen! So. Yeah."

"Right...'Cause having a guy follow you across the auditorium to check on you and make sure you're okay is something that has never happened in the history of your existence? Except—oh wait! It totally did right now!"

I roll my eyes and start adjusting levels on the huge mixer board.

He reaches behind his back to twist the knob. He's pulled his bottom lip between his teeth, and his head is shaking back and forth slightly. He's standing there, and I can see it all over his face—in his sad angry eyes, in the way he's holding his breath and giving me time to respond. He's practically begging me to acknowledge his point and apologize. But every single time I put one foot in front of the other, it seems like a misstep today.

I feel heavy and tired and frustrated and invisible and disgusting, and I just want him to leave.

"Yeah, well, cross me off your stage manager list of obligations, okay? 'Sound designer wasn't harassed by castmate: check.' Job well done."

He purses his lips and wordlessly nods at me in a sarcastic, heartbreaking way. I hear him sigh as he goes.

I throw my Sharpie across the tabletop as I watch through the glass. He strides down the house left aisle, and all I can think of is how much I want him to turn around. But he doesn't. And then he's vanished into the stage right wing.

The walkie-talkie on the table squawks, and I hear Brice's bright voice.

"Imogen, can you come and help me in the costume room if you have a chance?"

In moments of sadness or frustration or anger, it always blows my mind when some small thing happens to remind me that the world hasn't stopped turning.

I scoot the chair back so I can lay my face on the cold desktop. I force myself to take five deep breaths before I reach over and grab the walkie-talkie off the table.

"Sure, B. I'll be right there."

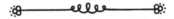

"There is no way this is going to fit her," I say, gaping at the dress—or should I call it a tent?—that Brice is holding up at the sewing machine, which is perched on a craft table in the center of the room. "I mean, it's way, way too big for Charity. This dress looks like it could nearly fit me."

Brice adjusts the hot pink dress on his machine and then steps on the pedal again. He has to shout to be heard over the hum. "Oh, the joys of period costumes. It's way easier and cheaper to make one of something and take it in over and over to fit new people."

He pauses to check his notes on the clipboard beside him.

"That makes sense," I say as I move another ensemble girl's dress to the "Fitted For Mics" rack.

"Of course it does." He clamps his pencil between his teeth and then sweeps Charity's hot pink ball gown around so he can take up the hem. He mumbles around the pencil clenched in his jaw, "Will you hand me a few of those pins?"

I grab the box and pull a safety pin out to twist between my fingers before handing a few straight pins over to Brice.

"So," I say, "I sorted out the dresses that I know will fit the packs, no problem. What else can I do? I don't want to go back out there with those idiots."

Brice laughs to himself and then turns to me, looking around, like he's checking for spies. "Oh, I don't really need much help," he whispers. He lowers his gaze and puts his hand up to his mouth like he's telling me a secret. "I'm pretty amazing at this, so..." He goes back to fiddling with the dress on his table. "Actually, false. Can you help me get this thing over the dress form?"

"Sure." I reach for the dress, which we drape over the headless, armless, surprisingly creepy torso on a stand. I really look at the dress for the first time. The entire show is done in an almost cheesy neon color scheme. It's like having fluffy princess dresses, but in bright green and highlighter yellow. Charity's statement dress is hot fuchsia and made in a corseted sort of style with lacing at the back.

Brice pulls in the excess fabric at the waist and examines it from the front. He mutters something to himself about having to take it in on both sides so the front panel will stay smooth. Without missing a beat, he shifts into full-voiced and chatty mode. "So the real reason I called you in here," he starts, "was so that I could totally spew some hot gossip and do my part to perpetuate the cultural stereotypes that I've been assigned."

I love that about Brice. He isn't trying to do or be anything but what he is, and he seems to be genuinely unconcerned with what that makes anyone else think. I wish I had that much self-confidence. I wish I had even half of that much self-confidence.

"Fair enough, spill it." I sit down on the floor near the bottom of the dress, and he flutters all around it, tucking and pinning and talking at breakneck speed.

"You're never going to believe this. Well, you probably will because, ugh, she's so freaking basic, but did you hear about your favorite stepsister and our leading man?"

I take a second so that my ears can catch up with my brain.

My brows furrow together. "No, what are you talking about? I mean, they're partners and library cuddle-buddies as of English class yesterday."

"Oh, it's more than partners. She's got Andrew—or Captain Tight Pants Junior as I like to call him—all sorts of wrapped tight around her finger—even tighter than his pants, which is significant. I mean, I almost feel like I'm doing him a cruelty by not introducing him to some relaxed-fits."

Immediately, my mind goes to last night when she was half-naked in the hallway flirting with Grant. Asking him about the Rally. Somehow, even when she was flirting with Andrew yesterday, I got the feeling she was just playing a game.

"Wow," I say. I try to make my voice sound like his. Interested and lighthearted.

"I *know*," Brice says.

I envy that he's able to talk about her so casually. Just a girl. A mean, attention-seeking girl, but pretty much just another girl.

I twist the safety pin I've been playing with back and forth between my fingers and soak up the feeling that is pouring out of Brice. Silliness and friendship and a little cattiness.

Four or five voices rush down the hallway, each of them speaking about some prop or light or scene. I make out one of the voices as Grant's.

They don't even look in the room, but I put my head down anyway, hoping to hide. I don't want to see Grant right now. Especially seeing as twenty minutes ago I was throwing my writing implement like a two-year-old having a proper tantrum.

Once he's passed, I bring my attention back to Brice in progress. "...Dead serious. She apparently asked Andrew all about the Rally next month, and when he visibly swooned and panted at her like a Rottweiler, she—allegedly—" Brice holds up open palms as if to say he's *only* passing on what he heard and that he can't be held responsible for the authenticity of his words. "—batted those eyelashes, and Andrew asked for her hand faster than a guy on *The Bachelor*. Can you believe that? The first day!"

"Uh, yeah, I can believe that. And did you know that she asked out Grant first and got rejected? You should have seen her the other night. She was prancing around the house in freaking booty shorts right in front of him. And me. Seems so desperate."

"Oh, she could be desperate," Brice says. "And we can think she's ridiculous. But *not* because of her clothes." He raises a finger to me playfully. "I'm afraid questioning a person's right to wear booty shorts is against my religion. Self-expression is holy."

I smile away the wisp of embarrassment at being so masterfully called out.

Brice grins and goes back to pinning and tucking, and then he checks his clipboard.

"You know," I say, "you're right. I shouldn't judge a girl by her hot pants. I'll try to remember that next time she leaves my pillowcase stuffed with candy bar wrappers or reminds me to bleach my handlebar mustache."

I stick the sharp end of the pin into my mouth and pinch it between my teeth for a second. The metal makes my teeth ache almost as much as biting into a popsicle stick.

Brice turns to me with big eyes and stares while he gathers his words. "Listen to me. You let me know if this girl comes in here and starts drama with you because if she does, she's got a cooter-punch coming from me. I can tell you that right now."

I look up at Brice with a smile just as I hear Grant march down the hall again, shouting to someone about spotlights. Guilt presses on me like a pin. It has been a *really* bad couple of days. I knew things would be weird when Carmella got here, but derail my whole life?

I was really ugly to Grant, who only wanted to check on me. And I was really unfair to Antonique who'd literally just held my hand during a panic attack. And I had an emergency session with TG after a breakdown over breakfast. I can't remember the last time I had a mood swing this extreme. It's been months for sure.

And I'm suddenly, absolutely afraid of my slipping grip.

"So, tell me. What do you think about my mister?" Brice asks, breaking my thoughts and pulling me back into the tiny room filled with the hum of his machine.

"Jonathan's really sweet. He seems like this super-quiet guy, and then he'll just randomly do something super-bold or funny or whatever. He's cool."

"Isn't he? I love that he's never what I expect."

I can practically see stars in Brice's eyes. It's adorable.

But it also makes me ache.

"But enough about me. You have some dishing to do, Miss Imogen. Ugh!" Brice lets out an annoyed growl, rips out all of his pins and starts again.

"Do I?"

"Well..." He speaks like he's making an apology for a toddler's hissy-fit at daycare. "As I recall, you got a little touchy on Sunday after dropping a little dollop of gossip, and I was wondering if you'd maybe taken a couple of chill-pills so that you could *finally* tell me the good stuff?" I have no idea what he's talking about. Thankfully, he continues, "You can't tell me there was an almost-kiss and not give me details. You just can't."

He claps his hands together, preparing to beg.

I tap the tip of my finger on the point of the pin.

It's not that I don't want to tell him. The idea of telling anybody about it, talking about it at all, does have some appeal. I sure didn't tell freaking George about it, and the only other person I would have turned to after getting rejected when I thought I'd try kissing Grant is...Grant.

But if I tell Brice, I'll have told him.

And then it will be a thing. And I won't ever be able to pretend it never existed.

I'm not sure if it's his eager eyes or the fact that I feel like I've shortchanged everyone in my bubble in the past eight hours, but I make the decision to speak.

"It was around New Year's. Not, like, New Year's Eve or anything, but it was sometime right after Christmas."

It was December 28th, sometime after 2:00 AM. My body knows the moment in the same way some people wake up just minutes or seconds before their alarm goes off.

I pull my gaze down and swallow the brick I feel lodged in my throat.

"I wasn't doing very well," I mumble into my hands. I look at Brice, hoping he'll be nodding at me to continue, but he's waiting for me to clarify. "It was around the anniversary of when my mom died, so I was pretty sad most of the time. Christmas is always really hard."

I check again.

He's nodding me on, thank God.

I push the pin closed and hold it between my thumb and first finger like a tiny vial.

"So, anyway, Grant was staying with me a lot during that time. Grant would make sure I ate enough or that I didn't lie in bed for days at a time. So my dad didn't mind having him around. Grant's kinda always been my one thing, you know?"

"It sounds pretty intense." Brice sits down across from me on the floor and puts his hands on top of my knees. I'm glad he does.

"It was intense. Things got bad. Like, they were fitting-me-for-my-custom-straitjacket bad."

"Well, obviously. Nothing off the rack." Brice smiles gently, but continues to pry me open with his eyes.

"And on this day, my doctor had prescribed me some sedatives, just so I could get some sleep. I wake up, all groggy and crazy-drugged out of my mind, and Grant is sitting on the side of my bed. And he's sort of crying."

"Like alligator tears or misty-eyed?"

"Misty-eyed. I look up at him, and he looks down at me and he just says, 'I love you.' Which, isn't, like, a weird thing to say. We say that kind of thing all the time, and we've been best friends since we were, like, so young. We're family."

I reach up and tuck a strand of hair behind my ear.

"Oh no." Brice leans even closer into me, and I nod my head at him and confirm his cringe-worthy hypothesis.

"Yep. I sorta sit myself up, face all tear-swollen, high as a kite on whatever they gave me, and I put my hand around the back of his head and I try to kiss him."

"Oh. My. God."

"I know."

"And so he pulled away?"

"Well, yeah, Brice, can you blame him? Some mangled-up, overweight zombie wakes up and tries to eat your face, wouldn't you?"

Brice doesn't laugh. And that makes him even more awesome.

"Did he say anything?" Brice asks.

"Well, once he pulled away, he sorta pushed me back onto my pillow. And I was already about to go under again, but I remember he sorta tucked in the covers and said, 'It's not time for you to wake up yet.'"

I pop open the pin and cross my arms as the memory washes over me like a bucket of cold water.

"Wow," Brice says. "I mean, on one hand, it was sweet that he knew you really needed the rest. But he said he loved you. Maybe you misunderstood. Maybe he does want more, but he just didn't want to kiss you because you were all hopped up on drugs and you wouldn't have remembered it anyway..."

"Yeah. Maybe," I say with a cynical snarl.

All I wanted in the whole world was more of him.

I wanted more of him so that maybe I'd *need* less of him.

But Grant was looking for a way to reject me without rejecting me. Gently and kindly and without shaming me into oblivion, he'd made his feelings clear.

I think the reason he never actually *said* "no, Gen, I don't love you like that, and I don't want to kiss you" was so that I'd never have to remember the moment he said the words that broke my heart.

Brice continues to look at me with his hands on my knee and his head tilted in sympathy. I look over my shoulder just as a parade of ensemble members cuts through the hallways to practice their opening entrance and Gild calls for the girls' dancing skirts.

"I better get back to it."

"Yeah," I say, "I better go wrap things up with Antonique in the booth."

Brice stands up and continues his work at the hot pink dress, and while his back is turned, I look down at the pin in my hand.

The left sleeve of my hoodie is caught on my watch, and I'm holding the tip of the pin against the pink of my skin. The point is pressing, right into the soft space between my thumb and forefinger on the palm of my hand, and it looks like my skin is being sucked down a drain where it touches. Just as the pressure threatens to pierce my flesh, just as the pin might draw the tiniest speck of red, I jump when Brice says, "Hey, can you hand me a pin before you go?"

Immediately, I stop poking myself and turn to see he's holding some folds of fabric in just the right position. I lean toward the mannequin, and hold the pin for him right next to his fingers. He wriggles his thumb and first finger free so that he can work it through the material and close it in place.

"Thanks," he says.

"No, thank you—for asking about my juicy gossip again. Not that I totally wanted to talk about it or anything, but it was nice to talk. In general."

"Anytime, cupcake," he says. "Oh, speaking of cake, do you and Grant want to come with Jonathan and me for late night pancakes after rehearsal?"

"Yeah, that sounds great." I surprise myself by asking, "Do you mind if I invite Antonique?"

"Isn't that your fish-kick?" he asks.

She is if she hasn't already told Gild she's quitting because her mentor went all crazypants today and abandoned her with a mountain of mic packs.

"Yeah. I think she'd really like to come."

And I'd like to say I'm sorry.

"Well, of course she can come," he says brightly without turning from his work.

I stop at the door and say, over my shoulder, "And next time I want to hear all about you and Jonathan, okay?"

He nods. Before he can return some pleasantry, I pull down my sleeve and close the door behind me.

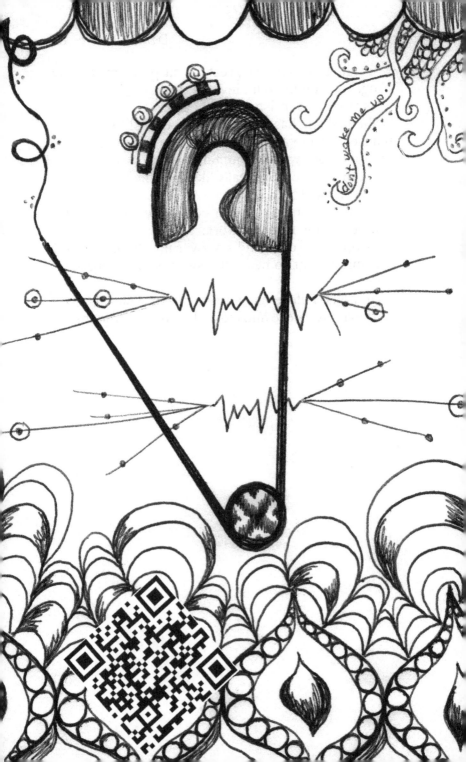

14

The hardest part about having pancakes with other human beings at eleven o'clock on a school night is that it would be considered rude to pour the syrup straight into my mouth.

Grant is across from me, stacking what's left of his sausages like Lincoln Logs. He's pulled little bits of pancake apart to look like what I can only assume would be mortar.

On the ride over, I apologized to Grant for being totally out of line. He said "it's okay" a lot, which left me wanting because I know the shape of his mouth when he's annoyed and I know his frustration is still creeping under the surface.

But if he wants to be okay, I can be okay.

It seems like guys just need the space to be a little bit "not okay" until they just, randomly, are again.

Next to me, Antonique asks Grant with a grossed-out smile, "What did that food ever do to you?"

He looks up at her from under his dark eyelashes, his face crooked from smirking. "I was thinking about the structural integrity of pork as a building material."

He gestures to his architectural project as if it's the most obvious thing in the world.

"I see your point," I interject. "That is a fine-looking piece of meat."

"Did someone say my name?" Brice asks, extracting his face from Jonathan's for the first time in ten minutes.

Jonathan rolls his blue eyes and drops his chin, smiling and shaking his head as we all start laughing. They look at each other and smile as Antonique and Grant continue to debate the best breakfast building materials.

While they're otherwise distracted, I take a second to look at each one of them in turn.

I glance at my Grant, who has always been there. Then I watch Brice for a second, and I think about how fun it is to talk with him and how nice it is to have a friendship that isn't complicated or weighed down with serious stuff all the time. As Antonique's laugh catches my attention, I look to her and see someone who I've known for two days and who's already seen deeper into my emotional closet than almost anyone. Jonathan saved me in English class and I don't know much about him, but I appreciate that he's a friend to Grant. And I appreciate that he's a love for Brice.

I sit back and press my shoulder blades against the vinyl booth.

I don't want to worry about who I am or how awesome it feels to be sitting with four people who actually seem to like me. Other than Grant, not one of these people would have been in my life this time last year.

There just wasn't enough of me for them to see.

I smile and shake it off as I pick up my mostly empty glass of orange juice and gulp it down.

It's now that I notice Grant is staring at me.

"What?" I mouth.

"What?" he responds. His lips move without making a sound.

He smiles and leans his body across the little table strewn with half-empty plates filmed with the remains of maple syrup. Our cash is piled up unceremoniously on our bill. I lean closer to him before whispering.

"I was just wondering how a girl who is as messed up as me managed to be here. With other humans. Who don't seem to hate me. Kinda makes me nervous I'll mess it up. I've gotta be honest—today really scared me. Getting so upset at you and reacting that way toward Antonique and Andrew. Every little thing was pressing every one of my buttons. And it's scary, you know? Like how did I feel so good on Saturday and feel so horrible now? I can't handle another bad spell."

Grant takes the last sip from his cup and averts his eyes. "I swear, Gen, sometimes I think you're addicted to being worried about stupid crap you can't even change. Like you somehow enjoy the familiarity of feeling OH-MY-GAWD-SO-TOTALLY-CRAZY."

My head pulls back, and his words recoil like a fist. He's trying to keep his tone lighthearted, but his eyes are searing and his lips are pulled thin. Something about his words and the way my day has gone makes it all seem very, very upsetting. I try to keep things light.

"Ouch. No. Grant, I'm okay. I am. I'm just also aware of the fact that I've got—at best—a fifty-fifty chance of blowing it with all of them and being alone and friendless again." I try to smile through my self-deprecation.

For the second time today, the edges of his mouth turn downward slowly. His face sets like concrete. "Alone? Seriously? Alone. Right, because—no, you know what? Forget it."

"Come on, Grant, you know what I mean."

His voice is low, but I know the others can still hear him. "No, Gen. I don't." He lowers his voice even more as we pretend that our friends only inches away aren't trying super-hard to ignore the tension growing on the other side of the ketchup bottle. "This is the same crap you pulled in the booth today! Don't apologize for saying stupid, thoughtless crap and then turn around and say the same stuff a few hours later! You know what your problem is, Gen? It's not your depression or your anxiety. It's fear. You're blinded by fear. That's your problem. You're blind, and you just don't see. Anything."

I feel an electric tug, right through my belly button, and my heart starts beating double time. The confusion. It's killing me. His whole presentation, his whole rant makes me feel like I want to hold him and tell him I'm sorry. And it makes me feel like he wants me to.

But I know that's a lie. I know that I tried once and I won't take a risk like that again.

How can he wonder why I'm scared when a huge part of why I am is because I never want to see his December 28th, 2:00 AM face again?

Grant stands up, sending his paper napkin fluttering to the floor. He bumps the table edge, and I watch as the contents of every glass jiggle. He turns away from the table for a second before looking back to the group and saying, "I've got to get going, guys. I'll see you at rehearsal tomorrow."

"Grant, you can't just walk home. Let me drive you," I say.

If I weren't with three other people and stuck in this booth, I would jump out and stop him.

He raises a hand as if doing so is the only thing keeping him from saying about a million other things he could never take back.

And I want to know what they are, but I also totally, totally don't.

"I've got it, Gen. Don't worry about it."

Without another word, Grant grabs his backpack off the back of his chair, and he's gone.

Once again, I'm just trying to connect the dots.

Antonique to Mom to panic attack.

Andrew to jealousy to treating Grant like crap.

Grant feeling invisible by my saying that I feel invisible...It feels like something's missing.

"Hey, love," Brice says from his spot in the crook of Jonathan's shoulder, "is everything okay?"

"Yeah. It's fine." I look away and throw my bag over my arm. "Look, I think I'm going to just head out, too. Um, Antonique, do you still want a ride?"

The last thing I want is to take her home, honestly. Only because I'm sure she'll want to talk, and there's no good way to tell her that I need her to shut it until tomorrow.

Jonathan looks up at me and shakes his dirty blond hair out of his eyes. "I can take her if you need to go, or I could always call Grant and make sure he's okay."

For a moment, I consider taking him up on it. All of it.

"No, really, it's no big deal." I turn to Antonique who is still a bit wide-eyed and anxiously twisting at her braids. "That is, of course, if you're ready to go?"

"Yeah, totally," she says. "See you two tomorrow." She waves timidly to the lovebirds, and I try to ignore the facial expression Brice flashes her that I assume means: good luck with her.

In the car, Antonique tries again to start a conversation. Her previous three attempts at making small talk have fizzled like dud firecrackers.

"Imogen?" Antonique reaches up and turns the air conditioner vent in the Grannymobile away from her and toward the window.

Attempt number four.

"Yeah?"

"Do you, um... Have I made you mad?" She asks this as if that would actually be a sad thing to her, and I almost burst into tears.

"No. No, absolutely not."

"Oh."

I scratch the crack in the plastic at the bottom of my steering wheel. "I'm sorry about today, Antonique. Leaving you with the guys and the mic packs."

She mutters okay toward the window, but I feel like I have to say more if I want to fix this.

"I don't want to make excuses, but I have almost no practice at being a good friend. Today was just the worst, all around. I'm really sorry."

"Can I tell you something?" she asks without looking at me.

"Okay."

"I'm weird and shy and feel the same way. Like, I worry that everyone thinks I'm weird, or that as the new kid, I'll never make friends here. I feel awkward and alone all the time. Just like you. Well, except I don't know what it feels like to have depression."

I try not to think about how she made the word "depression" sound like the word "cancer." I busy myself with looking in my mirrors and try to calm my stomach that is now tense with knots.

"It's awfully hard to imagine you being the awkward new kid. I didn't know you were a transfer."

"Yep. Just moved this summer. Crestwood is nothing like my old school."

"Yeah. It's pretty huge," I say.

"No, it's gigantic. Like, enormous. And everyone seems to already know all the people they plan to hang out with, and I just...It's really hard to find a group of friends, you know?"

I've been here forever, and I still don't have many. As a matter of fact, I'm pretty sure my first "group" of friends is about forty-eight hours old.

Antonique looks out the passenger side window, and I get a chill over my skin when I think about what I felt and wrote about her today.

Guilt rises in my throat like bile, and I nibble on my bottom lip as she gestures to which house is hers.

"Thanks for the ride," she says.

"It's not a big deal," I say.

I'm glad I had the distraction.

She grins at me and grabs her bag from the floorboard. Her eyes are bright in the darkness, and I feel like warm, happy feelings are shining straight from her smile. She peeks her head back inside the car door for just a moment and answers, "Yeah. It is."

’m bad at lots of things. Bad at walking through a crowded room alone and looking at something other than my feet. Bad at not pissing off my best friend. But I'm extra-super-seriously bad at sleeping when I'm anxious.

I will myself to stay in bed until my alarm goes off just on principle, and once it does, my phone pings again and a message from Grant pops up.

"Didn't want to text till you'd be awake. Have to go to school early for contest stuff. Don't need a ride. See you later."

So here's where I should text him back and apologize for being so annoying yesterday and tell him that I know I was ridiculous. The thing at the restaurant was just blown out of proportion, but the reason he snapped at me was because of what happened when I snapped at him in the sound booth. I know I struck a nerve.

I was cold and said things I don't even believe.

I'm big enough to say I'm sorry. But...

"OK" I type.

Great. Good job. You selfish, stupid girl.

I search through my closet for the least dirty pair of jeans to coordinate with the self-loathing I'm wearing.

Come on, Imogen. He deserves better than that.

As I grab my bag, I look at our texts. My heart cracks. I feel it. I hear it.

I risk my very life as I type while walking down the stairs.

"I'm sorry."

I watch, and I see that he starts to type. As I enter the kitchen, the little graphic disappears. He's stopped typing. Or deleted it. A reply never comes.

In the kitchen, I microwave two sausage, egg, and cheese breakfast sandwiches and find a note from Evelyn on the counter.

"Hi, sweetie. I had to run to an early morning yoga class, and Carmella had something early at school. Be sure to lock up, and have a great day! :)"

I crumple the note in a ball and toss it into the recycle bin. How can a morning completely absent of any physical human contact make me so completely irritated by people?

I toss another breakfast sandwich into the microwave for good measure.

It isn't until I'm walking up to the school that I realize I didn't have to deal with first period yesterday. I make a beeline for the counseling office so I can be sure Evelyn made the call about changing my schedule.

The receptionist has a pair of glasses pushed up on top of her head and another pair hanging from a beaded chain around her neck. At the counter, I don't wait for her to see me. I just sort of start talking.

"Hi. My name is Imogen Keegan, K-E-E-G-A-N, and my stepmom was supposed to call and leave word that my schedule should be changed. My first period. Some other English class, I don't really care, but I need to make sure my schedule is totally, definitely changed."

I throw my thumb against my teeth and start gnawing at my cuticle while she wordlessly clickity-clacks on her keyboard. "Your first period class is Mr. Reed's junior English."

"No, it *was* Mr. Reed's junior English, but now it should be something different."

"We do not have a change on file for you, and there are no notes about your stepmom calling about your schedule."

I rub my left hand against the pocket of my jeans. Maybe the thick seam will scrape away my nerves before I completely freak out.

"I can't go. I can't. Could you please call her? Maybe she forgot."

"There's no note," she says.

"I can't go to that class!" I hear my voice echo in the small office, and two teachers stop in their tracks in the mail room behind the front desk.

She blinks at me and makes a pissy little scowl with her lips.

"I am in the middle of other things right now, and frankly, it's not the first month of school anymore and you need to attend your assigned class. Or we can escalate this if you'd prefer." She reaches down and holds up a pad of paper that says "Discipline Referral Form" on the top, and I can see that I'm not getting anywhere with Miss Six-Eyes, so I take my soggy hands and my soggy eyes and turn to walk out the door just as the bell rings for first period.

While I was playing ninja in the hallways yesterday, trying to avoid Carmella during every single passing period, I figured out which hallway houses her locker.

Of course, since I came in by the front office, I'll have to walk down that hallway to get to the library to meet my class.

I walk on my tiptoes, my neck craning to see over the heads and shoulders of all of the kids who are taller than me and who are filling the hallways like a flood. I bump and push past people, and I don't even hug the wall. I need a clear view if I'm going to avoid her.

I start to imagine what Carmella will put me through today. Maybe she's going to lead them in a chorus of jeers as I enter, or maybe she'll have a bucket of mac and cheese ready to dump on my head in a more delicious version of a horror movie scenario.

"Please just leave me alone," I mutter to myself as I pull open the double door of the library. We're working on our research, and I scan the room for Jonathan after waving at Mr. Reed, who checks me off of his attendance sheet.

I look from corner to corner and I can't see Carmella's perfect hair or her perfect face anywhere, but there's Jonathan. He's snagged us a table tucked in the most quiet, isolated corner of the two-story library.

Thankfully, our table is tiny, but the chairs are pretty big. I'm comfortable when I sit—something I haven't experienced at school in a very long time. Jonathan's notes are spread out, and his hands are hidden under the table.

I glance over my shoulder again, half-expecting for Carmella to jump out from behind a shelf screaming something horrible at me, but I still can't see her anywhere.

"Where is she?" I mumble as I crane my neck. There's no chance of me focusing until I find her. I know she's here. Her mom said she'd be at school today.

"Who—Cinderella?" Jonathan asks with a grin spreading across his face.

I smirk and point my finger at him. "Don't call her that."

He laughs and reaches up to turn the page.

I can't help but steal a glance. I've felt something weird must be going on with his hands since I noticed he's always got at least one of them shoved deep in his pocket. I'm leaning over, trying and failing at being stealthy while looking for missing fingers, warts, or webbing.

"Miss Keegan?"

I let out a tiny scream and almost fall out of my chair when Mr. Reed says my name directly behind me.

He uses his hand to smooth over his hair—side to side, not front to back—and then he asks, "Have I already given you two a rubric?" He sets a sheet of paper on the table before we can answer. "Make sure you reference at least five print sources and cite them correctly on your works cited page. Do you two have everything you need?"

"Yeah. I think we're fine, but um..." I clear my throat. "Is Ella, my stepsister, here?"

Mr. Reed points to a Post-it note on his clipboard. "I received an email yesterday afternoon stating that Miss Cinder would not be in my first period class after all. I believe her mother called and requested a schedule change."

"She did?"

I'm not complaining, but what would have made Evelyn change Precious Princess's schedule instead of mine? How would she know that was the problem?

Oh God, I hope Evelyn hasn't, like, figured something out and is planning a George-ified intervention. I'll jump through his sixth-floor window, I am not even kidding.

"Apparently so," Mr. Reed says as he sniffles and tugs at the waistband of his ill-fitting trousers. I can't help but notice that they're so long he's stepping on the back of the hem. "Now, back to work, please."

He stuffs his clipboard under his arm and continues making rounds throughout the library.

I swear, little singing birds start flying around my head, and the entire room fills with rainbows and kittens. If this were a musical, and everyone in the library knew the choreography, and if we had a really amazing, bouncy, peppy score (something modern like Jason Robert Brown, not classic like Gershwin), I would gladly dance my way through this musical number and jazz hands my ass right to the top of the circulation desk.

"Congratulations," Jonathan says as I reach for my phone. I smile. My heart is paper-light as I text Grant the good news.

At some point this morning, he decided to answer my text after all: "*I know. Me too. Lunch in courtyard today?*"

"*Sure.* ☺" I reply.

I pull out my tiny white earbuds and turn on my "Try to Be Happy, Dummy" playlist.

Just a few hours without Cinder-comma-Ella, and I'm already feeling happier. If I close my eyes and focus on the music, I can almost convince myself she was never here in the first place.

"Okay, that isn't hopping or running or skipping, but it could be frolicking. Are you frolicking?" Grant asks as he stands to greet me in the courtyard with his sandwich in hand and his soda on the picnic table.

The sky is perfectly blue, and I'm still imagining a big dance number featuring all of the nearby squirrels and ladybugs. I glance at the mural as I walk by and do a quick sweep, top to bottom. I pick a two-foot wide section and scan it all the way down to the grass. I set down my tray and continue to circle the table until I'm on his side.

Grant reaches over and wraps his sandwich hand around my shoulders, hugging me into his chest.

I speak, muffled, into his shirt. "First, yes. I would call that frolicking. Second, hi. Third, yesterday was a really, really bad day. Really bad. And I'm sorry I took it out on you."

He leans his head down, and I feel his cheek resting against mine. He closes his arm around tighter. The smell of his grape jelly makes me grin.

His speech sounds soft as it whispers through my hair. "I know. I shouldn't have huffed off like a brat." His sandwich has the cutest little nibbles taken out of it.

"But you are a brat." I push against his shoulders, and he fakes a giant groan of pain and staggers back as if I've given him a roundhouse kick to the neck.

He brushes his T-shirt smooth (it uses Barium, Carbon, Oxygen, and Nitrogen to spell BaCON) and then comes back to the table to sit. I do the same. We're positioned on one side of the table, facing the south wall mural because we always look when we're here. He knows the drill.

"I really am sorry," I say.

"I know. Me too." He leans over to bump my shoulder and takes a huge bite of his sandwich. Mouth full of sticky peanut butter, he says, "So congratulations on a Carmella-free English class. How did that happen?"

"Well..." I pull apart my white dinner roll and smear my white mashed potatoes across the sections in my white Styrofoam tray. "They changed her schedule, I don't know why, but she's gone."

"I thought you asked Evelyn to call and change *your* schedule."

"I did, but Reed said that Evelyn called to change Carmella's instead. I just got lucky, I guess. Maybe Carmella had to find some way to replace her class on Post-Modern Industrialism in the Western World or something."

"What?" Grant lets his sandwich-filled mouth hang open with confusion.

Even when he's gross, he's not gross.

"Nothing. Whatever. Anyway, I am basically the happiest girl in the world. I probably won't ever have to see her again."

I'm distracted by some freshmen boys that charge out of the cafeteria and chase each other through the courtyard, jumping through a circle of girls who are sitting and eating in a big, bubbly ring on the grass.

"Okay, you do remember that you live in the same house. In adjacent rooms."

"Yes, Grant, I remember. But we've got rehearsals almost every night, and she's got dance team practice, plus you and I get here early, and—I don't know—I'm just feeling optimistic!"

"Oh my God." Grant stares at me and sets down the last bit of his sandwich.

"What?" I ask, looking over my shoulder.

"Oh my God!"

"*What?*"

Grant stands up and shouts across the courtyard, "Ladies and gentlemen! Imogen is feeling optimistic! Cake for everyone!"

"Oh shut your mouth, Thornton!" I throw a bit of bread at him and look around to make sure that he didn't actually get anyone's attention. He didn't.

"See anything new?" Grant asks as I turn my face to the wall again. Top to bottom, starting with that big red "C." Just outside my field of vision, I sense him turn his head to the wall. When my eyes get all the way to the grass, I let out a little sigh and let my gaze wander back to the top.

"See that blue dog up there?" I point above our heads at this pathetic-looking blue dog with a striped tail. "I thought that might be hers. Then I realized the stripes spelled 'Tommy Rules' so..."

"Not hers." He continues to stare at the wall beside me. The breeze blows, and I smell his hair goop, strong and boy-scented, like the smell of soap and cheap grocery store cologne and a little bit of something else.

"Definitely not," I agree.

I scan another large stripe.

"Have you ever considered that maybe she didn't paint anything? I mean, how do you know she even put something up there?" Grant continues to scan the wall.

"I just know. Her whole class did it before their graduation. It's not really her style to sit out and be a bystander when it comes to a public display of anything."

Or it *wasn't* really her style.

I drop my chin.

"It's been a tough few days, Gen, I know that."

"Yeah." I nod my head and mumble toward my chest, "You have no idea."

"Yes. I do." He turns on the bench and grabs my knees, forcing me to spin on my seat and face him. "I know that you're scared of change. We all are. And I know you don't know how you and Carmella are gonna share a family. But I know you're strong."

I brush my hands through my hair—avoiding his statement with conviction.

Grant reaches up and puts his hands on the sides of my face very gently. His more-green-than-brown eyes are full of fire. "You are stronger than you give yourself credit for. She does not have the power to hurt you unless you let her. And you are doing what you need to do to stay well. Seeing George. Journaling. Whatever. Do you know how hard that is? How many people never do that?"

"I guess so. And I guess if Dad's happy to pay for extra sessions, why not go? If one session is good, three is better, right?"

"Yep. It's multiplication. Math is never wrong."

He smiles. His hands are so soft on my cheeks. I notice the way his chest moves with each breath, and my eyelids close and open slowly as I look into his face.

My voice comes out softer than I mean for it to. "Very good point."

Also very good face.

Grant snaps his hands back into his lap so fast it almost makes me jump. The absence of his palms on my cheeks leaves them feeling cold. He glances at his watch. "Uh, so, no tech rehearsal tonight." He shifts his weight back and forth twice before I answer his non-question.

"Right. Do you wanna study for your science thing later? Your preliminaries for regional are tomorrow."

He hoists his bag over his shoulder. "Yep. We're the home school so our 'field trip' is to our own gym. How stupid is that?" He rolls his eyes, and I just almost die. He looks at me for a second, and then shifts his backpack to the other side and blurts, "Okay. I'll, uh, see you later." He takes off toward the building, and I sit there. My stomach lurches after him, like my whole body wants to be tugged along with him when he goes. A tug like gravity.

"Bye." I sort of toss out the word as the abrupt end to our meeting makes my head go crazy with all of the worst kinds of doubts.

Maybe he stopped holding my face because I have food in my teeth.

Or horrible school-lunch breath.

Or maybe he saw my eyes go all starry and worried that I was getting the wrong idea about his strictly platonic face-holding.

I close my eyes for a second to listen to my breathing and keep it slow. When I open them again, my eyes instinctively scan the wall one more time while I gather my bag. I notice a cluster of color near the base of the wall: tiny leaves are painted in the midst of their fall. Red, gold, and green, their concrete tree in a perpetual state of losing. The largest leaf, forever caught on the wind, is more green than brown, but definitely both.

For the first time, I smile as I leave the wall behind me.

"Okay, this malaria treatment is an alkaloid and comes from a tree called Cincho—"

"Quinine!"

"Okay, sure. Ummm..." I sigh and flip through the flashcards for another question that I can reasonably expect to pronounce properly.

"Come on, Gen, pick a hard one."

"Yeah, 'cause I know which ones are hard ones, right?" I know I sound snippy, so I tack on a half-hearted smile at the end and kick out with my fuzzy-socked foot. He's lying across the chair in my room, and his legs are so long that, from knee to ankle, they're on my bed, too.

"Oh! I know this one!" I say. My eyebrows shoot to the sky, and my face beams with pride. "The SI unit for power is named for the guy Watt! Bam! Scienced!"

"Did you just verb the word science?"

"Yes, Grant. I did."

He grins at me and gives me a little round of applause. "Well, then maybe you should come to the competition with me."

"Uh, no." I giggle. The grade on my last lab flashes before my eyes.

"And why not, Super-Genius?"

I go back to flipping through flashcards. "Uh, because most of what I know about science, I learned from your dumb shirts."

He laughs and I laugh, but it feels stretched.

The up and down is killing me.

A new mood every hour. A new version of myself to try and shove toward normalcy.

"Could you two keep it down in here?" Carmella purrs her request over my head.

I turn and see her standing in my doorway in a different pair of those dang booty shorts and a tank top. She must go shopping at that store in the mall that all the sixth grade girls are obsessed with because where else would she even get shorts that size?

"Carmella, will you please stay out of my room?" I growl at her.

"Ella," she snaps. "I know sometimes you have to hear things more than once for it to really sink in, but my name is Ella, okay?" She pushes her hand through her hair and then fluffs up the ends that are resting across her chest.

"Hey, hey, hey, no need to be rude, okay?" Grant's voice is so plain and steady. He's scolding her and still managing to sound like a nice guy. On one hand, I'm pleased to see him defending me, but on the other hand, he's having a really hard time turning away from her in her her effing United Federation of Booty Shorts Enthusiasts uniform.

"I didn't mean to sound snippy. It's just that I'm so tired from dance, and I really need my sleep. And I was just downstairs, and my mom says that Grant needs to go home now. It's already after ten."

She puts her hand on her hip, and I push myself up to sitting. Something about this day and the pendulum swing has me ready for a fight.

"Excuse me?"

"I didn't use a word you don't understand, did I?"

I try not to sound panicked, even though I am. "You and your mom don't get to decide when he leaves. My dad does. And as far as he's concerned, Grant is family, so why don't you get out of my room and stay out of my business."

I watch as Carmella's eyebrows twitch in surprise.

Beside me, I can feel Grant's surprise, too.

"Your dad makes the rules?" she asks. "How does he manage that when he's not actually here? I mean, I don't blame him. If I had to choose between presenting my opportunistic memoir to sad, old people in dusty library meeting rooms or being here with you, I know what I'd pick." She reaches up to scratch her side, and her fingertips lift up the edge of her shirt just the tiniest amount. A sliver of her tan, flat stomach peeks out from under the white tank.

That flash of skin is a middle finger. It's a declaration of war. It's a not-so-subtle message from her to me that she is what she is and I am what I am.

I stand. Slowly.

She's taller than I am, and even with her all the way over by the door, I feel her looking down at me.

"Get. Out." The words fall to the hardwood floors in two steady thuds. I don't raise my voice, but I've never felt so ignited. I've never felt so close to running across the room and attacking her like a sumo wrestler.

"Good night, Grant. Good luck at your competition tomorrow." Carmella smiles at him and turns around. I think she pauses for a solid three seconds, with her shorts barely covering her butt, just to be sure that Grant has time to see her before she pulls the door closed behind her.

My shoulders rise and fall with each breath; each inhale and exhale comes quickly. My sweaty hands begin to tremble, and I feel my jaw clench and release over and over.

My eyes burn and my world turns shimmery, but I forbid the tears from forming. I absolutely forbid it.

"Are you okay?" Grant asks. His face is concerned, and his eyes are wide, too. We're not confrontational people, but the air in the room feels like we were both just in some crazy bar fight. "Here, sit down."

I sit on the side of the bed and lie straight back, keeping my feet on the floor.

Grant mimics me and lies down beside me.

On the bed between us, I feel the heat radiating off of his hand, which is resting just millimeters from mine. For a second, I think he might take my hand, but he doesn't.

My voice is delicate in the aftermath. "I hate her. And how does she even know you're in this science thing?"

Her mentioning it makes me feel straight-up jealous.

His voice is cautious and quiet. "It came up during class today. She's just trying to bother you. I'm honestly surprised. I mean, she's being so rude to you. It's definitely not just in your head."

I let my head flop over to look at him where he lays.

"I *know* it's not in my head. Why would you even say that?"

"I just want you to know I believe you."

"Why *wouldn't* you believe me?" An ache settles by my temples. "Did you think I was just making this up? Did you think Crazy Gen was just jumping to conclusions again and that I'd just misread this poor sweet girl's body language or something?" I cover my eyes and turn my head away from him. "Maybe she's right. Maybe you should go."

Grant sits up and stares down at me, even as I look the other way. "Seriously, Gen? Are you serious right now?"

I sit up to match him and shift so that my back is toward the headboard.

"You know what, Grant? I'm exhausted. I've been kicking and screaming and fighting this fall for days, and I'm tired of it." I lean back, accidentally smacking my already aching head on the wall. I take in the pain and push it out to every nerve in my body. With my eyes closed, I let the words pour out of me like water. "Five minutes ago, she wasn't here. It was you and me, and it was perfect and good and right. And she poked her freaking face in here in those effing shorts and she's wishing you luck and now I have a headache and you're finally convinced I'm not just being dramatic and I feel alone even though you're here. And that's the actual worst thing. And everyone thinks I'm not trying, but I am. It's just that I'm exhausted. And nobody understands that."

"Actually, Gen, I do. And you know what? I'm exhausted, too." He starts quietly, but quickly picks up steam. "These swings don't just impact you, you know?"

He stands up and grabs for his things. He paces around the room and throws his stuff into his bag while he talks. "And sometimes, when you really get down, you stop fighting. Sometimes, you let it win—even for a day. And yes, sometimes—even for a day—it does feel like I'm fighting harder than you are, but I have never dropped the ball for you. Not for years. You are *not* the only one who's tired."

The tears I forced away are back with a vengeance. Filling my eyes and falling when I blink. I place my palms down on my knees and press hard. Grant pauses at the door. He hates fighting so much. "Just... nothing. I've got nothing. I've got my competition in the morning. I won't need a ride."

He clomps downstairs, and I hear the front door slam.

I stare at the ceiling, forcing my mind to wander, but the more I try, the more depressed I feel.

"Depressed."

I say it out loud.

Just a whisper-quiet declaration into the stillness of my room.

Nothing changes.

Sometimes I feel like my stomach will never stop aching. Other times, I feel like my head is being stabbed all over by the acuity of my sadness and that my eyes will never stop burning from excessive tear production.

Right now, I feel like every inch of my skin is covered with a single, giant bruise. My flesh throbs, and even breathing causes pain.

My mother's face flashes at me from behind my lids every time they close. Each blink reminds me of her laugh and her smile.

I will myself not to blink, to avoid her.

Exhausting.

It is absolutely and unfathomably exhausting to swing back and forth between despair and things-are-okay-look-at-how-awesome-and-normal-I-am.

The swing is the worst part.

Every time I feel a little bit okay, a tiny little pinprick of light flickers inside me and I wonder if it will stay.

But inevitably, the breath of my sadness blows it out. Every time.

I roll over, toward my bookcase. Up on the top shelf, the hand-painted, ceramic picture frame holding the photo of me and my mom catches my eye. She wrote my name across the top in her beautiful swirling script. In the photo, she's holding me on her lap on the morning of my first day of kindergarten. I'm wearing a T-shirt with a giant, smiling sun on it, and I'm looking at her with the most joyful admiration.

I can still feel the gentle tug of my hairbrush as she guided it through my baby-fine hair at bedtime each night. We sat in this room and sang show tunes and played dress up. She would prop me up against my pillow and read from my big book of fairy tales in a hundred different voices.

When she'd reach the end of a story, even though I knew it was coming, I'd always stop her and ask, "Mommy, what happens now?" It was one of our favorite games.

"Well, they have a happy beginning!"

I would wriggle with fits of giggles, arguing, "No! The princess has a happy *ending*!"

She'd kiss my forehead and smooth my hair before turning out my light. Silhouetted in the doorway, she'd say, "You're right, Princess Immy. She'll have a happy ending, just like you."

If only that grinning Imogen had known she was looking at a liar.

I walk over to the shelf and reach to turn the framed photo face down, stifling her smile that cuts me like a blade.

Click.

My eyes move toward the storybook tucked in the corner on the same shelf.

My fingertips tingle as I stare at the spine.

I imagine the chill of metal cool against my skin. The push until, in one instant, the pressure is gone and the pain slips in and out through the whisper-thin opening.

Behind my headboard, on the other side of the wall, Carmella's music flips on. I hear her adjust the bass to make it louder. The cup of old water on my nightstand ripples as the wall rattles my room.

So much for her needing to go to sleep.

I cough and rub my hands over my arms and roll away from my shelf.

Grant's going to pick her.

Maybe it won't be today or tomorrow and maybe it won't even be *her*, but someday soon, Grant's going to realize he's a prince and he deserves far better than a messed-up, overweight stepsister. One day he's going to realize he's been wasting himself for a long, long time.

Grant's words ring in my ears over and over and over.

Exhausting.

It's exhausting being my friend.

And he's growing tired of it.

Let Me Go.....

18

After trudging through three forgettable class periods, I decide to take advantage of our open campus lunch and leave for some comfort food. I check my phone to see if Grant's texted, but there aren't any notifications. I almost send one to see how he's doing in his on-campus "field trip" today, but I change my mind.

Almost ten miles from school, I'm hunched over my grease-soaked bag of comfort. I drove far enough to pretty much ensure I wouldn't run into anyone from school out to lunch but close enough to get back before my next class. The crinkle of waxed paper wrappers echoes in my ears as I polish off my eight thousandth chicken nugget. I wipe my hands on a napkin and turn to a clean page in my journal.

When are we gonna get a fat princess? How about a princess with bad acne and crappy posture and the mouth of a sailor? Probably never. Every. Single. One. Is the same. Totally hot. Totally predictable.

Snow White has the attention of seven little men, not because she's the only one who can reach the top of the bookshelf, but because she's a porcelain-skinned, ruby-lipped knockout.

The Little Mermaid got a prince because she shut her trap for five whole seconds and looks fierce in a bikini.

And Cinderella? She's a girl who clearly demonstrates to the prince that she's got lots of experience on her knees and doesn't mind getting dirty.

Carmella and those chicks would run in the same clique, that's for sure. And they're the girls who get it all... Who get happiness.

Something to strive for? Something that one can attain with enough passion, faith, and positivity?

Yeah, right.

Happiness isn't a choice. And people who say it is are just lucky enough to not really need to choose it.

Real happiness? You show me a barrel full of chicken nuggets and ten different sauces, and I'll show you real happiness.

My shirt feels tighter around my middle after my indulgence, which reconnects me to myself. Suddenly the smell of stale cooking oil is all over me—in my hair and on my hands. I wrench open the door, and as I pull myself out of the car, I feel like my skin could burst open and spill my sickness all over the concrete. As I walk to the garbage can, I gag. The smell of the trash mixed with the sight of the flies all around it is too much. The grease is too much. The heat is too much. I double over and heave beside the can—a self-fulfilling prophecy.

I climb back into the car and close the door, but I know what I've left on the concrete. A puddle of revolting filth that doesn't come close to matching what I still feel writhing just under my skin.

I pull out of the parking lot as fast as the Grannymobile will take me. I'm desperate to leave just a little of my own disgust behind me.

I spend the drive back to campus in silence, which I don't realize until I turn into the back of the school parking lot and my blinker sounds more like a hundred-soldier death march than a delicate click. I drive to my spot: 93-B. Every year, juniors and seniors buy reserved spots as a fundraiser. I got my spot as part of a fine bit of negotiation. Moderately hideous car—two years of premium parking.

I slam on the brakes, and my tires squeal as my body lurches forward. There, in my parking spot, all shins and elbows, is Grant. He's seated on the concrete, his earbuds in, and his head rests on his arms, which are crossed around his knees.

In one snapping motion, he springs out of his coiled form, wide eyes and long legs, striding to the side of my car, so I can pull in and not run my best friend over while doing it.

I get out quickly so he doesn't have to watch me struggle. And also so he won't smell the deep-fried odor that's soaked in my seats.

Suddenly, he's hugging me tightly. Really tightly, next to my open car door.

"Graaahnnn."

It feels like he's practicing some wrestling move.

"Graaahnnn, Icannndbreatheee."

"Oh, sorry. Hey." He pulls back, keeping his hands on my arms. He purses his lips into a frown before saying, "Gen, I'm really sorry I got on your case last night. I was tired because of the show and my physics stuff and everything. And when the competition broke for lunch and you weren't in the courtyard, I came out and saw your car was gone, and I texted but you didn't write back, and I was just worried."

I pull my phone from my pocket. I didn't realize I had it on silent. He's wearing one of my favorite shirts today. It's black with a giant bone on the front and the words: "I find this humerus." I can't help but smile.

"No, I was way out of line. I'm out of control. It's Carmella being snarky and Dad being gone and Evelyn being annoying and the show opening soon, and I've just been, y'know, crazy."

"No." He bends his neck and hunches over a little so that he's looking at me eye-to-eye. He reaches up with both hands and cups my face in his warm palms. "Don't say that. You're not that. I should have been more sensitive to how intense life is for you right now."

My skin ignites with fire as he suddenly removes his hands and takes a small step back.

He's gonna have to stop holding my face like that, or someday when we both least expect it, I'm going to pounce on him like a lion in wait and tear his clothes right off with my teeth.

"And I should have been less cantankerous," I say.

We step away from the car, and he shuts the door.

"Why aren't you inside? Isn't your science-y stuff in the gym all day?"

"Yeah. It sucks. They're doing the Beta Team's reviews right now, and it took over an hour to get through Alpha Team's so I knew I'd have time to come find you over lunch. I hate to admit that I was worried things got worse for you last night and something bad had happened."

Bad.

That generic thing that people say when they don't want to say what they really feared.

He reaches down and picks up my arm to loop it through his. I look down to our feet, which have fallen into stride. I never noticed how tiny he has to make his steps when we walk together.

"How's the competition? Feeling good about making the top three?"

"Well, it's hard to say, but I came in sixth for round one. Lake View's team is killing it. I'm not sure if I'll be able to pull it off."

"Ugh, I'm such a jerk. You're out here checking on me and worrying about me, even when your own big thing is crashing and burning."

"Hey, sixth place isn't exactly crushing defeat!" He grins. "It's really okay." He winks as we reach the edge of the parking lot. I stop and turn him to face me.

"No. I get caught up in my own stuff, but that's not fair."

"Oh, please. Will it make you feel better if I say I forgive you?" We step up on to the curb, and I shift my bag to the other shoulder. My favorite smirk creeps onto his lips and his secret dimple comes out, and dammit if my heart doesn't bounce.

"Yes." I grin. "Forgive me?"

"Gen..." He pauses coyly. "I will never forgive you."

"Hey!" I say as I lunge for him. The scent of his hair stuff fills my whole head and makes me dizzy.

"Never!" He reaches out and taps the tip of my nose. Just then the bell rings. "Oh, crap! I've gotta go!" And he's off running—actually running—back toward the school.

"Have fun at your not-really-a-field-trip!" I scream at him.

He takes it up a notch and is now running backward, never losing stride. "I mean it's at school! What the crap?!"

"Okay, guys, I have a few announcements! Listen up!" Grant is shouting, trying to get the attention of the cast and crew before rehearsal. The actors, however, are still too enthralled with the sounds of their own voices to shut their yaps.

"*Hey!* That means you." He gestures to a clump of chorus members who instantly melt into their seats. "Thank you." His authoritative scowl drifts back into a glowing smile.

"Mrs. Gild will be out to talk with you in a minute. She's working out the blocking on scene four right now, but as it doesn't concern most of you, I'm going to get these announcements out of the way. So the coming week of rehearsals is really important. None of you should be absent or ineligible or sick or covered in head lice or infected with leprosy or anything that would keep you off the stage for the entirety of Tech Week."

I look around and watch as everyone stares up at him and hangs on his every word. I make a mental note to tell him again how proud I am of his making stage manager this year.

"We'll have rehearsals every night, through Thursday, and then, as you know, Friday, Saturday, and Sunday is our show! Yes, you will all be required to strike the stage after Sunday night's closing. Yes, everyone will stay to help clean the dressing rooms, green rooms, and anything else Gild asks us. We have just three shows, then we're out. If any of you have questions, feel free to track me down, though it will probably be difficult if I'm wearing my stage blacks backstage because, as you know, when the lights go down, every techie wearing all black becomes invisible."

I let out a chuckle, but I'm the only one.

As the crickets chirp, everyone in front of me turns around to see who the sad soul is who thought Grant's lame punchline was actually funny.

But his enthusiasm won't be deterred. "Okay, then. Go forth! Check your props! This is your last day without costumes! We're getting started in ten minutes!"

The rest of us offer the traditional echo back to him. "Thank you, ten!"

Minutes later, Antonique and I are sitting at the soundboard while the cast prepares for Gild's first declaration of the day. I automatically recite Winnifred's words right along with Charity, who is running lines on stage. Antonique smirks at my delivery, and I have to admit it feels kinda nice to have an audience.

"Are you getting excited? I can't believe next week is Tech Week," Antonique says as I'm fiddling with the gain on mic two, which has been giving me fits since yesterday.

"I know. Hell Week is more accurate. It is so intense," I say. "And opening night is a rush. The pressure can be so heavy you feel like it might squash you."

"Oh, I can imagine," she says. "I already feel like I'm going to barf, and it's still days away."

Her face looks like she might actually throw up.

"That's not weird, but remember, throwing up in the sound booth is strictly prohibited."

She laughs. "Good to know. Hey, I thought we had closed rehearsals?"

I follow Antonique's gaze and see Carmella traipsing down the house-left aisle of the auditorium. She's wearing her drill team practice uniform, and her ponytail could literally not be higher.

On stage, the cast is working through some bumps in Act II, which have been giving them trouble for days. I know Carmella may think she's the golden girl, but she does not want to be the person who interrupts Mrs. Gild's rehearsal. Doesn't matter who the Princess thinks she is—Gild's gonna rip her to shreds.

Carmella takes a seat on the aisle about five rows from the front and watches her apparent boyfriend, Andrew, flit around the stage.

I reach up and depress the button on my headset that connects to the other techies and, most importantly, to Grant.

"Grant, you have your ears on?"

I hear a faint click before a slightly digitized version of Grant's voice starts crinkling in my ear.

"'Course, Gen, what's up? Everything okay?"

"Kinda. I don't want to raise the alarm and trigger Gild's werewolf transformation, but Carmella just walked in and sat, like, five rows from the front."

"Seriously? Gild didn't notice her? Where is she?"

"I guess not. She's up against the stage trying to start Act II. She's got other things going on."

"I'm on it."

My headphones go dead, and I look over to Antonique who's sitting beside me in front of the mixing board, peering through the thin pane of glass that separates us from the rest of the auditorium. Her eyes are just as big as mine.

Seconds later, Grant emerges from the stage right edge of the proscenium arch and hugs the wall as he descends the small staircase.

Miraculously, Mrs. Gild is still barking orders at the cast. The general busyness of the moment masks Grant heading toward where little Miss Perfect is sitting.

"Oh my gosh, what is he gonna say to her?" Antonique asks.

Get out.

Go away.

Be gone, foul demon.

"I have no idea, but I really wish we had some popcorn."

I watch as Grant leans over and tells Carmella something that makes her respond by placing her hand on the back of his neck. *Why? No! Grant, you are doing it wrong.*

I feel Antonique's head snap in my direction. I guess she was looking for my reaction, which is decidedly not awesome.

Her hand. Her hand. Her hand.

As Grant walks away, Carmella gets up and starts heading back up the aisle. She's approaching the back of the auditorium and walking in the direction of my booth.

"Ugh! Ah! Would I be showing signs of weakness if I hide under the console?" It comes out as almost a shriek.

"No, no," Antonique replies, thinly veiling her own panic. "You're fine. She's gonna walk right past. She's just gonna keep walking. Oh, yeah, no, she totally saw you."

"Oh my God," I say as I pull my chair up to the table as close as it can go and pray for invisibility powers right effing now.

She taps the door, but it's cracked open a little so she just pushes it further in.

"Hey, sis," she croons.

"I'm working right now, Carmella." I don't turn my chair around.

"Ella. My name is *Ella*. And I know. I just stopped by before dance practice to see Andrew—my boyfriend—but then Grant and I got to talking. He's awfully cute. I'll have to find some time to get to know him better."

She purses her lips just a little. She looks so calm, and I hate myself for feeling panicked. Feeling scared. Who is she, and why would I cower in her presence? Where's the beast version of me that told her off last night?

Long gone, best I can tell.

I try to steel myself against her. I straighten my posture and push back my shoulders.

"Yeah, rehearsals are closed to outsiders. So..."

"I get it," she says. "So is this the little room where they hide people that are considered too hideous to be on the stage?"

My shoulders slump.

"Whoa, whoa, whoa, what's your problem?" Antonique asks, braver than I am by far.

"I'm pretty sure I wasn't talking to you," Carmella says as she shifts her weight onto her other foot and crosses her arms. "You're a freshman, aren't you? I can tell by how much you resemble a brick wall."

Carmella reaches up and runs her hand down her chest.

Antonique's fortitude has run out.

"Imogen Keegan! Where is my sound cue?!"

Mrs. Gild is screeching from the stage at me, and I have no idea where they are in the script or where she needs me to be.

"I'm sorry!" I yell. "We had a situation back here! So sorry! What's the cue?"

But it's too late. Gild is marching up the aisle, and she looks furious.

I turn to the door where Carmella had been standing, but she's fled, just in time to miss out on what would have been an incredible rant.

"Imogen, you have got to be on this!" Mrs. Gild's face is beet-red.

"I know, I'm sorry, my stepsister came into the booth and I—"

"We have closed rehearsals, Imogen, you know this. I'm disappointed that you had someone here without speaking to me first. Don't let it happen again."

Mrs. Gild calling me by my first name leaves me feeling like I've been kicked right out of her family.

"Oh, but she wasn't here for me. I mean, I didn't invite her. I wouldn't. I—"

"I do not care why she was here. She was in *your* booth. Period. We quite literally do not have time to discuss this further, so get your head in the game. We need you. Do *not* disappoint me again or Antonique will be the one in the chair on opening night."

Without waiting for my response, she is gone, heading back to the cast who are all glaring through the glass at me with their hands on their hips or their eyebrows raised in unison.

I look toward Antonique and say with all the urgency I can muster, "We can't miss a single cue from here on out. You know that, right?"

"I know," she says. "I can't believe that girl's your sister."

"Stepsister," I correct her. "Not my sister. Not my sister at all. I'm so sorry she said that to you."

"I'm sorry she said that to *you*. And also—" Antonique turns a page in her script to find the spot where the actors have sprung to life.

"Yeah?"

"Don't listen to her. She's just a girl. As insecure as the rest of us."

I scoff. "I don't think she's insecure at all."

"Of course she is. Maybe not the same way as me or the same way as you, but she is."

"Whatever her personal issues are, they don't give her the right to treat me—to treat *us*—like crap."

"Nothing gives her the right, but it might give her a reason," Antonique says.

I consider the truth of her statement and try to imagine a scenario in which Carmella would have ever felt the way she makes other people feel, and I come up empty.

I nod my head and say, "Maybe," before we both turn our full and undivided attention back to the script.

Final dress rehearsals are really horrifying. Normally sane people lose their damn minds, and people who have been on top of their game for weeks suddenly drop lines, miss notes, and can't keep it together. I am grateful for my pharmaceutical regime right now because during such a stressful period there is very little room for error. Or craziness.

The sound, costumes, lights, and props are each small blips on the whole of the production, but when they all start coming together, it's magical. When the house lights go down and the blues, reds, and greens of the stage lights flick on, it's like being transported to another world.

Despite my best and most diligent efforts to loathe them, the cast is doing pretty well considering how insufferable some of the leads are. Andrew and Charity have nice enough voices, but I'm having a really hard time ignoring how ridiculous they are off-stage. Andrew acts like a leader, but he's not. He's a follower, just like the rest of us.

Hell Week blew by before anyone could blink. We rehearsed until midnight and prayed our parents wouldn't be mad, and we still managed to go to our classes and keep our eyes open so that we could stay eligible. The intensity of the week combined with my last two confrontations with Carmella meant that, somehow, we stayed out of each other's way. Evelyn tried to spring a few unnecessary gatherings on us, but since Carmella and I agree that we'd rather drink bleach than spend time together, we managed to hold her off. It struck me as a little weird that we were technically working toward the same goal in that regard.

Walking into the theatre a couple of hours before the curtain rises on opening night, I feel like I'm stepping into a holy place. Something about the ghost lights always haunted me—but knowing that the glow is constant has always comforted me, too. The auditorium is pitch black, except for the weak glow of the single bulb standing alone. Grant leaves me and goes to get all of the lights turned on as I walk through the wings, fingertips brushing the velvet wall of curtains.

The heaviness of the fabric, rich and aubergine, pulls at the ceiling, creating a frame for the stage. Layers of black paint have covered the floor, year after year, sealing off the sweat, blood, and tears of so many casts from so many shows. I follow the glow-in-the-dark stripes of tape and find myself standing at center stage.

I look to the back of the room and stare into the glass window of the sound booth. I remember being on my dad's knee, sitting in the back of a booth like that one. It was the "best, free seat in the house," Mom always said. It was the perfect spot for watching her as she danced across the stage in whatever community theatre show would have her. My dad swears that it was an easy decision for them to leave New York and come back to her hometown to raise a family. He says she never thought twice about leaving her dreams to shelter mine. But now I know that the reason she spent so much time in dinky little shows on tiny little stages wasn't because she was desperate for attention. It was because she had to. If she wasn't in the city, then fine, but that wasn't going to keep her from the stage.

My vision blurs a little, and I turn my head to the left. In the space beside me, washed in cool blues, I imagine my mother. I envision her delicately twined into a shape both strong and graceful. I can picture my dad, seeing her, such a lovely, braided figure, extending right up to the clouds. In my mind, she turns to me, and for a moment, her eyes meet mine.

Slowly, I lift my arms, arcing, softening, placing them in the same aerial position as hers. I mimic her shape, just as I did when we danced together with my dad as our only audience. With the mildest of grins on my lips, I turn my head, hoping to see an approving smile on the apparition of my psyche, but instead, in the wings, I see Grant. His mouth is slightly agape, his eyes focused on my form.

A breath catches in my chest, my arms still raised, and I notice a quick intake of air from him as instantly my eyes are blinded by light pouring in, white and hot, from dozens of can lights all around the stage. My arms shoot back to my sides, quick as an arrow, and I look toward the back of the house as Mrs. Gild enters. I look for Grant to explain to him that I was just messing around, stretching or something, but he's gone.

The curtain wavering slightly is the only indication that someone had been standing there at all.

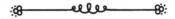

Opening night unfurls before us.

Grant is dapper as ever in his stage blacks. The SM patch I gave him has been neatly ironed onto his right sleeve. He keeps popping in and out of view as he gets ten million last-minute things accomplished. The cast is running around like a flock of headless chickens, and every few minutes, a new half-dressed character darts past my vision as Antonique and I wait in the hallway with our box of batteries.

"Looks like everyone's been checked," she says, looking at the clipboard.

"Good. We're about to do circle, and then we've gotta get back to the booth before they open the house."

"Happy opening, ladies!" Mrs. Gild approaches and puts a hand over my shoulder and Antonique's. Her white hair is tucked and pinned up onto her head, creating a soft nest of curls. She's wearing a pair of flowy black pants and a flowy black tunic that's embellished with rhinestones. One thing I'll never take for granted in the theatre is how acceptable it is to wear head-to-toe black.

"Wow, Mrs. Gild, you look beautiful," Antonique says.

"Yeah, you look great," I agree.

"Thanks, girls," she says. "Spread the word. We're gonna circle-up out back."

"Sure thing," we say.

Mrs. Gild heads to the area outside past the scene shop, and Antonique and I split up duties. She heads to the wings to notify the crew there, and I head to the dressing rooms to tell the rest of the cast.

As I peek my head into the hall outside both rooms, the smell of hairspray almost chokes me to death.

"Circle-up!" I shout over the sounds of shoes and sprays and clicking compacts.

Dozens of voices, high and low, scream back at me their confirmation, "Thank you, circle!"

Just a few minutes later, the entire cast and crew is in a gigantic circle just outside the stage doors. The neon dresses look amazing, like giant colorful candies. My heart is pounding, but not in its usual way. It's clamoring with excitement, not dread.

"Take hands, guys." Gild crosses her right arm over her left, and we all do the same.

On my left is Grant, and on my right, Antonique asks, "Am I doing this right?"

"You got it. Just cross arms and hold hands. This is one of the best parts." I smile at her.

As I stand in the circle, I look from face to face. Brice and Jonathan are on the far side of the circle, sandwiched between a dozen girls in bright poofy dresses. While I'm not terribly invested in much of the cast, there's a friendliness that grows over time when we're all working so hard toward the same goal. For the past two years, I stayed in the shadows as much as I could. But after things got better for me last spring, I really tried to open up during the second-term show. And experiencing the sense of family—even though it usually only lasts for a short while—is something I'd never trade.

Mrs. Gild begins to speak, and every voice falls silent. "Guys, we're ready to put on a great show. I am so proud of each and every one of you. We're already a few minutes behind so I'm going to go ahead and pick tonight's speaker. I hope you'll all agree that I chose an excellent right-hand man in Grant Thornton. Kick us off, would you, dear?"

"My pleasure." He beams.

I beam by association. I am so incredibly proud of him.

"Gang, we're going to rock this show! All I want to say is trust yourself. You know the show. You trust your fellow actors and techies. All that's left is to have some fun. Let's do it!"

As soon as he finishes, Grant squeezes the hands he's holding. I'm on his right, and Gild's on his left. As we feel the squeeze, we pass it on to the hand of the person on our other side until the little squeezes of happy energy and trust make it all the way around the circle and they both end up back at Grant.

"Got 'em!" he says as I return the squeeze from the other side into his crossed left hand. "Good show!"

Then we all raise our arms and turn our bodies until we're untangled and we break the chain. I turn to Antonique and put my hands on her shoulders.

"Ready, fish-kick?"

"Circle is so awesome," Antonique says, with her eyes wide and her smile wider.

"It really, *really* is. Let's go."

Antonique is totally starstruck by the entire experience. As we shut ourselves in the sound booth, she looks over her notes again and again. She is trembling as we do our final checks.

"Close your eyes," I tell her.

Antonique is clammy and sweat collects on her brow, but she closes them anyway.

I open the sound closet door and pull out her opening night surprise.

"Okay!"

Her eyes pop open, and she breaks into a huge smile as I position the second, big, giant rolling chair next to mine. A pair of thrones. She beams brightly and sits down beside me as we settle in for some audience watching.

In front of us, the auditorium is packed with parents and siblings and friends. Moms stand up and take pictures of the empty set, and kids hold up their programs and take selfies on their phones. The hum of the audience is one of the most important sounds in the theatre. Backstage, I can imagine the actors standing, waiting, hoping the crowd will be good. Hoping it'll laugh when it's supposed to. Hoping they'll make whomever they brought to see them proud.

In my ear, I hear Grant calling for ready signals.

"Sound: ready," I say to him, and even though it's silent, I swear I can hear him smile at the sound of my voice.

Antonique reaches over and puts her hand on top of mine. I'm startled, but instead of yanking my hand away, I just give her hand an encouraging squeeze.

"Here we go," I tell her as I adjust my headset.

The house lights come down, and the audience gets still and we're both silently listening for our cue to go.

"Good show," I whisper.

"Good show," she replies.

A deep breath.

Curtains up.

O n Sunday, the morning of our final performance, I wake to the sound of three text messages arriving on my phone at once.

I lean forward to grab my cup of water from my nightstand and swirl some in my mouth. I forgot to close my blinds all the way last night, so I can see the breeze rattling the remaining leaves on the tree in the yard. I give a big yawn before falling back on my pillow to read my texts.

"(1/3) URGENT: All cast and crew of OUAM. We will be having an emergency full company meeting at 11:00 AM in the auditorium. This meeting is mandatory, and you must al-

(2/3) -l be in attendance. There has been a situation, and we need to be in the same room to discuss how we want to proceed. The decision to carry on tonight's perform-

(3/3) -ance or to cancel it needs to be discussed. Please respond to this text, indicating that I can expect you at 11, or I will be calling you 1 by 1. -Gild"

Whoa.

As I'm typing my reply, my phone rings in my hand. Grant.

"Hey."

"Hey." His voice sounds deep and fragile, like he just woke up.

I wipe the sleep out of my eyes and try not to think about how poufy and messy and perfect his hair probably looks. "What the hell's going on?"

"I don't know. Mrs. Gild hasn't told me anything else, so I'm in the dark, too."

"Well, let me finish texting her, and then I'll call you back, okay?"

I hear him yawn on the other end, which makes me yawn, too.

"Don't bother, I've got to get ready. Pick me up at 10:40?" he asks.

"Sure, see you then."

After disconnecting, I reply to Mrs. Gild's text.

"I'll be there. Hope everything's okay, Mrs. G."

At 10:58, after endless speculation in the car, Grant and I are no closer to guessing what could possibly be wrong, and we enter the auditorium without a clue.

The house lights are up and the stage lights are off, so the castle stands high above us looking mostly sad and fragile. Almost all of the cast and crew are already assembled, so I make my way down the aisle, finding a spot on the same row as Brice and Jonathan.

"What's going on?" I whisper to Brice.

Jonathan leans forward, speaking over Brice's lap. "She hasn't said a word yet."

We shrug at each other as Grant files in after me, and I silently take a headcount. Actors are notoriously late; teenage actors are even worse. The fact that we're all here on time is an ominous sign. Well, almost all of us are here. There's one person missing. I begin to look around for who it might be.

"Good morning." In the most amazing, dramatic fashion, Mrs. Gild emerges from the stage left wing. She's wearing loose grey pants and a long shirt with grey, purple, and blue flowers all over. Her glasses are down on her nose, and she looks tired. "Thank you for coming so early and on such short notice. I'm afraid we have some unfortunate news, and we have very little time to decide what to do about it."

Mrs. Gild's stark white hair, which is usually soft with curls, either around her face or piled on top of her head, is pulled back, tight and smooth into a tidy bun. She does not look pleased. "Last night, one of our own made some unfortunate choices, and we, as a company, must decide how, or if at all, to pick up the pieces." She clears her throat and looks down to the stage floor. When she looks up, I wonder if she's going to change her mind about telling us at all. "Our Winnifred, Miss Wells, attended a party last night where alcohol was consumed by minors."

Her words are carefully curated, and she rarely misspeaks. I'm listening to every syllable, desperate to discover what disaster is about to befall our little show. I scan the room quickly and see that Charity is definitely *not* in the house.

"Unfortunately for her, and for all of us, she was drinking, and at around two-thirty this morning, she and four other Crestwood students were arrested for public intoxication and public indec–" She pauses to clear her throat again. "Also, possession of alcohol by a minor. I don't tell you this as fodder for gossip, but to impress upon you the seriousness of her offense."

Holy balls. Public indecency. What was she doing, walking–

"Was she walking down the street naked?" Grant leans over to whisper in my ear, completing the thought that was already racing through my head.

"Excuse me. Mr. Thornton, Miss Keegan, I could really use your attention right now." Mrs. Gild is glaring at the two of us. She's already so mad this morning she doesn't even have the playful glint in her eye she usually can't hide when she's scolding one of her theatre babies. Obviously our whispers weren't quite as quiet as we'd intended.

"We're sorry. Uh, sorry." Grant mutters our apology, while I drop my eyes.

"So we are in quite a predicament. As you all know, the show is already sold out. Which means that we've already collected payment for all 988 tickets, which, of course, is a great amount of money for our program. Canceling the show is, frankly, a costly embarrassment. Conversely, as you know, Miss Wells did not have an understudy, which puts us in a very stressful position." She raises an eyebrow before letting a layer of cattiness drip into her tone. "Usually, getting through a mere three performances without our leading lady being arrested isn't quite so difficult." Her lips are pursing in frustration. She's obviously and rightfully pissed.

"We must decide—right now—what our options are and what we plan to do."

One of the girls in the ensemble chimes in, "What do you mean 'what we plan to do'? There's nothing to do. Charity got herself arrested, and now we have to cancel the show."

"So, is she, like, in jail? Or is there a chance she'll be released this afternoon, and can still make it by curtain so the rest of us don't have to pay for her mistake?" Brice asks with a perfectly timed swivel of his neck.

Mrs. Gild holds up her hands and nods as she takes in the frustration of her kids. She bends down and sits on the edge of the stage, pulling up her knees to sit cross-legged in front of us.

"Unfortunately, even if Miss Wells were available to be here this evening—and she is not—she would not be allowed on school property or be allowed to participate in this school function. I don't think it would be out of line to presume that all of the students in question will be facing a disciplinary hearing when the administrators get into the office tomorrow morning."

"Well, if she can't do it and no one else can do it, then what is there to discuss? We have to cancel," remarks one of our spotlight guys.

To the surprise of everyone on our row, Jonathan pipes up. "Unless maybe we can brush up one of the other actresses. Maybe someone can fill in? I mean, do any of you have her parts memorized?" He shakes his head to shift his sandy hair out of his eyes and looks toward the faces of the girls scattered around the auditorium.

One of them shrugs and says, "No. I mean, we know some of the music from hearing it all the time, of course, but her lines? No way. No one has her lines memorized." The other girls nearby nod in agreement.

Even though it's only one performance, I feel my stomach sink. I really wanted to do the show one more time. This sucks.

"Well," Mrs. Gild sighs, "I suppose I knew that would be the case, but I thought it was important to meet with you and discuss it first so that we'd all be in agreement. I'm more than a little angry that one member of our team will have caused all of the rest of you to miss out on your final performance. I'm truly sorry."

Grant nudges me in the side. Hard.

"Ow! What?" I whisper-shout.

He looks at me, with his eyes as wide as jawbreakers, and he nods his head up toward the stage.

"Why are you looking at me like that? What?" I am trying to keep my voice down after being scolded once already by Mrs. Gild.

He leans in close, his breath hot in my ear, and says, "Gen, you totally know the whole script. Every line. Every cue. Not to mention the fact that you've had the whole score memorized since you were a kid. And, on top of that, you can sing."

Now my eyes are the ones resembling dinner plates.

"You must be out of your freaking mind, Thornton." I hit him playfully on the leg, but I'm not really playing. "And you better keep your trap shut." I cross my arms before adding, "And you have no idea if I sing, you've never heard me. I don't sing."

"Oh, please. Nobody is saying you're headed for a Tony, okay? But you sing. When you're studying and you don't even know you're humming along and you think nobody is listening. But I'm listening." His face flushes with color, and I look down at my hands as my face starts to warm, too.

He listens.

"Mr. Thornton and Miss Keegan, I sincerely hope that you two are deliberating about some brilliant scheme that will pardon our department from the disgrace of returning all of that ticket money."

Despite my certainty that Grant would never, ever betray me in such a way, I see him slowly coming to his feet. I grab his jeans pocket and almost rip it completely off trying to tug him back down. He responds by pulling my clawed fingers off of his pants and holding my hand tightly in his. When Grant starts talking, everybody turns to listen.

"Guys, I have an idea. Maybe. Well, I don't know about you, but I really think that we should do the show tonight if we can, and I think I know a way that could work. It might be our only shot."

Oh my God, Grant. Please don't make me kill you. I don't want to spend the afternoon with naked Charity behind bars. My fingers are turning purple in his grip.

The murmurs of curiosity are rushing across the surface of the room. My insides are trying to claw their way out of my skin. I'll murder him. I swear I'm going to actually murder him.

"There is someone who, from being in the sound booth and being a musical junkie, knows the show, inside and out, who knows all of Charity's lines, all of her songs, and who'd make a great Winnifred."

I finally rip my fingertips away from him and rub them until the tingling starts to subside.

The cast and crew sits waiting, their collective mouths dangling open in anticipation.

"Antonique, do you really know it all?" Andrew, the Prince, has turned around in his seat and lifted himself up on his knee. The entire company turns from Grant and stares at Antonique with expectant eyes, and she looks like she's just been shot.

Jealousy blossoms within me, and I feel my throat get tight as, once again, I'm overlooked for a title I didn't even want.

Antonique stammers and looks over her shoulder for me as conversations break out all over the auditorium.

"Oh, she'd be such a good Winnifred!"

"She'll look really cute in Charity's dress."

"What do you say, Antonique, wanna be my stand-in princess?" Andrew smiles crookedly at her, making his most princely face, and I feel my jaw clench together.

She's trying to object, but no one is listening.

Why wouldn't they hope that the cute, fit, angel-faced freshman would have the chops to know the show inside and out? Why would they ever want it to be me?

I look down at my hands as Grant tries to calm all of the chatter. "He meant me," I say too quietly for anyone to hear.

Grant looks down at my soft words and gives me a small smile. He holds out his hand, and I take it and stand.

"He meant me." This time, they all hear.

The room goes quiet. I feel like I've just ripped off a blanket of invisibility and they're all seeing me for the first time.

"Oh, thank God," Antonique says. "I was trying to say that I don't know the show like Imogen does. I certainly don't know the songs. Grant wasn't talking about me. He was talking about Imogen. And I think Grant is absolutely right. You can do this." Antonique looks at me with her soft, dark eyes, and the whole room is waiting for me to make my case.

"Look, I don't want to do this. Don't be confused. I'd much rather be sitting in my little black box in the back, pressing buttons and pretending I'm on the bridge of the Enterprise. But I don't know. It might work."

I look at Grant, who nods at me, and I take a second to study his face. His shoulders are back, and his chest is puffed out with pride. I look down and see that our fingers are still woven together between us.

"I'm not, like, a great singer or anything. I don't really know when the last time was that I sang, out loud, for people. It's been since I was a kid, but I can carry a tune and..." My eyes start to dart back and forth from face to face. Without meaning to, I start counting them and then I remember how many seats Gild said we have to fill and my palms are slick and my heartbeat is cranking out a rhythm that would put the drumline to shame. I feel my throat close and I just want to swallow, and without finishing my sentence, I sit down.

No one moves. They all just sit there and look at me with wide eyes and downturned brows. They nibble at their lips and fingertips, and a few freshmen chorus girls actually have their hands folded together in a shape like praying.

I lift my chin and look at Grant. "What was I thinking?" I whisper. "I can't do this. I have to run sound, and I can't seriously do this."

"Gen, you can." He sits down beside me and continues to talk as if we're the only people in the room. As if there aren't about a billion eyeballs watching us like some primetime reality show. "Seriously, think about it. Antonique can run sound. You've said yourself that she's brilliant at it." Two rows in front of us, I see Antonique's head bow with humble pride. "And like it or not, you know the part. It's you or nothing. Please, Gen. Just sing through a song once with the accompaniment, and if you can't do it, you can't do it. Please?"

My heart is bruising my ribs from the inside, but it keeps beating, which is more than I expected.

I laugh, hoping to diffuse the tension, and bring the blood rushing back to my head and limbs.

I turn to face the rest of my row, mostly Brice, even though I know everyone else is still listening.

"Guys, I-I don't even know. I mean, the costumes. The costumes would never ever...I—"

Brice chimes in beside me and states without flourish, "Gen, I can make those costumes work. A few seam rippers, and I can take 'em right out. I'd never let you hit the stage looking a mess. You know that I can do it. And so can you."

Antonique turns in her seat, looks me straight in the eye, and says, "You can do it, Imogen, and you've taught me so much. I can run all the sound cues. I really can."

I want to run. I want to melt into this auditorium chair and disappear into the fabric.

I'm not scared of the music or the lines.

I'm scared of the embarrassment.

I'm going to totally embarrass myself.

Grant stands again and says to the group, "Look, it's a decision for all of us to make if Gen's willing. Those who'd rather have Imogen play Winnifred than cancel the show, raise your hand."

First Grant's, then Antonique's, followed by Brice's, and soon, the rest of the auditorium.

Mrs. Gild hops down off the stage and walks up the aisle toward me. As she approaches, her voice gets softer and she addresses only me. "Well, Miss Keegan. I suppose it's all up to you. I would, of course, like to hear you at the piano, but assuming you'll agree, I guess I'm asking–we're all asking–if you'll do this for us so that we can have our closing night. If you'll at least try. It's only one show."

The softness of her voice and her gentle hands on my arms almost make me want to cry, but the eyeballs boring holes through me stops the urge. I speak.

"Okay."

I'm hit with an instantaneous need for a Prozac and about five million candy bars.

Mrs. Gild offers me her arm. She gives a nod to the accompanist sitting on the front row, and he goes to sit at the piano. "Everyone, there's lots to do, so..."

She tries to usher everyone off, but she loses steam. She knows there isn't a single chance in all of the universe that the kids aren't going to watch this unfold.

I feel like I'm in a funeral march down the aisle. I'm either about to be the nail in the coffin of this dying show or be its final breath of life.

We get to the piano, and Gild whispers, "Can you do this, honey? You don't have to if you can't."

Strangely, I think maybe I can.

I take a deep breath and look at everyone washed in bright white light. Their faces are painted with excitement and nervousness and hope, and I feel myself ache with doubt.

Suddenly, the house lights switch off.

After a second of confusion, we all look back and see that Grant has gone to the controls and lowered the auditorium lights. When I look back to the rest of the cast in the seats, I see them, but only vaguely. Their shapes are cast in blue shadow, and I can't make out their expressions.

I feel my heart slow behind my ribs.

I clear my throat and turn to the pianist and give the slightest nod. He sets off on Princess Winnifred's first number, and miraculously, surprisingly, and adequately, I sing.

I'm no superstar. But I'm better than nothing.

The kids in the audience jump up in squeals of applause as I finish the first verse. There's no time to hear me sing anything else.

I turn to Mrs. Gild, and her face spreads into a smile. She looks happy and relieved. She looks proud. She reaches out and grabs me, pulling me into a giant hug.

I breathe in her scent—like perfume and powder.

Half-a-second later, she pulls away and snaps back into work mode.

She begins barking orders with a broad smile on her face. "Ladies and gentlemen! We have a lot of work to do! Brice, take whomever you need to help you prepare costumes. Actors, be ready to run lines with Imogen as soon as we finish at the piano. Grant, check with Antonique to make sure she has everything she needs. Cast, we'll all be doing a cue-to-cue with Imogen as soon as she can, and let's try and do a run through at about one. Curtain is only seven hours away, people! Let's all work together and go out with a bang."

Mrs. Gild is delegating and sending her cast and crew off in a hundred different directions faster than I can breathe. She turns back to me. "Thank you, Miss Keegan. I'm sure this is going to be a night we'll not soon forget." She gives me a little wink and says, "Let's get you ready to be royalty. We have an opening for a princess."

t's six hours to curtain.

The cast and crew scatter, and people I barely speak to (or who barely speak to me) are patting me on the back and telling me "thank you" and "you can do this" and I'm freaking out because it seems that no one really cares much about how good I am at what I'm about to be doing. They just care that I'm good enough to let them have their final hurrah.

"Mrs. Gild, can I step out for a second?" I ask her as she's passing notes to the dozens of people who are clamoring for her attention.

"Sure, hon, but make it quick. I want to be sure we know what's what on the parts with harmony."

I stop by my seat to grab my bag before shoving through the side doors into the hallway. The air is so cool I'm instantly relieved by the change in temperature.

I pull my phone out of my back pocket and dial my dad's number. When I hear the click and the sound of his voicemail instead of a ring, my heart sinks down to the floor.

I almost hang up, but at the very last second, I decide to speak.

"Hey, Dad. It's me. I—You said you wanted me to call you whether it's up or down, and honestly, I don't know which one this is. But the short version is that the girl lead couldn't do the last show, and so, um, I'm going to fill in for her. I'm freaking out. And I just really wanted to hear you tell me I can do it. But, anyway. I'll probably be too busy to answer if you call back. So just...it's okay."

I try not to sound mad or disappointed because, truthfully, I'm not. It's just a fact of life right now that he's not here.

He's not a bad dad. He's an amazing dad, and he loves me and I love him and I know that he's doing every single thing he can do and I'm glad he's following his dreams and that he finally wrote his tragic little memoir and that somebody, apparently, gives a crap.

But he's not here.

He's just not here.

"I'll tell you all about it when I can. Be safe. Love you, Dad. Bye."

I tap the screen and turn at the sound of the auditorium doors opening behind me. Grant walks out and straight to me while I'm digging through my purse for one of my quick-acting anti-anxiety pills.

"You hanging in there?" he asks.

"Not really sure, actually."

Grant walks to the water fountain and presses the lever for me. I swallow my dose and then wipe off my mouth while staring at him blankly.

"I just want *you* to know that I know you can do this," he says. "I know it, and I know this is going to be scary, but this is good. Don't you think so? Doesn't it feel like one of those things in life you're supposed to do?"

He's reaching, desperate for me to not be mad, but he's right. Somewhere deep down, this doesn't feel like a stretch. Like somewhere along the way, I should have known that a dramatic, turning point moment would have to happen in my life. And maybe this is it. I cling to the hope that this is it.

I look up into his more-green-than-brown eyes and tell him, "Yeah. It kinda does."

It's five hours to curtain.

My head is pounding. The blocking and notes and information have been pumped into my brain steadily for long enough that it should be oozing from my ears.

"Where's Andrew?" Gild screams to no one in particular. "We need to run the scene before 'Happily Ever After.'"

"Here I am," he says, as he jumps up on the stage from the floor like some creepy theatre ninja.

Gild is distracted again, and I'm looking over my notecard and then Andrew is grabbing my hand and pulling me toward the middle of the stage. He moves me into position roughly, and it doesn't seem mean. It just seems like he's accustomed to moving and positioning and controlling everything he wants. Come to think of it, maybe he and Carmella are a pretty good fit.

"We start over here," he says with an awkward flick of his hand.

I'm standing center stage, looking into Andrew's annoyingly blue eyes.

My brain clicks into focus as he says his lines, and then he's got both of my hands in his, and he's speaking so sincerely that I'm utterly distracted. I never realized he delivered his lines with so much conviction. His hands feel super-strong. Like textbook-tearing strong. I glance at my notecard, crumpled in his grip, before I reply and then I almost reach up and punch him in the side of the head because his hand is gently touching the bottom of my chin.

Oh, crap.

I notice my legs quiver just a little bit—though to be fair, that could because they're screaming obscenities at me for requiring them to stand and move for the past several hours, which is not our normal way. But whatever the reason, I realize that I've forgotten one, little, tiny, minuscule moment that happens in the show: Prince Dauntless kisses Princess Winnifred.

The tiniest kiss. It's seriously supposed to be a peck. I've given my Grandma a bigger kiss than this. But still.

Andrew is going to kiss me.

Well, he's just going to have to kiss my corpse because I am about to die.

He's pulling closer, and then he suddenly breaks character and says, "And then I give you a little kiss before exiting stage left, cool?"

Uhhhh.

"Cool," I say.

'Cause the first time in my whole life that a guy kisses me gets planned out, complete with stage directions, every day. No big deal.

Andrew and I just stand there awkwardly while we wait for more instructions. Behind us on stage, set pieces are getting reset and I can hear Brice shouting something at one of his costume girls through the open double doors at the side of the house.

My eyes dart anxiously around the room, and then when I glance at Andrew, I see him just staring at me. I half-expect him to make some horrible comment about how he's so upset he has to kiss me or that he'd rather have his teeth extracted, but he never does.

"So..." He scrounges for something to say. "Are you nervous?"

I shift my weight from one foot to the other. "Are you kidding? I starred in a musical on six hours' notice because the lead got arrested for drunkenness and indecency just last week. This will be a piece of cake."

He laughs.

"And I know all about cake," I say, hoping that, if I make the fat joke first, he won't do the same.

"Oh. Right. Okay," he says awkwardly.

"So..."

"Yeah."

I look down at the index card, already bent beyond recognition from being rubbed and folded by my hot, sweaty hands.

Andrew reaches up and rumples his hair. There's nothing at all special about the smell. "You're doing good, by the way." He bobs his head along with his own comment. "I think it's pretty kickass that you're brave enough to do this. I mean, I'm really good, but I've been practicing for weeks. If I had to do it on a few hours' notice, I probably wouldn't. You're tough."

"Tough. Yep," I stammer. "Tough, toughie, tough." Please, brain. Stop. I don't know exactly why I'm being so weird. Maybe because he's so good-looking or popular or because he's dating my arch-nemesis. I bring my hand to my face and rub my eyes instead of hitting myself in the head.

"No, really, you're a tough cookie." He reaches up gently and awkwardly punches my shoulder. He's almost being weirder than me.

"Well, it's true," I say. "I've never met a cookie I didn't conquer." I pat my belly and instantly regret it.

He chuckles, just a little, but I'm pretty sure it's because he thinks I'm funny. "No, I mean it," he says. "You surprised me. You're gonna do great. Maybe not as great as me, but..." He flashes a smile that I never imagined I'd be on the receiving end of.

"Well, I hope so. I don't wanna let everyone down."

He reaches up and puts his hand on my shoulder, in the same place where he punched it before.

"You won't," he says.

I think I believe him.

It's four hours to curtain.

Brice has me in his web as he's snipping and sewing pieces of costumes together and apart and together again. He's recruited several girls from the ensemble that are willing to help him get the job done, and I find myself in the dressing room with a rack full of clothes. He is making shooing noises and pushing the girls out, assigning them tasks as he shoves. He then reaches in his bag of tricks for some pins.

He's talking so fast and I'm staring at my cue card, and I totally miss that he's asked me a question.

"Helloooooooo, Imogen, punkin, are you ready?" He's holding up the hot pink garment with black trim along the corset edges, and he's waiting for me to duck my head inside so he can slip it over my body.

Fear rises in my chest, and I feel my skin dampen. What if after all this conjecture and after agreeing to do this awesome thing, I'm not even able to fit into her costumes? What if they have nothing in the whole costume closet that fits and therefore nothing I can take the stage in at all?

He pushes me behind some heavy clothing racks filled with costumes and turns his back. For a second, I'm not sure why he's put me in my own little corner, but then I realize, it's because he wants me to get dressed—and first...undressed. He reaches down and then slings a plastic bag over his shoulder.

In it, I find a pair of extra-large nude leggings, a pair of big, black, booty shorts, and a nude-colored camisole with a long, slimming torso that comes down almost over my hips.

I take a deep breath and rip off my jeans and hoodie and wrestle myself into what amounts to a big nude body suit.

"Okay," I say. He turns to face me, but he doesn't really look at me as he holds the dress up high.

In another out-of-body motion, I step under the heavy folds and the dress comes down around me. He spins me toward the back corner of the room, tugs on a zipper, and pins the fabric where he'll need to make adjustments.

I feel him tugging again, and a cold knot forms in my stomach.

My chin falls to my chest and I feel my eyes start to well up. "Brice, it's not gonna fit, is it?"

He steps in front of me and lifts my chin to look at him. "Honey, I'm going to try to not take that as an insult."

With his hands on my waist, he turns me around and marches me toward the mirrors. My mouth falls open. I'm miraculously contained by the soft layers around me. The dress is on. It is zipped. It is tied and pinned. And I look like a freaking princess. I'm Princess Winnifred.

Granted, a two-hundred pound Winnifred, but a princess nonetheless.

It's two hours to curtain.

I've been onstage and offstage. I've walked through every set piece and held every prop. Brice has decided that his team can handle makeup for the rest of the cast and that he's going to help me. This is good because I wouldn't have the first idea where to start.

Thick heavy makeup is smeared all over my face. Soft bristled brushes deposit wisps of powder on my skin, and dark kohl is used to ring my eyes. My hair is being straightened and curled. My lips are swabbed with color.

He pauses for a moment, and then in the mirror, as he steps to the side, I see them.

My arm. My scars.

I haven't looked at them, thought about them, worried about them, but now, with only a couple of hours to go, my arm is all I can see.

"Brice!" I hear the panic in my voice, and I feel the dress start to squeeze against my lungs. The edges of my vision start to turn grey as I try to breathe.

"What?" Brice asks without really looking at me.

"Brice, I need you to find me some sleeves."

My pulse beats faster and faster as Brice douses me with a fourth coat of hairspray.

"You look hot. Don't worry about sleeves, really. You look great."

I reach up and place my hand on my chest, and I can feel that my heart is pumping out of my skin. I look down and watch my ribs heave as I struggle for air.

Brice isn't looking. He doesn't see.

"Brice!" His name comes out in a desperate crack. "I can't breathe." The corset of the dress is wringing my lungs out, crushing me like a vice grip, and I really can't breathe. I can't breathe at all. "Brice, I need you to find me sleeves."

My eyes fill with tears, and I tip my head back so that they won't fall.

Full on panic sets in as Brice puts down the hairspray, and confusion and worry finally fill his face.

"Brice, I need you to give me sleeves. I need sleeves."

"Honey, we don't have sleeves. You need to calm down."

"Brice." I sound like a child. I can hear the tremble in my voice. I hold my arm up, showing him my scars only an inch from his face.

He looks at my arm and then lowers it to my side. And wraps his arms around me while I sit in the chair. He shushes me, and he doesn't even worry that he's flattening the hairstyle he so painstakingly teased.

"Look at me. Listen to me." He puts his face as close to mine as my arm had been to his nose. "Breathe." He smiles at me and soothes me with his voice. He waits for a second and then says, "Here."

He reaches over to the vanity top and picks up a makeup sponge and a pallet with a rainbow of flesh-colored cake makeup. He begins to daub the flesh-colored crème onto my arms, and slowly, I watch as my scars disappear. With every layer of color, my breathing slows. With every press of the sponge, the scars grow fainter, and I feel my heartbeat return to normal. When he's done, he spritzes it with setting spray and coats me in a fine layer of translucent powder.

He's daubing the sweaty part under my nose and humming under his breath. As quickly as it came, the panic recedes. I stare at him. His precious, pixie face and his sweet tiny nose. I start to cry, but he wags his finger in front of me and says, "No, ma'am. I don't have time to redo that makeup."

He blows me a kiss and then vanishes into the hallway on a mission to turn another simple schoolgirl into someone else.

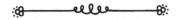

It's thirty minutes to curtain.

The entire cast and crew (minus Charity, of course) is holding hands in the back, arms crossed, and Mrs. Gild is trying, and failing, to hold herself together.

"So I just want to thank you all again for going so far above and beyond the call of duty today. Every single one of you stepped up. Not just Miss Keegan over here." She looks across the circle at me, her eyes all glisteny. Grant leans into my shoulder just slightly. Brice on my other side pulls up his leg behind us and kicks me in the butt. I smile.

She continues, "You've all made this possible, and you all should be proud. And no matter what happens, you're going to get through it together. Even so, I think it's only fair that Miss Keegan has the chance to speak before we pass the squeezes and go make our final preparations. Imogen?"

Again, I feel the weight of all their eyes. I feel the expectation and the fear.

"I don't really know what to say." I swallow. "I may screw this up. Royally." I flash a cheesy grin, and they all giggle. "This isn't something I would ever do…normally. But I just…maybe normal isn't actually my best option, so I guess I'm gonna put on my big girl panties and just get out there. It was really amazing having all of you be so totally there for me this afternoon. So thank you."

They all give me little smiles, and I squeeze both of the hands I'm holding.

I watch and wait as they each pass the gesture around the circle in opposite directions. I feel Brice squeeze my hand, but nothing yet from Grant's side.

"Oh, great, did I ruin the circle?" I ask.

"Nope, I've got it," Grant says. "I just wanted to make the last squeeze a big one."

He squeezes my hand, and then we all unwrap our arms and I feel bodies start pressing against me until I'm stuck in the middle of the cheesiest, most ridiculous, overly dramatic group-hug since grade school.

And it feels awesome.

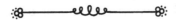

It's five minutes to curtain.

Beyond all comprehension, we're about ready to start.

After years of avoiding the mirror like a plague, I find myself staring into my reflection again with only a few moments before we begin.

There's a single knock before Grant opens the door and enters dressed in his stage blacks with his headset over his messy hair.

"How are you feeling, Gen? You're going to be great. Are you ready?"

It seems he might be almost as nervous as me.

"I'm...I guess I'm okay. I mean, there's no stopping now, is there? And of course, I figure if I fall down dead from embarrassment, you'll be the one to blame, so I can at least take solace in that." Adrenaline is coursing through my veins, and my attempt to lighten the mood has left a quiver in my lips that I can't seem to shake.

I stand and face him, all decked in my dirty, swampy Act I garb.

He looks me in the face like he's got something important to say, but he can't find the words.

I open my arms wide, and he breaks into a smile. His eyes look relieved and worried all at the same time. He wraps me in a hug that almost crushes me in half, and I look up into his face as he looks into mine.

"I'm so unbelievably proud of you," he says.

"Thanks." I pause. "I'm so scared."

He moves his hands toward my face, but stops short.

"Makeup."

He smiles and uses one gentle finger to tilt my chin up so that I'm looking in his eyes.

It feels like an electric current pulsing between us—or maybe a magnetic pull.

That gravity.

His gravity.

That makes me spin and keeps me right where I belong. He looks at me for longer than I expect, and I can't shake the feeling that he's not doing or saying the thing he came in to do or say.

"Just go out there and stare into those lights. Let the glow drown out all of the audience members, and put on a great show—for me. Pretend that it's just me and maybe your dad. And your mom. All the people who love you and want you to have this moment to shine. Break a leg, Gen. I've got to go. We're at places."

He drops his hands and turns in one motion.

I nod my head, forcing the tears back behind my well-adorned eyes, before reciting the traditional echo, "Thank you, places."

The first few numbers don't involve me. I'm standing in the wings listening to the audience laugh and clap, and I'm pretty sure I'm going to pass out. I review my lines and try to keep it together, and I remind myself of where I'm supposed to go when I enter. Cross downstage, say a few lines, and then, of course, just belt my face off. I keep waiting to lose consciousness as the songs drone on and on, and I feel like hours have passed while I wait.

And then I blink, and I'm suddenly certain that I've missed my cue. I hear the Minstrel repeat his line.

Oh my God, that was my cue.

I inhale deeply, as if I might never breathe again (and that may, in fact, be the case), and I step on to the stage.

The lights, bright and blinding, shield me from all of the faces looking up at me expectantly.

I adopt the posture of the woebegone princess, soaking and covered in seaweed from her unconventional entrance through the castle's moat.

The audience chuckles.

But not at me.

At Winnifred. This princess who's skin I get to share tonight. I take it in, and as I say my first few lines, I soak up the adrenaline. I feel like someone else.

My heart swells, and my head focuses intently on the words my fellow actors are saying. I'm basking in the blazing-surface-of-the-sun-like heat of the stage lights. I melt away and carry myself across the stage as somebody other than Imogen.

I laugh as her. Joke as her. I'm confident, as she is. I am unafraid because she is.

I'm singing, hitting each note—or at least getting pretty close. And I'm remembering more words than I'm forgetting. My brain is both completely focused on my stage actions and, at the same time, completely distracted by the absurdity of my presence on the stage at all. I glance out into the bright white of the lights. Suddenly, with my arms reaching toward the sky, my smile painfully tight, I realize that I've finished my first song.

For the briefest of instants, I imagine my mother sitting in the audience of a show she'll never see, watching her daughter sing a song she'll never hear, and applauding her triumph. I can hear her clapping and cheering in my mind.

But the clapping isn't hers. It belongs to the crowd.

Their cheers and laughter and whoops of approval grow and swell, and it all crashes into me like the heat of an open oven door.

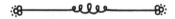

I sprint through the wings and find Brice standing there, holding my next costume piece. Without a second thought, I rip the dirty potato sack dress down past my shoulders. No one backstage spares a single glance for me in my camisole and bloomers. I literally don't have time be insecure or to even care that, technically, I'm in my skivvies in the same small space as fifty other people. Brice drops the next costume over my shoulders and whips me around, tying things tight and tapping me on my shoulders while I head back to the side of the stage.

I've taped cue cards to the walls on both sides so I can glance at them each time I have to enter or exit. I double-check myself to be sure I know what's happening, and then I walk back out into the blistering lights.

I'm in the home stretch of the first act. All I have to do is get through the most embarrassing dance number in the history of the world. When we worked on it this afternoon, I kept saying, "Don't worry. I've got a plan. Don't worry." And I managed to convince everyone that there were more important issues to address.

But now I'm standing around dozens of other girls dressed as princesses, and they're about to start this huge dance number, and I know there's no chance of my dancing it. Even worse, the whole point of the scene is for Winnifred and Prince Dauntless to out-dance the other couples.

I'm about to lose a marathon dance-off against twenty girls and *also* ruin the plot of this sixty-year-old musical in front of almost a thousand people.

The music plays, and the couples start their choreography.

I feel like a deer ready to be run down on a highway, and I catch a few wide-eyed glances as I stand there, center stage while the rest of the girls dance.

I feel the mask of Winnifred slipping down as the fear climbs up my spine.

And then Andrew is at my side, with his hand out for mine. He starts making up words, loudly, so they're heard over the music. "I don't know the steps to this one either. Let's just show them a Royal Freestyle!"

And then he throws himself to the ground in a breakdancing move, stands, takes my hands, and starts jumping around. The audience loves it. The room shakes with laughter. I hesitate for a second, looking out into the audience at the hidden, shadowy faces.

And then I start jumping and bouncing and laughing, too. I'm instantly out of breath and red-faced. Thank goodness my stalling took up part of the song because, when it's over and I step backstage, I fall to my knees and almost hyperventilate.

Stagehands walk through, whispering, "Ten-minute intermission, guys. Ten minutes."

"Thank you, ten" echos around me.

"Jessica, grab Imogen a bottle of water," Andrew demands before checking on me one more time. "You okay?"

He's on his knees beside me, and his face is just as sweaty as mine is. He's smiling, and he takes the bottle of water and opens it for me.

"Yeah. Thanks," I say. "You really saved me out there."

Somehow I feel surprised about it, which means I don't have much faith in the guy, but he really stepped up.

"Don't mention it. Dust yourself off and get your game face back on." He smacks me on the left shoulder as I stand and take a giant gulp of water.

The cold burns as it sloshes down into my growling stomach. I haven't eaten since the Crestwood High School Theatre Troop Booster Club moms brought sandwiches around noon.

"Where's Imogen?" I hear Brice's voice calling through the wing. "There you are! We've gotta get you changed. You good?"

"I'm good."

"Of course you're good. You're freaking fabulous."

He smiles at me, and I laugh so hard my cheeks ache.

As everyone sets for Act II, Brice ushers me into a corner and helps me out of and into smy dress. My heart is still flying, and I can feel that my face is fire engine red and drenched in sweat. He reaches up and dabs at my face as if on cue.

"And here's a little more powder to set your lipstick so Captain Tight Pants Junior doesn't get red all over his face."

There it is. I had forgotten. Again.

"Oh my God. Brice, I totally forgot. I can't actually kiss Andrew Bates. I mean, I really can't!"

"You can and you will. Now get back in there." He swats me on the butt as I walk to my entrance and check my cards one more time.

I trip on my way into position, but the crowd just laughs because it seems like it fits the character. There are a couple of scenes, and then it's almost time for my solo and the most embarrassing moment of my life to unfurl in front of a live audience.

I'm going to kiss Andrew Bates.

And my first kiss ever is going to be this scripted thing happening between two people who aren't even real.

The lights cook my brains like scrambled eggs, and I feel my costume is soaked with sweat even though I'm no longer dancing. My brain's on autopilot, and I move into position and my mouth says words, I guess, but I can't really be sure.

I hear Andrew's voice and my voice, and then I'm looking at his face, but not really because I can't remember what I'm supposed to do next. And then my solo, after the kiss, is about to start and I can't remember the first line of my song, but as the music starts, I begin singing which means apparently we kissed, but I really can't remember anything about it, even though it must have happened.

Every single thing seems to whiz by me in a blur.

In and out of the wings, costumes flying, laughter, and the sound of dozens of voices singing all together.

And then, we're bowing. I feel like one of those people who talks about having split personality or whatever and losing time because, if somebody offered me a million dollars in cash to tell them the details of how I moved my body and said words and sang songs over the past several hours, I would walk away broke.

We're all holding hands, and the parents and grandparents and kid siblings who were dragged to the show are all clapping and cheering and whooping for us. At the end, my castmates shove me toward the front of the stage and gesture for me, giving me a special little moment in the limelight.

The feeling of the applause soaks me to the core. I feel like if someone struck a match, the sound of their praise would ignite and I would go right up in flames.

And I briefly wonder, who are they celebrating?

The uncouth but lovable character in the show? Or the hot-mess teenager who—as Mrs. Gild announced in her curtain speech—just learned the part today and filled in at the last minute so the show could go on?

I think, just maybe, they're clapping for the both of us.

Either I survived my stage debut or the afterlife looks a lot like a high school lobby following a musical performance. Parents and students are rushing about. Castmates are half-in/half-out of costumes, hugging friends and family, and I'm looking around, saying thank yous to strangers who are being so terribly sweet.

As many of my cast and crewmates greet their parents, I wish I had my phone with me—that it wasn't tucked into a pocket of my jeans on the floor of some dressing room. I wonder if my dad got my message. I didn't think I'd care, but it would have been nice for him to have seen it.

"Oh, Imogen, *darling*! You were brilliant. Just wonderful and amazing!"

I recognize Evelyn's voice before I turn around. I spin and look to her left, to her right, over her head. A hopeful grin is stretched across my face.

"Is my dad here?" My brain knows he's not, but I can't stop the hope from crawling up the back of my neck as I crane to look over the crowd.

Evelyn's smile slips for a moment, but she picks it up before it can fall all the way. She shouts to be heard over the packed lobby.

"No, honey, he's not. But he got your message, and he wanted me to come and get it on video! And of course we wouldn't have missed it for the world! We just loved it, didn't we, Carmella?"

My eyes widen to golf ball size as the beauty queen emerges out of thin air. She is wearing a black dress, sleeveless and about two inches shy of dress code regulation. So, basically her uniform.

"Mother. It's Ella." She rolls her eyes and then continues, "And, yes, it was...hilarious. I just laughed and laughed and laughed. You were a huge success. Totally...huge."

I swallow hard, stalling, but I can think of nothing to say.

"Darling, it was just wonderful! I'm so proud of you. I only wish your father were here to see it."

"Me too," I say, still a little off-guard to see the Cinder women standing in front of me.

"It was excellent! Just *wonderful*, dear!"

"Thanks." My eyes dart between my two inherited family members, and I manage an only slightly more gracious "Thank you for coming, Evelyn."

She looks so sincerely proud of me, but something about that just doesn't click in my head. It just doesn't make sense. I'm not hers.

"I know you've got the cast party, darling, so we're gonna head on home. You were amazing." Evelyn gestures to Carmella, who continues to scan the crowd for someone who'll give her the attention she needs.

"I'll be right there, Mother. I need to say bye to Andrew first."

Evelyn nods and leaves me to be devoured by her big bad girl.

The second her mom turns around, Carmella steps right up to my face.

The familiar panic pushes blood through my body, and I hear it pump in my ears.

People are moving all around us. Hugs and squeals and flowers fill every extra space. She leans forward and whispers in my ear. "I want to make it clear that I didn't want to be here tonight. I only came because my mom made some big deal about how you need to feel supported and this was something for you to be proud of. But don't be confused. You made a fool of yourself up there. And if you're not embarrassed, you should be."

"Ella?" Andrew and a fresh batch of actors flood out of the stage door.

I feel stupid. I feel like I cannot continue living with this girl in my life. And I don't know how to make her go away. I don't know how to make her disappear.

As Andrew rushes over to Carmella, my friends find their way to where we've been standing just to the side of the ticket office.

Grant and Brice come up behind me, and each take an elbow before showing me a big, beautiful bouquet of supermarket flowers they scrounged up at some point this afternoon.

Bright yellow carnations and a few red roses are mixed with pink and purple flowers that almost look too bright to be natural. But I don't care. They're the best flowers ever.

My heartbeat slows down as they take turns giving me a hug. Behind them, Antonique and Jonathan wait for their turns.

I'm insulated in this moment. I'm physically surrounded by people who have my back, who support me, and that matters. Much more than I expect it to.

Carmella watches, red-faced.

"I didn't know you were coming to the show," Andrew tells her.

"I wasn't gonna come, but then my mom made me when she heard that Imogen here was going to be dressing up and pretending to be a real girl."

Andrew catches her attitude for half a second. I see it as his eyebrows twitch and his eyes flick to me. He tries to blow past her quip. "Yeah, well, the kid did all right, don'tcha think?" Andrew looks back toward me and grins.

Grant bumps into my hip with his own and says into my ear, "More than all right. You were amazing."

I turn to him and smile while I hold the bouquet up to my nose and breathe in deeply.

Carmella's face is being carved in two by her plunging eyebrows, and her lips are drawn up so tight, I can barely make them out.

With every moment of affection, with every moment of support, with every second I don't run away crying, I see her shrink in front of me. And I love it.

I give her a smile.

This seems to trigger her full-on flip-out because all of the sudden, her posture changes, and she steps away from Andrew and once again confronts me by bringing her chest right up next to mine.

I grimace at her again.

"It was amazing, all right." She clenches and unclenches her fists and spits out her words through gritted teeth. I've never seen her so spun up before. She turns her face toward Andrew without backing away from me. "I thought it was particularly amazing that you managed to kiss this pig right on the mouth and not vomit on the stage!" She snaps her face back toward me. I step back, stunned.

"Whoa!" Grant roars at her, stepping in front of me.

"Nope!" I hear Brice begin mumbling under his breath and see him try to push forward, but Jonathan holds him back.

"Ella, what the hell is wrong with you? You should go," Andrew says.

I am completely shocked at the sight of her losing control. I don't know how to respond, so I just stand there.

She tosses her hair and reaches up to straighten the top of her dress. "Well, I have to leave, so, whatever. And Andrew, we're officially over, okay? If you want to waste your time with these losers, so be it."

I fully expect her words to hurt, but I don't feel the sting.

Honestly, she's just acting straight-up crazy.

I look to either side of me and see Grant and Brice and even Andrew all standing there, poised in protective positions—chests puffed out, heads shoved forward, ready to defend me—and I almost feel a little sick.

I appreciate them, but what kind of girl lets a guy, or three, do all the fighting? I take in a little breath to steel my nerves.

"Excuse me." I reach around Grant and move him out of my way, bringing myself right to Carmella's face.

"Gen, you don't have to—"

"Grant, I don't need you to save me," I say, putting a hand on his arm and giving him my most assuring look. It's not about him. It's about me.

I turn around to face her, head on.

"Carmella, I'm done." I swallow nervously and almost bring my hand to my mouth, but keep it pinned to my side. "I don't know what it is that made you decide that I don't deserve to be treated with even a sliver of human decency, but this has got to stop."

Her face looks like it's made of stone. I might as well be talking to a wall, but I continue anyway.

"Look around you, 'Ella.'" I finger-quote her name. "Right now, I've got all these friends on my side, and no one—no one—is standing on yours." I grit my teeth. "Where are your friends, Carmella?"

Her eyes are absolutely glaring, shooting fire or lightning or poison. And as I pause for a breath, I recognize—in a way that most people wouldn't—the shimmer of hot angry tears building in her eyes. I consider walking away right then, but I have one more thing to say.

"You say I should be embarrassed? I'm not. You don't get to decide when I'm embarrassed. And I'm no expert, but if you just got dumped by your boyfriend for insulting this loser fat girl playing dress-up in a princess costume, *and* if that loser is pretty soundly putting your narrow ass in its place right now, maybe you're the girl who should be embarrassed. I'm done."

All around us, faces are turned to me.

I feel like I'm ten feet tall and made of steel.

Cold.

Unfeeling steel.

I swallow as the sound of talking in the lobby fades to a low murmur.

Carmella looks like her eyes are made of glass, and then she pushes her shoulders back and she looks invincible again.

"Yeah," she says with quiet defiance. "You're done."

She looks around at the group of people standing behind me. I watch as her posture falls and she shifts her weight from side to side, but only for a moment. In a split-second, she's standing tall again, and her smile is plastered back in place.

With a flip of her hair, she struts away.

I don't blame the boys for watching her go. Jiminy Christmas.

Antonique walks over to me and puts an arm over my shoulder. "You okay? That was awesome. I didn't know today was Imogen the Brave day, but I like it."

"Yeah, I think I do, too," I say as I try to smile at the little circle that's surrounding me. I turn to Grant, who nods, and I feel the weight lift from my shoulders.

Jonathan sets the world back in motion when he says, "Let's go tear this show down so we can get to the cast party. Text me if you need directions to my place." Many of the kids who've been hanging around the lobby head backstage to work on picking up before we leave.

Brice walks up to me with a big pout on his lips and claps along with every word, "You gave it to her." I think he wants me to be proud. "Are you ready to turn back into a pumpkin?"

I pick up the edges of the dress and twirl it a bit. "It's a little pink...and I wish there were sleeves, but I've gotta tell you, I really did feel like a princess. No wonder Cinderella was so pissed at midnight. Not only did she have to run off without her man—"

"But she had to give up the dress, too. I know. Such a tragedy." He giggles and grabs my hand to give it a squeeze. "I'll be back there when you're ready."

The lobby has mostly cleared out, but Grant hangs back and, when I turn, he gives me a little smile as I walk to him.

"Are you going to kick me if I tell you how pretty you look?" he asks.

I laugh. "Not today."

"About before—I wasn't trying to save you. You know that, right?" His eyes are full of worry.

"Yes. I know that."

"Okay, 'cause I wanted to be sure you didn't think that I didn't think that you could stand up for yourself."

"I think I knew how because I've watched you save me so many times." I laugh. "And don't worry. Just because I saved myself this once doesn't mean you can't totally fight dragons on my behalf sometimes."

Before he has a chance to respond, I turn and head backstage, leaving Grant with his hand in his hair and a smirk on his lips.

Out of costume an hour and a half later, I'm face to face with dozens of red plastic cups being hoisted all around me. Jonathan's house is pretty massive—perfect for a party. His parents have decorated the living room in a modern, minimalist design with low, white couches and low, white tables. All are covered with sweaty teenagers. Still others, including myself and my little crew, are seated on the floor.

"To Imogen! The overnight princess!"

"So awesome."

"You killed it, Imogen!"

They gulp from their cups and pass around the two-liter bottles to top off their sodas.

It's only as Andrew is walking toward our little cluster on the floor that I remember the horrible awkwardness from before. When he told off his girlfriend for being rude to me, a virtual stranger. Well, I'm not sure if we can be strangers if our mouths have touched, but whatever. And as that thought pops into my head, I feel a mix of sadness and relief that I have absolutely no memory of the kiss ever happening. So much of today is a blur. Even my run-in with Carmella seems like a distant memory.

"Hey, you!" Andrew says through a goofy grin.

"Hey."

"I just wanted to say that you did a really, really great job today. It was totally boss sharing the stage with you." He rakes back his hair again, and I try not to laugh at his popular-guy-speak.

"It was, uh, boss working with you, too."

"I'm sorry about what Ella said after the show. That was not cool." Andrew's face slips from doofus to genuine, and I almost don't recognize him.

"You don't have to apologize for her," I say.

"Yeah, well, she was supposed to be my girlfriend. I guess I expected too much?"

"She's supposed to be my stepsister! And all I ever expected was for her to not call me a pig in public!" We laugh, and he holds up his red cup to me.

"So we're cool?" he asks.

"Totally," I say, and I clink cups with him.

Across the room, Jonathan is pointing to a shelf by the fireplace. I grab a handful of popcorn and walk over to where he's halfway through explaining the display.

"—no, really. They're all paper. This one took me three weeks to get right."

Jonathan is holding a dragon with dozens of individual scales and talons as sharp as toothpicks. Beside it rests a tiny paper bird with feathers so delicate, it looks like it might fly away.

"You made these?" I interrupt.

He sets the figure back on the shelf as if it were made of glass. "Yeah, I like origami."

"You must have really steady hands," I say without thinking, just as Jonathan shoves his left hand back into his pocket.

"Of course he does!" Brice steps over and wraps his arms around Jonathan's waist. "But how about you let me show off for a while. I've been practicing my billiards skills."

Jonathan's parents let us use their awesome game room, and we play what I'm sure is meant to look like pool, though we can barely manage to break. Laughter swirls around us as we sing along to the indie-pop songs that flow out of speakers in every room.

The party swells, and I truly feel victorious–I did good.

The clouds that are always just a few paces behind me seem to have backed off. They seem less threatening. Less heavy.

My little circle sits in the living room, near the fire, laughing and talking about the close calls in the show tonight. A few botched lines and a few exits through the wrong door and virtually no choreography, but on the whole, they're proud of me.

And I guess, though it surprises me to say it, I'm proud of myself, too.

onday morning comes too soon, but the warmth in my heart from the joy of last night still glows. I pull into the school parking lot feeling like the world is a bit brighter and less cruel. I feel like, somehow, yesterday's boldness binge has steeled me and filled my veins with strong stuff. Grant and I spend the ride recounting our favorite moments of the night. He loved when I was singing, and I loved when I wasn't falling or dying or blacking out.

"What on Earth got into you yesterday?" he asks.

"The show or the thing with Carmella?"

"Both, I guess." We haven't spoken about the things I said to Carmella in the lobby. I think Grant and I both wish I hadn't felt the need to defend myself like that. But I also think we both understand why I did it—what I hoped it might accomplish.

"I dunno. It was a weird day." I clear my throat and change the subject. "So regionals for your science competition are on Saturday morning."

"Yep," he says. "They'll let me know if I earned the scholarship this Friday."

"Awesome. I'm sure you did, though. I don't have a doubt in the world."

He smiles.

"And you're sure you don't want me to try and come to watch on Saturday morning?" I ask.

"No, you should stay and get ready for the dance with Antonique and Brice. It will be fun."

"Fun for who?" I laugh, and he shoves me sideways as we walk.

In the courtyard, he veers off so he can meet with his team before school. We make faces as we part, and he heads across the yard.

I have a few minutes, so I walk along the mural wall and head to a table where I don't usually sit. Once settled, I pull out a package of Frosted Cherry Pop-Tarts. When I start to tug the zipper of my bag closed, I notice the pattern of swirls on paper that I don't expect to see.

I pull out my journal and examine it. It's open to a page I wrote a while ago, and the spiral is folded backward so the pages are open, exposed.

I don't remember leaving my notebook in any position but closed since the first time I wrote in it, but I shrug it off, close the cover, and stick it back into my bag.

I have time to listen to a few songs and scan the mural for a bit before I have to head in for class. While I sit and soak up the morning light, I lean my head back and squint into the sky, white with clouds. I can't make out even a trace of blue.

"Hey, Imogen!"

I look over my shoulder and see two freshmen girls I recognize from my keyboarding class. The taller one says, "Good job last night!"

They don't stick around to hear me shout thanks.

That warm, filling feeling of pride comes back in full measure. It wasn't the performance of a lifetime.

I'm not a star, but I did okay. And I felt closer to my mother than I can ever remember.

With a smile, I push off the bench and head off for the double doors.

Strutting. I think I'm strutting—just a little bit—as I head down the main hall. Dozens of students are lining the walkways, milling around before the first period bell. I smile at faces I don't know, and it occurs to me that I don't usually pay much attention to things above floor level as I walk.

I turn down the hall that houses my locker.

Did she just point at me?

I'm being crazy. Of course she didn't point—wait, I know that guy just pointed at me.

Stop being paranoid.

I continue down the hall, picking up the pace, but my rushing makes me breathe heavier, and soon, it seems like more faces find mine and more people whisper to each other behind their hands.

These aren't the whispers of people who saw the show. These aren't smiles like the girl who said hi in the courtyard. This doesn't feel the same at all.

Pink spots flood my vision, and I realize that my eyes aren't playing tricks on me. The hallway near my locker is covered with violent pink. I'm sure it's nothing to do with me, but the staring doesn't stop. In fact, it's getting worse.

My locker is completely covered with the hot pink fliers. I close my eyes in a desperate attempt to disappear.

One step at a time, nearer and nearer, the pages slowly come into focus.

There are several different versions. Some of them are photographs of me during the dance number last night. My arms are mid-jiggle, and my face looks like I'm in the middle of a bathroom emergency. Some say, "Escaped from the psych ward!" One has a picture of me holding my arms up while I sing, and big red slashes have been drawn up and down my wrists in bold marker.

I try to breathe, even as the grey starts ringing my vision.

Some of the fliers look more plain. They're just handwriting.

I step closer.

My handwriting.

Copies of pages from my journal are all over the hallway. I shiver and cover my mouth. My mind starts imagining all of the secrets I've written in those pages. Feelings and fears and hurt that I've tried to put into words.

But I quickly realize that none of the pages are about me. They're all about them. Words I've written about the kids in my classes. About cool kids and smart kids. About normal kids. About Brice and Antonique and Andrew.

About Grant.

Moments of frustration and jealousy and insecurity, spewed onto paper.

Just moments.

But now they're on the walls.

They're all I can see.

IMOGEN KEEGAN'S REAL THOUGHTS ABOUT HER FRIENDS:

Antonique really needs to think about what kind or reputation she wants. Because if she's content to be a body with no brain, then by all means, she should keep flirting with half-naked guys just because they looked at her funny.

Andrew doesn't have much in the way of brains, but apparently he uses the few neurons he does have to flirt with freshmen and laugh at people.

I start to pull pages off my locker, and as I remove the layers, I feel the eyes. All around me, they're connecting dots and realizing that I'm the girl who must have written it all down.

In a panic, I spin around to face dozens of my peers. Some walking and laughing, others standing still, unashamedly gawking. A few look ready to rip my head off.

And then, I see them.

Brice, Jonathan, and Antonique are at the end of the hallway.

They all have a pink page in their hands.

I watch as Brice holds up the paper. He stares at me, holding the page, and I'm frozen. My heart is beating so fast it's causing my ribs to ache. Jonathan reaches up and puts his hand on Brice's shoulder, whispers something, but Brice shrugs him off and wads the paper up into a ball. He drops it on the floor, spins on a dime, and walks away without looking back. I look to the wall and see the words I know he's reading.

Brice and Jonathan make me sick.

I gasp. A sob catches in my chest, and my eyes cloud with tears.

The bell rings, and the students all begin moving toward their first classes. Kids shove into me and bump me against the wall, and then, without a warning, the bodies clear and I see Grant.

He's reading the pink sheet in his hand.

I'm frozen, staring at him. Willing him to drop it, unread. Slowly, as if he knows I'm standing there, he lifts his gaze.

His eyes lock onto mine.

We don't blink. I'm about to run to him when he closes his eyes slowly.

And then, he turns from me, and walks away.

My silent tears are gaining speed, collecting and falling like bombs. The only sound I hear is my ragged breathing and my heart pounding like a jackhammer.

I look over to the locker and put my hand on one of the pink pages.

Grant would be a better friend if he'd stop trying to fix everything all the time. He thinks he's so perfect. He's always swooping in, saving his best friend, the perpetual damsel in distress, but it just makes it obvious that he's got an out-of-control savior complex.

I rip it off the wall as my vision gets spotty and I start breathing too fast and too hard.

I sense that my feet are moving. They're not actually glued to the floor. My lumbering quickens, and soon, I am jogging down the hallway. My sagging body jars with each footfall, and my lungs begin to burn. Slamming through the double doors, I move as quickly as I can, cutting through the parking lot to my car. I throw my bag in the back, shove in behind the wheel, and pull the seatbelt across my shoulder. It digs into my protruding belly, and I slam my fists against the steering wheel. A guttural shriek of frustration and sadness escapes my throat, and I bury my face in my hands.

When I stop screaming, I turn my key.

The thread I'd been holding onto—that made me feel normal—has been ripped away. I've lost my grip, and I'm falling.

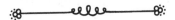

In my next coherent moment, I'm racing up the stairs of my empty house. My sobs have shredded my throat. My breathing is so erratic I'm feeling lightheaded. I storm into Carmella's bedroom and see a few boxes still in the corners on the floor. I approach her desk where her computer is on, but sleeping. I tap a key, but it's password-protected, so I turn around and stomp to her night stand. There's nothing of interest.

Stupid. This is stupid. She'll surely have covered her tracks, but at the same time, there is no one who could have done this but her. No one. I head for her door and stop short. Beside her mouse is her all-in-one printer. The scanner lid is still up. I reach for the paper tray and close my eyes.

In one fast tug, I rip out the drawer.

Three sheets of hot pink paper still sit on a thick stack of plain white sheets. I toss the tray on the floor as a sob breaks out of my lungs.

I leave her room and turn into mine, slamming the door shut.

I don't want to think. I don't want to see anyone, ever again.

Even though Evelyn isn't home, I drag the ottoman from my big chair over to the door to barricade myself in. My tears dot the fabric.

I reach into my bag for my phone, and my hand brushes against my notebook. I think that, somehow, I thought it would have vanished into thin air, but it hasn't. It's in my bag. It was in my bag today. It was in my bag last night, while I was still at the cast party, when she was desperate for a weapon. She found one.

I pull it out and flip through it in a blur. I stop as I see a single green Post-it stuck to one of the pages— the one page in the entire book that contains a harsh word against Grant. That one page.

Her handwriting is heavy and sharp.

"DONE."

I sob and toss the book to my bedside table and pull out my phone.

No calls yet.

But they're coming.

For a second, I want to call my dad. I want to call him and tell him what Carmella has done.

But then I think of all the things I said last night after the show, and I hear my dad's disappointed voice in my head and realize I'm trapped.

Instinctively, I tap Grant's name and then disconnect. I can't talk to him either.

Right above Grant's number is the emergency number for Therapist George.

It only rings twice.

"It's Imogen." My voice is ragged and filled with only air.

"Are you okay?" George's voice sounds different on the phone. Deeper maybe. I can't hear any of the light in his office. I can't picture the cufflinks that make him seem real.

"I..." I can't think of what I want to say.

I can't tell.

I can't tell George or anyone what happened.

What she did will come back to me. I'll get in trouble somehow. They are my words. It will all be my fault.

"Imogen, talk to me. What's going on?"

"My mother was wrong." The words are spoken before I have time to think them through.

"About what, Imogen? How was your mother wrong?" I hate the urgency in his voice and the way he keeps saying my name. I hate the way he's restating my questions.

"About life. About everything."

"Okay, I'm listening."

My thoughts are scattered and rushing through my brain in all directions. "She had a childish point of view. Like, she used to call me her 'Happily Ever After.' Like I was the cherry on top of her sundae. She actually bought into the bullshit idea of happiness and had the privileged point of view that everyone could have it."

Tears are streaking my face, and my phone is slipping over my skin.

"And you disagree?"

"Yeah, I do."

In a wave, I feel the heat of anger and resentment wash over me.

It comes on so quickly that I feel light-headed as my temperature rises.

"Even if you manage to have it for a moment, who says you get to keep it? I mean, the way I see it, I had happiness once. And she was smashed across a highway by a semi-truck. So don't tell me that happy endings come to those who're looking 'cause if anyone deserved a happy ending—if anyone had done everything right—it was her."

"Imogen, why don't you come in and see me. I can clear my schedule for you. Just come on by."

"I don't want to see you, George. I don't want to see anyone."

His voice dwindles to nothing as I pull the phone from my ear and disconnect the call.

I turn my ringer off and shove my phone under my pillow.

I sit on the edge of my bed in the dark for a long time. Hot, fresh tears roll down my cheeks, and my body is trembling again, wracked with great heaving sobs.

Outside, the compassionate sky has dimmed. The white clouds that blocked out the sky all morning hang heavier now. They seem to press down on the space above my head, as if every raindrop they're holding onto is just waiting to fall once my tears run out.

I felt proud for standing up to Carmella with an army behind me.

An army of people who should have known better than to align themselves with someone who doesn't deserve them—someone who has written and thought horrible and senseless things about them in the moments she couldn't control her feelings.

I get up from the bed, and empty candy bar wrappers fall to the floor. I've all but emptied my secret sweet stashes. I've eaten from the stockpiles under my desk, in my sock drawer, in my rarely worn dress shoes, and now, behind the books on my shelf. I reach behind the few paperback novels I keep and grab the last of my treasures. In a few chomps, it's gone.

As I stand in front of my bookcase, a shiver passes over my skin that has nothing to do with a chill. An old itch that I instantly crave to scratch.

All of this anger and sadness. All of these tears. They've been forced on me. I didn't choose them, and I can't contain them. I didn't ask for this life. I didn't ask for a dead mom and a disease I can't control. I shift my eyes to the painted picture frame, and once again I reach up and turn it face down.

Sorry, Mom. You wanted a girl who could do it all and be it all. You wanted beauty and talent and compassion and strength, but you left and you just took it all with you.

How could I ever be those things now?

"Those are the things you were supposed to teach me."

The sound of my voice in the quiet room seems to trigger the falling rain.

I listen as it falls against my window.

I can't control all of the hurt and rage.

But there is a pain I can control.

My breathing slows, though the tears don't, and I reach up to the top shelf. I pull down the storybook full of fairy tales. She read it to me so many times, I'm sure I could still recite the whole thing.

I collapse on the bed with my book. I hold it to my chest and smell the worn pages. I open it and see the secret hidden there.

On the inside cover, in a neat little square, boxed with bright colors, my mother wrote,
> "*For My Happily Ever After,*
> '*The End' is just*
> *the beginning!*"

I run my hand over the script, but her ink is not the secret I seek.

I trace my way down the page and wrap my fingers around the cold, sleek metal.

The single blade I've been hiding gleams in my palm.

Just one cut. I just need one.

I push up my sleeve and run my finger across the six faint ridges.

The metal on my skin is cold, and I press. Press. Press.

Until I'm in.

I can't explain the feeling.

It hurts. Of course it hurts.

But it's *my* hand that's doing the hurting. My pressure, my force, my will.

My teeth are gritted together, but my trembling has stopped. It's not like I wanna die or anything.

But I want control over my pain.

I want to know that the stinging and slicing isn't being inflicted upon me, but is of me...It is me.

The second I stop, shame fills the wound.

I look down and press my hand against my arm. I try to press it back together.

I swore I'd never do this again. But...I also kept a blade.

I pull my sleeve back down.

I slide the steel back between the pages and drop the book on the floor.

I reach under my pillow and retrieve my phone.

Three missed calls and twice as many texts.

I knew it was only a matter of time.

Grant's first text says, "*I'm not happy right now. But I also need to know you're okay. Tell me you're okay.*"

His second seems more urgent. "*Gen. Your car is gone, and if you went home, fine, but please let me know.*"

And then there's one from Evelyn. "*Honey, are you okay? George just called my cell and told me you were upset. I'm on my way home. It will be okay, honey.*"

No.

It's not okay. And I don't want you to come rushing in and throwing out words you don't understand, Evelyn. I'm not your daughter, and this isn't your problem.

I turn off my phone.

I swallow a pill.

I fall back onto the bed, arm pulsing with pain, and it all crashes over me again.

And I let it.

No resistance.

No false strength.

The wave of my grief bears down on me and begins to pull me under.

I don't struggle. I let it pull me down into the deep.

24

My consciousness ebbs and flows. I try and ignore the bodies and voices that come in and out of my room. I wake when the rush of fear and anger fills my head, which reminds me to take another dose. I register only broad brushstrokes of feelings before weariness and grief and chemically induced calm come again to claim me.

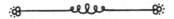

I know it's Tuesday because I hear the trash truck drive down our street before the daylight has even crept in. Grant came last night, but I didn't respond when he shook me and begged me to wake up and talk. I wanted him to be angry and to hate how broken I am. I wanted him protected and rid of his most toxic relationship.

He started out softly. He said soothing things from the edges of my room. I listened as he paced, his voice and demeanor changing with each word I refused. He didn't touch me. He didn't sit beside me.

He only walked, back and forth, until finally, his voice splintered and cracked with anger and hurt.

Maybe, if I push hard enough, I can give you the distance you've always deserved but never been brave enough to take.

I lay with dead weight on my pillow until he left.

Even as the space between us grew, his steps dwindling into the absence of sound, my whole being wished for him to prop himself in his regular chair and whisper into my darkness. I felt like a magnet, reaching for its match until it's pulled just a millimeter too far and then it reaches for nothing at all.

He didn't stay.

Stupid, worthless bladder.

I open my door without making a sound because, even in the worst of times, a girl's still gotta pee.

I take one silent step before the bathroom door swings open wide, making me jump.

Carmella is ready for bed.

We stare for a moment, but say nothing. As she stands there, I stand here, until I manage to pull my foot back in my room.

"I'll hold it," I mutter as I slam the door shut.

The next time my eyes open it's dark outside, and the time after that, it's light again.

Wednesday. I peek under my hair to see that Evelyn has cracked my door open. Beside my bed are three peanut butter and jelly sandwiches. I roll my head the other way and sob into my pillow.

How dare she try and comfort me? Mother me? She'll never be my mother.

I don't have a mom.

I have two women who should be or could be but won't ever be my mom.

Both of them have no idea who I am.

Evelyn has only ever known me as a disturbed, sad, broken thing.

And my mom only knew me as a tiny, mirrored bird. I never had my own song to sing; I only mimicked hers.

She wouldn't recognize me now. She never would've wanted a daughter who hurts herself more than she helps herself. She never would've wanted a daughter who cries more than she smiles.

I wish she were here to comfort me. She might utter sweet shushing sounds and tell me it would be all right.

She'd be lying, but I'd take it.

Because that's what daughters do.

They believe in the hopes and dreams, however false, their mothers have for them.

I hear Evelyn in the hallway. She's talking to my dad on the phone. She's telling him that she's not sure what to do, but that the doctor said a few days wouldn't be out of the ordinary.

She tries to convince him to finish his trip and not to come home.

It sounds like he agrees.

I wish I felt surprised.

I wake to feel warm water on my left arm. I force myself to be still and quiet as Grant cleans my thin, pathetic wound. I can't see him. I don't change my breathing or move the pillow from my face, but I know it's him.

I can smell his hair. I can feel the specific way he sits on my bed without making it creak.

But I can't feel him. His gravity is gone.

All that's in me clamors for the familiarity, but there is no pull from him. All this time, I was sure that our connection was all from me: loving and wanting and needing.

But as tears slip onto the pillow beneath me, I know I was wrong. We both held an end of the rope, and now he's letting go.

I hold my breath and almost choke trying to keep still, even as sobs fill my chest. When the cut is clean, there is only silence. And then, right on the raw skin, I feel delicate pressure. Two soft spots, warm and gentle. Lips. I hear his kiss as he pulls his face away and runs his fingertips down to mine before pulling the sleeve of my hoodie back down to my wrist. I search my nerves for the electric charge that always accompanies his touch. I will my spine to shiver. I wait for my heart to take flight.

But it's broken. And maybe, if he's lucky, we are too.

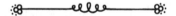

It's morning again. The stupid birds won't leave my window. It's like they don't know that Cinderella lives in the room next door, and I have no desire to sing with them or knit them little bird hats or ever hear music again.

They've been too loud. They've pushed me too far into awake-ness.

The jangling of the doorknob indicates my privacy will soon be violated, so I retreat further into my pillow and blanket enclosure.

I feel the bed sink beside me.

"Seriously. Leave me alone."

My voice is raw, broken, and unused.

"Come on, Gen. You can't send me away. I'm a total mushroom." His voice is painfully tender.

My heart flutters for half of a breath in my chest, but as I exhale, it calms.

"Grant. Please, just go. I don't want to see anyone right now."

"But, Gen, I'm your very favorite mushroom of all time. You don't mean that."

I will not take the bait. I will not help him set up a stupid punchline. We don't need comic relief.

"Please, just go."

"Mushroom!" he shouts.

"Oh for God's sake, fine!" I flip over suddenly and pull the biggest pillows away from my face. "Why are you calling yourself a mushroom?"

"You know me, Gen! I'm a fun-guy!"

I hold my deadpan face for as long as I can before attempting to retreat behind my pillow, but he got me.

His stupid joke and his beautiful face and the bandage on my arm and all at once I start to laugh and cry. I look up and see the corners of his mouth are turned up, but that's not his smile.

For one random moment, we both freeze. His sad eyes are dull, and they watch a tear fall down my cheek.

The moment lasts for the rest of my life, until slowly, he reaches up and wipes the tear away.

Radiating out from that spot, throughout my body, my skin tingles like I've been tossed in a fire. The return of that spark locks my walls into place.

"Don't," I say as I lean back on my arms. "You cannot talk to me like this. All sweet and funny. You shouldn't be here. You should be somewhere, angry."

"Oh, I'm a little angry. And hurt, Gen. This whole thing sucked. But I'm smart enough to know that you don't take a quote out of context. I don't care about the stupid posters. I got mad when you pulled away and shut me out."

Fingers of guilt wrap around my spine.

"I came in here and tried to pull you out before you'd fallen too far, but you just threw in the towel and disconnected completely."

I disconnected.

"And," he continues, "you can't do that. You can't. Ever. You can never stop fighting because if you lose you, I lose you."

He starts to say something else while my mouth stays shut, but the words catch in his throat and he looks down at the carpet for only a second. He reaches up and brushes my hair back from my face.

"You are my best friend. The best friend that any person could ever, ever have."

Best friend. Friend.

I swallow and use my brittle voice again. "But I'm not. I'm selfish. I miss things. I mess up."

"Yeah, and you also make me laugh and make me feel like I'm better than I am and teach me about strength."

"But what if I broke us?"

In less than a breath, a smile—his real smile—breaks across his face, and his eyes stare straight into mine as he shakes his head, laughing.

"Oh, would you stop being dramatic? Nothing's broken. A little bruised, maybe, but not broken. Never broken. Not us."

I throw myself forward without thinking and wrap my arms around his shoulders, resting my head on his chest. His arms circle me tightly, and his hands trace small swirlies on my back. The floodgates open, and the tears pour out like lava, burning my eyes and clearing out everything in their path.

I consider words like "I'm sorry," and "Thank you," and "How are you mine?" but before I can speak, my mind empties and my breathing slows and the eruption finally stops.

I pull away and wipe my face all over my sleeve.

"So what happened?" I ask.

"Well, I didn't realize you were gone till after first period. Jonathan skipped second to drive me over and drop me off. The front door was locked, but I sat outside until Evelyn got home."

I have no idea what to say. Nothing sounds right in my head, so I keep my mouth shut.

"Evelyn was really worried, obviously. I told her you needed a little space but to call Dr. Rodriguez and TG and your dad. She was really, really upset. She kept asking what happened."

"Well, she's never seen me like this without Dad here. Probably freaked her out."

"It freaked *everyone* out, Gen. It's scary." His voice is stern for the span of one word.

I sit up straight on my bed. "Oh my God, you didn't tell her what happened, did you? With Carmella? It would just make everything worse."

"I probably should have, but I couldn't. And by the time I walked by your locker again, every flier was gone. It was like it never happened. I told Evelyn that someone said mean things to you about the show. But that's it."

"And Carmella? I've barely even seen her at all."

"I mean, she's been at school. I haven't said a word to her—and I won't—but she hasn't said a word to me either. I ran into her in the kitchen last night, but she just turned around and walked back out. Whatever that means."

I grab a cup of water and swirl a big gulp around in my stale mouth.

"So have you talked to my dad? I heard Evelyn talking to him. I know he didn't bother coming home."

Grant looks away, and I'm instantly suspicious.

"His phone was off when George tried calling him. And when he turned it back on, Evelyn, George, and everyone pretty much had things under control. He wanted to come home immediately, but everyone convinced him you were stable. It wasn't until yesterday that I saw your arm."

He pauses, and I hear his voice tighten around words he doesn't want to say. I look down at the sleeve of my hoodie.

"How did you know?" I ask.

"I just had a feeling. I pulled up your sleeve, and I had to go call him."

"Oh, God." I lean back and look at the ceiling. I can picture it now: my dad talking about betrayal and trust, how I promised I'd never cut again—like it's that easy.

"Seeing your arm like that again really scared me." His voice is tinged with confusion and disappointment. He pauses, giving me space to respond, but there's nothing I can say. "He just got here. Right now." Grant pulls his phone from his pocket to check the time. "I begged and pleaded for him to let me talk to you before he busted in here. He gave me exactly five minutes."

"I guess time's up?"

He nods.

I look at Grant's face and remember his lips on my skin. I think of my dad running to catch a plane and worrying about the girl he'd find when he got home. I think of all those peanut butter sandwiches.

"Thank you for taking care of my arm." My jaw clenches. "I'm just really, really sorry. And I am glad you're here because you probably shouldn't be. But you can't just let me hurt you because you want to make me better. You shouldn't just forgive me because you want another chance to play the hero."

His eyes change before me. They seem to pull away, and his brow knits together, just slightly. A whisper of hurt is etched on his face.

"Gen, I wish you could believe me when I say this: I don't want or need to be a hero. And only broken things need fixing."

I open my mouth to speak, but close it again. I want to tell him that I'm more broken than even I really knew.

And it scares me.

"They've said I can crash on the couch downstairs. So I'm going to. Turn your phone back on and text me if you need anything."

"I know you wanted to check on me, but it's okay, really."

He looks at me with a face that is hard to understand. His eyes are gentle, but his brows are furrowed. His jaw seems clenched, the muscles twitching beneath his skin, but his mouth is relaxed and he bites his bottom lip for just a second before he answers.

"I'll stay," he says.

He turns and walks out the door.

I take to straightening myself up in my bed. I prop myself against my pillows and pull my hair back into a neat bun just as the door creaks open slowly.

My dad looms in the doorframe. He is tall and lean and dressed in a perfect college professor costume, but it's actually from his everyday wardrobe. His face is dotted with great blue eyes that always seem to shimmer. But not now. His skin is grey, and his cheeks are scruffy and hollow. His hair is rumpled, and his shirt is untucked.

He plants himself at the edge of my bed and places his hand on my leg.

"Hi, Dad," I say feebly.

"Hey, Immy."

I can't look at him. I know that the second I do, I'll burst into tears, and for some reason, I just don't want him to see me like that. I don't want him to see me fall apart again. I don't want him to think about the girl he carried down the stairs in the middle of a nervous breakdown not even a full year ago.

I set my jaw and focus on a spot in the center of his chest.

"Oh, baby girl." He scoots over and sits against my headboard, pulling me under his wing.

At least now I don't have to see his eyes.

"I'm sorry, Dad."

"You don't have to apologize to me."

"I do. You had to come home early because I can't hold myself together. Even when I try."

"Coming home to make sure you're okay isn't a burden, Imogen. It's my job."

"Is it?" The question comes out in a much more accusatory tone than I mean it to, but the ball starts rolling and I decide to let the honesty flow. "Dad, I don't blame you for needing a break from me. If I were in your position I'd probably need to get away too. I can't imagine what it feels like to have a daughter that has been broken and sad and angry and damaged for as long as I have. I probably couldn't stand to be around me either."

He sits me up and tries to catch my eye. I avoid him for as long as I can until he finally draws my attention up to his face.

"Listen to me. Yes, watching you hurt is harder than you could ever imagine. You're absolutely right. I hate it. I hate to see you in pain. But I'm not escaping you."

The flicker of peace he brought into my room threatens to go out.

"Immy, you had such a good summer. George said you were doing great. And when my publicist said there were places willing to pay me to come and talk about grief and the book, I thought the timing was right. I didn't know what you were going through, and I didn't plan to miss this."

"I know you didn't plan it, Dad, but how could you go and make this whole new career out of writing about her and talking about her to other people when you barely talk about her to me?"

I feel my chin begin to quiver.

My father swallows and runs his hand over his scruffy face. "I don't know if you've ever really thought about it, but I don't know anything about losing a mom. I know how to lose the mother of my child. How to lose my best friend. But I don't know how to say the right things to you. Sometimes I look at you, and all I can see is pain I can't heal. And it guts me. And it's horrible. But I'd carry all your pain and all of mine if I could. I love you so much. I would do anything to take that pain from you."

My eyes have filled with tears, and even though I don't want him to watch them fall, I know that he sees them there. I reach up and wipe them away.

"This hurt..." He gestures to his own chest. "is never going away. Ever. And neither is yours. But that doesn't mean life is over." He points at my heart, too. "Every single hour of every single day I pray for the moment that you realize she left behind so much more than just pain."

My breath catches in my chest, and I breathe it out slowly into my lap.

I look at my pillowcase. The stitching is coming apart in one corner, and I tug at the thread.

He stands up and begins to walk to the door.

"But what if the pain's the biggest thing she left behind? Sometimes it feels like it's taking up every bit of space I have," I say.

When I lift my chin, tears stream down my face. I don't see the point in holding them back anymore.

He looks at me with tears of his own and says in his voice that's always so full of music. "Someday you'll have to let some of that pain go to make room in your heart for something even bigger."

*E*ven though I begged and tried to remind him that I had just spent the past four days in a depressive episode, Dad insisted that if Therapist George said returning to the school routine was healthy, then I had to give it a try.

George. That miserable traitor.

I surprise TG by telling him that I feel like I can get through the weekend without him. I make an appointment to see him on Monday.

This Friday morning, I'm fully committed to avoiding everyone I know. I enter through the door by the Math building and cling to the walls. As I turn to pass the main staircase, I see Antonique's face through the crowd. I try to turn away before we make eye contact, but it's too late. She looks at me for a moment before dropping her gaze and heading up the stairs.

Blink. Blink.

The disappointment settles in my gut as I open and close my fists, and I suck in a deep breath.

I'm so stupid.

I rush to the library and make a beeline to the table upstairs in the back. On my way in, there are no jeers.

No taunts. Life has moved on at Crestwood, and no one seems to remember the giant, sobbing girl from Monday morning. Except for the people I care about. I doubt they're gonna forget.

I don't have to wait long for Mr. Reed's class to come filing in. Students scatter all across the space. I wait for Jonathan, hoping to see a friendly face, but I don't see him anywhere. I hear bits of conversation about all kinds of things. They talk about their projects, the big Fine Arts Rally tomorrow night, and about who saw who making out in the equipment closet. Nobody is thinking about me at all until Mr. Reed takes role. There's a long quiet stretch after I answer "present." Or at least it seems that way. Almost every face is turned toward mine. Except for Andrew's. On the other side of the library, I see him staring straight ahead and twirling his pencil.

I don't blame him for ignoring me. I'd ignore me, too.

Tucked in the back, I set my chair so I'm staring toward the window, and I can't see who might be looking or not looking at me behind my back. I try to think about where Jonathan and I were in our research before I was gone, but I don't even know where to start.

"I finished the archetypes project." Jonathan's voice carries over my shoulder. "It's all ready to turn in. You just need to put your name on it. Reed's oblivious. He won't figure out that you missed most of the work."

He walks up to the table, one hand deep in his pocket, and with the other, he pulls out his chair and sits down.

"Thanks," I say. My voice sounds deflated and sad in my ears. There's a deep quality and a coating of shame that I hear dripping off of every word. "Jonathan, I know everyone is mad at me. I know Brice is mad at me. You should be mad, too. I really—"

"Stop," he interrupts. "Brice is...frustrated. But I don't want to talk about him. I was late because I heard you were here today and I wanted to get something out of my locker for you."

"You heard I was here?"

"Brice saw you creeping through the parking lot this morning."

I don't blame Brice a bit for not saying anything. I wouldn't have either.

Jonathan reaches into the outer pocket of his backpack and cups something between both hands.

"What?" I ask.

He opens them, letting it fall to the table before returning his hands to his lap.

Sitting in front of me is an origami flower made of hot pink paper.

That paper.

I look closer and see the harsh black lines of permanent marker and can make out a few cruel words and bits of my own handwriting.

"I pulled down all of the fliers after you left. I shredded them all by hand. Except one. This one."

Confusion settles between my eyebrows, but based on context clues, I'm relatively confident this is meant to be a comforting gesture, so I settle on an awkward, "Thank you. For...destroying them."

"If paper-shredding were a superpower, I could definitely be a hero." He reaches up and places both of his hands flat on the tabletop.

I can't stop myself from looking. I try to force myself to stare at his face, but after a few seconds, he says, "Do you know why I spent an hour shredding them? Or why I spent my time folding this flower?"

I shake my head.

"You've noticed my hand, haven't you?"

"Yeah. I mean, no." I nod slightly. "I've wondered."

"Imagine this." He holds up his hand between us, showing me his palm. "Imagine waking up one day and being overcome with the crippling fear that your hand is dying. You know it doesn't make sense. You know that hands don't just fall off and die, but you're sure—with every fiber of your being—that your hand is actually gonna fall off. The more you move your hand, the closer you are to losing it."

I feel my eyelids open wide and I try to keep my face neutral, but I know that there's something I don't understand.

"Imogen, I know what it feels like to have anxiety take control of your life. My OCD came on like a light switch, and it's the most frustrating, painful, confusing thing that's ever happened to me."

I watch his Adam's apple bob as he swallows, but I can tell he's not finished, so I keep my mouth shut.

"For almost a year, I tried to keep my hand totally still. I'd sit on it or even wrap it with a bandage so it wouldn't move. I thought if I hid my hand, I'd hide my problem. But then the disuse atrophy got really bad. Eventually, I got help. I got medicated. I started using my hands in certain environments."

"Like being a stagehand," I say.

I've never thought for a moment that I was the only person with problems, but that didn't help me feel less alone. Days of forcing myself to breathe and count while cowering in the bathroom in junior high school made me feel alone, even if I knew it wasn't true.

But here in front of me sits Jonathan. His hand is open, unflinching between us. It looks normal and he looks normal, but Jonathan knows what it feels like to not have control of feelings—to not have control of fear.

"I had no idea," I say, my face as full of compassion as I can ask it to be.

"I didn't tell you. Which, come to think of it, was probably pretty crappy of me. I knew you were going through some crazy shit, and I probably should have told you, in specific words, that you weren't going through it alone."

"I don't blame you. Really. I get it."

"I know you do," he says, shifting his focus back to the pink paper flower.

The venom of her words and mine screams to me from the folds. I turn from them to face him again. "You didn't have to tear those down for me. Especially not after what I said about you and Brice—even though what I wrote...that's not what I think." I backpedal and reach for simple gratitude. "I just...Thank you."

"I didn't just tear them down for you." He smiles. "One of the most effective parts of *my* treatment has been learning origami. Using my hand in controlled, repetitive movements is good for me. Plus I like taking something that's flat and dull and making it more alive. It's my way of making something cool out of something that sucks so totally bad."

Jonathan reaches over and spins the flower where it sits.

"I just really needed to find a way to use the worst thing in my life to make my life better."

The flower is this beautiful symbol of his strength, but it looks an awful lot like a memento of one of the worst moments of my life. I'm glad it made him feel better, and I know it's supposed to make me feel better, but it only makes me sad.

I force a smile and take the flower from the table, putting it into the pocket of my hoodie.

"Thanks for telling me," I say softly.

He looks down at the table and places his tortured hand on mine.

"It sucks. But you can make pain beautiful...if you try."

I swallow hard and push the shimmer out of my eyes as Jonathan squeezes my hand once before shoving his own back in his pocket.

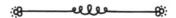

At lunch, Grant and I walk outside out of habit, but I don't want to eat in front of the mural today. I decide not to argue, but as he takes his regular spot on the bench, I don't sit beside him. I walk around and sit across from him, with my back to the mural.

"I'm not going to Gild's class last period," I declare.

"Gen, come on."

"No, I can't. I can't face the others. Not after what I wrote about them. Maybe you're over it, but clearly, Brice isn't. Antonique probably isn't. They have every right to be mad at me, but I can't handle *seeing* them be mad right now."

He awkwardly gnaws at his carrot stick, and I can tell that I'm right. They are mad. And he's not arguing hard enough to convince me otherwise.

"I went by this morning and told Gild that, since I missed so much class this week, I had work to make up. She wrote me a pass to the library for later. She said you guys aren't doing anything anyway since all anyone wants to do is talk about what they're wearing to the stupid dance tomorrow."

Grant looks up and over my head. I see his eyes do a long vertical pass on the mural.

When he puts his eyes back on me, he looks tired and sad. His eyes don't sparkle, and even his hair seems flatter.

"Gen, please don't tell me you're not coming to the dance with me now? The Rally is a big deal—it's always been a big night for us. We make that night special and fun, and I'm sorry, but I don't want to miss being there with you."

"How could you ask me to go? How could I be at a dance with all of those people who know what I did?"

"Gen, you didn't *do* anything."

He reaches across the table and puts his palm out flat and open. I stare at it and consider everything it means if I take it. It means I have to take a step forward. It means I can't keep dwelling on these past few days. It means my right to wallow in self-pity runs out.

I lift my hand and place my palm on top of his.

"How can I go and wear some stupid outfit and not be the butt of another joke?" I ask him.

His sad eyes have already changed in the seconds since I took his hand. They seem lighter already—more hopeful.

"Y'know, we don't have to go and wear costumes and be weirdos. It's a formal dance. We could always dress like normal people."

The bell rings, interrupting us, and I realize there's not much left to say that can be squeezed into two minutes.

"I'll meet you at the car after school, okay?" I say.

"Okay," he says. He shakes his head slightly as he walks off.

Something in his body language, the way his chin is tucked under as he bites his bottom lip catches me off-guard and I realize he was waiting for me to say something. "Grant!"

He turns around to face me and opens his arms in question.

"The scholarship thing! Did you hear about it? Did you make the top three?"

He smiles and nods at me.

"Why didn't you tell me?" I ask while kids start pouring through the courtyard to get to their next class.

"You didn't ask," he shouts into cupped hands. He doesn't look mad or even disappointed. He just says it. Like it's just this fact of life that he's accepted as easily as the sky being blue. He's accepted that I'll be consumed by my own drama and forget his.

My best friend is satisfied to be an afterthought. And the idea of that makes me sick to my stomach.

How can I love Grant so much more than I ever manage to show him?

No wonder he keeps that door blocked off. Why would he want to be in love with someone who loves their drama more?

A whisper slips past my lips and is lost in the sound of the kids passing by. "I love you more."

"What?" he hollers through the flood of students. He jumps up to see me, and I laugh.

"I–congratulations!" I scream over the crowd.

"Thanks!" he shouts. He lets the corner of his mouth tip up, and he heads to class.

I drag my backpack against the steps as I head up to my room after school. The sound of four days of homework echoes through the hallway.

I push open my door, and for a second, I think I've entered the wrong room. I see my bed, my walls, my bookcase, my posters, but it's barely recognizable.

Everything is clean.

Just then, Evelyn pops out of my closet door and almost jumps out of her skin.

"Oh! Imogen, honey, you scared me."

"Scared you? You're the one in my room. Why are you in my room?"

My face is pinched with anger and confusion, and I resist the urge to scream at her to get out. I drop my bag and take an inventory of key places. My eyes dart to the top of my bookshelf—my book is undisturbed—to my nightstand drawer—I just refilled my candy stash before leaving today—to my jewelry box—she better not have touched my mom's old stuff.

"I...I wanted to tidy some things up for you—"

"You touched my things?" My voice is calm but questioning. What was she looking for? Was she trying to find dirt on me? Was she looking for my journal? Did Carmella tell her?

I feel my pulse quicken, and I hate–absolutely hate–that my body is always so quick to react. Heartbeat, sweaty hands, lump in throat. I hate that I'm so obvious. Even to myself.

She takes a step forward and puts her hand on the side of my arm. "Hon, I wasn't trying to invade your privacy. I just figured today would be really tough on you...going back to school and everything...And, well, I read that having a clean space can help bring about a fresh start."

She smiles at me, and her eyes are so concerned and gentle that I almost want to forget my perpetual annoyance and wrap my arms around her waist and bury myself in her warmth. Almost. But I don't.

"Oh." I notice how my millions of hoodies are folded on my chair and how all of the little papers from all over have been stacked neatly on my desk.

She watches as I look around the room. "I hope you're not upset with me. I just didn't know how else I could help. I always clean up Carmella's room for her, especially when she's upset or when things are rough for her."

"Things are ever rough for her? That's pretty hard to imagine. I mean, her life is obviously perfect."

"No, Imogen. It's not. You don't think she stomps around here with a grumpy face because she's happy, do you? Think she's happy that her parents got divorced or that I remarried? You think she would have left the only school she's ever known–halfway through the fall semester–unless she had to? Unless she believed it was the only way?"

"Only way to what?" Evelyn seems to have pulled open a freshly healed wound. I'm sure that I'm invading something, that I shouldn't be hearing these words and she shouldn't be saying them, but before I can change the subject, she speaks again.

"There are mean girls other than the one you think I maliciously planted in the room next door, Imogen." I swallow hard and bite my lip to keep from interrupting her thoughts. "I'm not blind. I know you two haven't had the smoothest transition to living under the same roof, but I think you both are missing the big picture here. Both of you have been through a lot. So much. Too much. Divorce and death and rejection and loss. It's a shame you only resist each other instead of embracing the built-in support of being a family."

Evelyn shakes her head as if she has just realized that she's spilling her daughter's business. I can practically see her bite her tongue.

"Anyway, about your room, I'm sorry if you feel it was a violation. It's just one of those things that makes me feel like I'm contributing something."

"No. Thanks. You didn't have to."

"I know I didn't, but I wanted to. I'll just head downstairs, okay? Would you like me to bring you a date and walnut bar? I made them today."

She twists her fingers together in front of her bright white tank top. Her skin is so tanned next to the shirt, it makes every freckle pop.

"No, I'm okay. I've got a lot of work to pretend I care about doing," I say.

"They're vegan," she says with a broad, toothy smile. Like this will be the key selling point.

I stare at her blankly.

"I was thinking I'd make some brownies later...the boxed kind. Eggs and everything..." she adds.

She needs this moment even more than I do. I can see it all over her face. "Okay."

"Okay," she says. She smiles proudly and pats my arm again before closing the door behind her.

I flop down on my bed and get out my journal for the first time since the afternoon that everything fell apart. I'm not sure why I don't want to write in it. I just want to try and look at my words through Carmella's eyes. I flip through the pages and try to imagine her thumbing through it. As I skim, I feel my face warm up with embarrassment. There are so many words on these pages that I meant to write but never meant to be read.

Who actually parades around in skin-tight dresses and super-short skirts? It's so obvious. Doesn't 'Ella' know what people say about girls who dress like that?

I feel a cold knot settle in my stomach.
Maybe she does know. Maybe she knows well.
Maybe it sucks for her that people have commentary about her body, the same way some people have commentary about mine.
I turn the page and see the bit that she copied about Grant. She didn't care that the next million sentences I wrote about him were good things. Of course she didn't care.
I flip again and see Brice's name. And then Antonique's.
I pull out my phone and start texting.

Two hours later, I'm sitting on the edge of my bed, trying to remember all the things I want to say. Grant helped me catch up on homework while Evelyn made the brownies—she added extra chocolate chips when I told her my friends were coming over.

I hear the front door open and the stairs creak as they approach. I stand awkwardly to greet them at my bedroom door.

"Stop standing like that," Grant says, reaching for a brownie for the seventeenth time. "You're being weird."

"Thanks for the pep talk," I grumble. "And you'd better drop that brownie."

Brice enters with his arms crossed, and behind him, Antonique is looking small and hidden despite her height.

"Thank you for coming," I stammer. "Please, sit somewhere."

I gesture awkwardly around my room as they search for spots to perch. Antonique sits on the other edge of my bed, and Brice makes his way to the ottoman by the big chair and the brownies.

"I have brownies!" I say suddenly, and I grab the plate and hold it out to each of them in turn.

"I did not come here for carbs. Say what you've gotta say," Brice says as he turns his chin away from me.

"Uh, right." I set down the plate, and Grant grabs two brownies and starts chowing on one. I give him the stink-eye, he shrugs, and then I refocus.

"So. First. I'm so sorry for the things I wrote...about you and other people...in my journal. I only wrote those things because of how I was feeling. I mean, I know it sounds stupid, but I wrote things when I was feeling insecure, and instead of lashing out at you in person, about things that weren't really even about you, I vented on the page."

The three of them are just staring at me, watching and waiting. They're not interrupting. They're letting me get this out. And I have more to say.

"I know that we haven't known each other for very long. Antonique, you've only been in my life for a few weeks, and Brice, we only became friends late last school year, and so maybe you don't really know all the parts of the puzzle. But, the truth is, I get a lot of poison out onto these pages—and it helps. But I want you to know that these single, out-of-context fragments of thoughts were plucked from pages and pages that aren't what you think."

I take a breath and open my eyes. I guess I'd been holding them closed.

"Grant, will you hand me my notebook?"

He reaches across the bed and hands it over to me. I flip through the pages and find what I'm looking for. I start to read.

I read words from out of the very core of my heart. And saying them aloud, hearing them for the first time, startles me. I can't keep my eyes from welling up as I speak.

"Brice and Jonathan make me sick. Watching Brice love Jonathan, and watching Jonathan love Brice back—in the same way—makes me so jealous it almost breaks me in two. I watch them sometimes when they're being all cute and snuggly, and I wish I could feel that. They're so lucky. Loving someone is easy. Finding a path through this mess of life that will allow them to love you back is hard."

I glance to Grant. He's looking in his lap and playing with the strap of his watch. I don't have time to stare, but I want to believe that his cheeks are flushed.

I turn the pages.

"Antonique isn't just gorgeous. It's not hard to see why she gets attention, but it isn't just because she's pretty. She's kind and open, and I feel like I have a girlfriend for the first time in my life. That means something. She will never know how precious her friendship has been to me."

I clear my throat and can't make myself look up from the notebook, so I just close it and stare at the floor.

"I know that it must have hurt to read that stuff, and I understand if you don't want to talk to me anymore. But I needed you to know that the stuff Carmella put up on those walls isn't really how I feel. When I saw my own words staring back at me, I lost it. I was embarrassed, sure. Those pictures were gross, and I couldn't believe my private thoughts were on display, but more than that, I was scared. The idea that my pain and anger could separate me from the truest friends I've ever known was horrifying."

I lift my eyes and try to give them space to respond.

Antonique has been looking straight at me, and as she scoots closer to where I'm seated at my desk, she says, "I was really worried that what you wrote was all you thought about me, and I was worried that the person I felt closest to at Crestwood wasn't really my friend at all. That's why I didn't talk to you about it before now. It's why I didn't call."

"No," I say. "It wasn't on you to call. I just hope you can forgive me."

She gives me a nod, and her braids swing back and forth.

I hold my breath and wait.

Brice hasn't said anything, and I fear that when he speaks, he won't be so forgiving. I try to accept the silence. I try to keep my mouth shut and let him take his time. But more words just tumble out.

"Whatever you want to say, whatever you need to vent, just say it." I steel myself against the worst.

He stretches his neck back and forth while tilting his head toward one shoulder and then the other before he takes a deep breath and says, "I was really mad at you. But not even because of what you wrote. I mean, to be honest, I've expected a lot worse to be said about me since Jonathan and I got together, but whatever. I was mad because you let this rude girl reduce you to nothing."

His face is stern, and his voice is powerful. He holds nothing back.

"And when I looked down the hallway and watched you collapse from the inside out, I just got so frustrated. I wanted you to march down that hall to me and tell me how stupid she was, but there you were, melting. And I just couldn't stand it. So I walked away."

"I get it," I say. "I'm so sorry."

Brice leans forward and uses two fingers to gesture from his eyes to mine before growling, "Gah!" He grits his teeth and starts to pull away, but then he reaches over and grabs the sides of my arms. "Listen to me. We worry 'cause we care, but somebody has got to tell you this: You deserve to be treated better."

"I don't know how to make her stop, Brice. I would, but—"

"No," he interrupts, pointing his finger straight at me. "I mean, yes. People should treat each other with kindness, but I'm not talking about them. You can't fix them. I'm talking about *you*. You deserve better treatment from yourself. I'm sorry if that sounds harsh, but you do."

My eyes glisten, but I blink away the tears and turn back to the three of them.

I don't know what else to say.

I look at each of them, and then I just sorta lift my shoulders and open my hands.

Brice holds out his arms to pull me up. He wraps me in a giant hug, and Antonique comes up beside him and squishes me, too. Grant closes up the circle, and I feel him rest his chin on my head.

"Aaaaaaaand break!" I say, giggling, as we all separate.

"Now for more important matters," Brice begins. "What is this garbage Grant tells me about you wearing a lab coat to the Rally tomorrow night? Because, no. This is a dance. This is Homecoming for Art Kids, and I'm sorry, but I forbid it."

"Oh, come on—" I smile at them, but everyone seems to be in agreement.

Brice continues. "Ah, no. You and Antonique and myself are going to meet here tomorrow around lunchtime, and we're going to get you dolled up. That's all there is to it."

"Brice, you can't be serious. I'm not up for playing *Cosmo*. You already had your chance to give Lady Chubbs-o-Lot a makeover during the musical."

"Gen..." Grant walks over to me, and I'm suddenly super-aware of how close we're standing, while we're in front of Antonique and Brice. I feel my cheeks bloom with fever, and he doesn't seem to notice. "Come on. Let's do it right. Once."

They're all looking at me, and I can tell that there's nothing I can say that is going to change their minds. I look over at Antonique, who has been quiet the whole time. She raises her eyebrows and her shoulders in a shrug.

"Fine. Fine, fine, fine."

"Do you want another group hug?" Brice asks with a maniacal grin on his face.

"No!" I laugh. "And now you all have to get out! Tomorrow is going to be a long-assed day, I can tell already, thanks to you guys. So let me get my freaking beauty sleep, okay?"

"As you wish," Brice says with a grin.

"See you tomorrow," Antonique says to me as Brice offers her his arm.

"Hey," I say as I grab Grant's wrist while he walks toward the door. "I need to read you something, too."

"Gen, you don't have to."

"I know. Just shut up." I pick up my notebook and flip to the part I want him to hear.

"I give Grant a hard time for always wanting to make things better. For wanting to be a fixer. But the truth is, he is the one person who never makes me feel broken. When I'm with him, no matter how many pieces are lying on the floor, I feel whole. It's not just that he acts like he doesn't see the cracks. It's like they're not there. Not to him." I close the book and drop it on my pillow. "So what you read...that's not it. I just needed to tell you that."

"I know, Gen."

I look down and see that I'm gripping his "Reading is JAWESOME!" shirt at his waist, right below the book-loving shark with gnashing teeth. I keep waiting for him to speak, but eventually, the quiet drives me crazy.

"Congratulations on your scholarship. I knew you'd get it. Tomorrow is the big competition. Are you ready?"

"Yeah, I guess so," he says. He reaches down and takes my hand from his shirt and cups it between his palms. "I'm nervous."

"You'll do great. You're the smartest guy I know."

"Yeah, well, we'll see." He crinkles his nose, and his eyes squint with mischief.

"You text me. As soon as you hear anything, okay? Promise?"

"How about I promise to text you *if* I have good news at the competition?" he says as he crosses his heart.

"Okay. I'm so proud of you. You're going to be amazing."

"Maybe." He drops my hand, and we stand there for a second. And I just wish I could bottle the shade of his eyes.

"I'll talk to you tomorrow." He walks out, closing the door behind him.

"Goodnight," I say to the empty room.

It feels like I always speak too late.

After tugging on my nightshirt and pajama pants (the ones covered in giant candy logos), I put on my bravest face and head downstairs to Dad and Evelyn's room.

"Can I come in?" I ask to the open doorway.

"Of course, honey." Evelyn is sitting in their oversized bed, propped up by a bazillion pillows. A cooking show plays on the TV on the opposite wall, and her bedside lamp casts a warm glow around the otherwise dark room.

"Where's Dad?" I ask.

"Oh, he's in his office. He's got a big meeting with his agent in the morning. They've gotta figure out his UK rights."

"Ahh. Right." I look around the room and consider going in to interrupt him, but I think better of it. "Evelyn, I wanted to say thank you again for the brownies, and I'm sorry for snapping at you in my room earlier. It was a really nice thing to do. So thank you."

"Honey, of course." She smiles mildly. "I should probably have asked first."

"No, it's okay. And, anyway, I guess that's not the only reason I came down here. Umm. Tomorrow night is the Rally thing at school. It's, like, a big dance or whatever."

"I know about it. They sent fliers home. I wasn't sure if you'd be up for it."

"Well, I'm probably not up for it, but I'm going anyway. Going to school functions together is sort of a tradition for Grant and me, so he really wants me to go. So..." I swallow hard, but the lump in my throat won't budge. "I said I would go, but the thing is, my friends want me to dress up, and I hadn't planned on that, and I don't—"

Evelyn reaches over and pats the bed beside her, but I don't move.

"I don't really have anything to wear."

I stood in my closet before coming downstairs and looked through everything I have that could possibly be considered a dress. The last time I wore one, it was a size sixteen. Nothing else I have even comes close.

My stupid eyes are filling up with stupid tears and I am trying to will them back into my stupid skull, but they fall anyway.

"It's just that, I'm kinda big..." My voice wavers as my cheeks start to flush. "And I don't exactly fit into every dress off the rack in regular stores. So I don't know if it's a futile endeavor or not, but...I'm willing to try. I know that it will be hard to find something pretty in my size...but..."

My head dips into my hands as the tears fall.

I'm so embarrassed. Asking my size-two stepmom to take me on an emergency plus-sized dress run in the morning. This is horrible.

I'm startled by Evelyn's arms around me. She pulls my hands from my face and looks at me with her own tear-filled eyes and says, "Darling, don't you even think about worrying. Don't you even dare. We've got tomorrow, and we're going to figure something out. It's a promise."

"Thanks, Evelyn."

She hugs me again, and I glance over at my dad's side of the bed, made up and undisturbed. I remember his side of the bed used to be Mom's side of the bed. It makes me wonder if he started sleeping on Mom's side because he missed her or because he wanted to be sure that nobody else ever slept there again except for him.

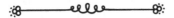

Antonique and I clamber back into the house with bags on our arms and French fries in our bellies at five minutes past four on Saturday afternoon. Brice and Evelyn have been scheming all day on something for me to wear, and Antonique was charged with keeping me out of the house. We're barely through the door before I hear Brice squawking to me from my bedroom.

"I'm scared. Should I be scared?" I ask her.

"Probably," she says.

"Come sit," Brice demands. "It's hair and makeup time."

He immediately begins working on Antonique's makeup while I check my phone for the billionth time in the past few hours. After Grant's initial *"Going in"* text this morning, I haven't heard a word.

I'm super-bummed because, even though I have tons of faith in him, maybe things aren't going well. I wish I could be there cheering for his nerdy domination.

"Why is your face glued to your phone?" Brice asks from the floor where he's sweeping Antonique's braids up and pinning them into position.

"I'm just waiting to hear from Grant about his big science competition this morning." I scoot nearer them, and Brice shoves some bottles and tubes of beauty products across the carpet toward me.

"Oh, yeah, I forgot about that. I'm sure he's doing awesome," he says. "Here, put on this moisturizer for me and then this primer."

The light is still coming in, but it will deepen soon. The days aren't lasting as long as they used to, and we'll be finishing our makeup by the crappy overhead lighting for sure.

"Imogen, your dress is going to be so amazing. Grant is going to just collapse," Brice says as he applies something to Antonique's eyes.

"Oh, I'm sure he'll remain conscious. No need to worry."

"I'm serious! It's so you."

"Well, I wouldn't know, would I? Can I please see it now?"

"Patience, my pretty."

Before long, Brice has finished his second masterpiece of the evening. My longish hair has been loosely curled and pulled back off my face. He's swept it to one side and adorned it with this great, embellished hair clip that looks like the traditional comedy/tragedy masks, but they're covered in shiny, black crystals. My eye makeup is dark and smoky, but still bright. Way less depressing than my normal look. I've got sheer, glossy, pink lips and a pop of color on my round cheeks.

From the neck up, I look pretty stinking cute.

And it feels nice to think so. It does.

The time has come for me to put on my dress.

We enter the spacious dressing area inside the giant master bathroom. The skylight in the ceiling shoots the last bit of sunshine over the tile floor.

"Hi, darling. I'm so excited I might die!" Evelyn is standing like a creeper in her closet next to a long garment bag hanging on the top of the door. "I want you to cover your eyes with this." She holds out a black silk scarf.

These crazy bats have hidden my dress to make it a surprise.

But whatever. I'm in theatre. I'm a sucker for dramatic flair.

I resign myself to the experience while Evelyn begins to maneuver, and I feel her fiddling with my clothes. I almost reach out and push her away as this woman starts to unzip and tug and pull silky things all around me.

"Whoa, what are you doing?" I try not to jump away from her—I know I'll fall down and crack my head on the bathtub since I can't see anything.

"I'm just helping you get this on. Now stop fussing."

She pulls my tunic off over my head. Here I am, standing physically exposed with a girl I've known for just a few weeks, a boy who's been my friend for less than six months, and a grown woman that I've made a real effort to ignore for most of the past year. But I don't feel uncovered.

And despite my fears, I'm getting excited.

I want to love this dress.

I feel the heavy weight of it come over my head, and I start to piece together what I know. I feel the roughness of lace. I feel the heft of layers. And I also feel a familiar weight on my shoulders.

Oh, man, what if they stick me in something stupid? I don't want to look stupid in front of hundreds of kids who all look beautiful.

I start waving my hands around at my side. "Can I please see? I'm so nervous."

"Why are you nervous? Don't you trust me?" Brice's voice cuts through the echo-y bathroom, and he and

Antonique sound like they're sitting on the edge of the tub beside me.

"Oh my God, Imogen. You look incredible," Antonique says.

I hope this dress is barf-colored because I am so worried I'm about to be sick all over this thing. I put my hands on my stomach and try to press away the ache.

I feel the bumps of a corset-shaped piece around my torso, and I feel a familiar hug of fabric around my hips.

Oh, no.

Oh, please tell me Brice doesn't want me to wear the costume that was immortalized on posters calling me a nutjob.

Hands on my waist turn me around to face where I know my friends are sitting.

"One more thing," Brice says. He bends my arms and pulls them through tight sleeves—or I guess they're long gloves that come up above my elbows. I wiggle my fingers through the open end.

Oh God, if the sleeves make my arms look like bratwursts, I'm going to melt into a puddle of shame and die.

Brice gasps. He's already gushing, and I haven't seen it yet. Evelyn finishes fastening up the back and pulling the laces, and I'm almost ready to pop when she says, "Imogen, dear, you look exquisite. Take a look."

I reach up and pull off my blindfold and find myself standing beside her full-length mirror.

At first I think I'm going to panic.

I *am* wearing my costume from the show.

Sort of.

I see that the body is the same; the top is a corset, and the laces have drawn me in around the middle. There is still black piping all along the seams, but there are these incredible fingerless gloves made of stretchy black lace, and my giant wobbly arms are tucked inside them. Wrapped around the skirt of the dress are layers of black lace strung on a ribbon and tied around the back. The edges aren't hemmed, and I can still see some of the pink coming through, but the effect is amazing. It's like this hot-pink princess dress with a little bit of edge. It's awesome. I feel pretty. Oh. So. Pretty.

I'm almost disappointed that Brice didn't cue up the song for me. What a missed opportunity.

I smile. I look at myself, at my shape, at my body, and I smile.

Brice turned this smelly old costume into something amazing.

I look in the mirror and see Evelyn ducked behind me. The absence of my mother slams into me like the truck that took her. Putting on dresses and tying my bows. I wish she were here to do those simple things. I shrug the feelings away as Evelyn spins me around in my perfect, angsty-chic dress. I look at her and say, with more sincerity than I can believe, "I'm so glad you're here. Thank you. Thank you so much."

"You look beautiful."

"Brice! How did you pull this off? How did you possibly do this? And please, dear Brice, tell me this has been dry-cleaned."

"Evelyn and I talked when I first got here this morning, and I remembered how fabulous you looked in this costume. I knew that with a few layers of lace and those fabulous gloves from the Halloween store, I could make this dress look a little less Winnifred and a lot more you. I texted Gild, and she said that as long as I put it back to normal afterward, I could alter it for you to wear. Oh, and of course. Ew."

He stands up and goes to put an arm around Evelyn. "And since Evelyn bought all of the material and I put it together, I guess we get to share the glory." He turns to her and says, "I'll be the 'Fairy' and you be the 'Godmother!'" He starts laughing, and we all giggle with him.

I look in the mirror again and can't make sense of how grateful I feel.

This could have been bad. A very bad situation. Too tight, too short, too sleeveless, too many things could have gone wrong.

I look down at my lacy black gloves and set my hand on my left forearm. "It's perfect," I say to no one in particular.

"I wish I could see you out there in those pretty lights with all of your friends," Evelyn says with a smile. "I'd love to see both of my girls out there together actually."

I feel my jaw go slack, and my eyes dart to Brice and Antonique, who look similarly freaked out.

"Carmella? You mean, she's going? I didn't even consider that she might be going."

I glance sideways and see my chest flushing red in the mirror.

"Well, she spent the night with some friends last night, and they're all getting ready over there, which is great because it gives me a chance to clean up her room tonight, but anyway, yes. She is on the dance team, so..."

I'm sure I look like I've been slapped in the face with a bag of bricks.

I summarize my new revelations. "Dance is part of fine arts. Of course she's going."

"Is...that okay?" She pauses. "Are you okay?"

"Oh. Yeah. Sure," I lie.

I'm great.

"Okay, then." She smiles. "Maybe you girls can take a picture sometime tonight? I'd really love a shot of the two of you together. I don't have one yet."

A picture with Carmella. And me in a dress. Just shoot me.

W e're almost ready to go. Brice is putting his suit on in my closet, and Antonique is changing in my room. I'm putting on the finishing touches—my mom's earrings—and as I step onto the landing, I notice a box just at the top of the stairs. About a foot long and half as tall, I recognize the shape of it instantly. A shoebox. It has been wrapped in black paper and topped with a shiny black bow. My name is scrawled across the top in silver marker.

I crouch down to tear open the package, and when I've exposed the logo on the side, I can't help but grin. I pull it open to reveal a pair of bright fuchsia low-top Chucks. Tied to the double set of pink and black laces, I find a handwritten gift tag:

Imogen,
I hope that these shoes work with your new dress. I considered buying you a new pair of heels but thought better of it. These look like you. The real you. The joyful, thoughtful, beautiful you that I can't wait to know better.
With love,
Evelyn

I look again at the hot pink shoes. I squeeze my eyes shut, and my mother's face swims in my vision. I can see her sitting on our back porch, sipping on iced tea, watching me twirl in my amazing dress. I notice that in my imagination Evelyn is sitting beside her. I can picture my mom reaching over and grabbing Evelyn's hand.

She would be so grateful that I have Evelyn here to watch me grow up.

I should be, too.

"Antonique?" I call. "Check out these shoes."

She's already exiting my room.

And she looks incredible.

She's wearing a bright emerald-green dress that, if it's possible, makes her look even more tall and elegant. The dress is sequined, more at the top and less toward the bottom, fading into sheer folds of the same green hue. Her braids are piled loosely on the top of her head, cascading a bit in the back, while her skin is bright and glowing. She looks strong and striking.

"You look amazing," I say.

"Where did you get those shoes?" she squeaks. "Brice!"

"No! Wait! Let me put them on first!" I giggle at her excitement, and she makes me plop down on the top step and tie on my new, fabulously pink sneakers.

When I finish, I look to the bottom of the stairs where my dad is standing. Staring.

"Dad?"

He slowly climbs the steps toward me. He looks like he's floating and not even using his legs. His mouth hangs open a little, and a smile blossoms on his face.

"What are you doing here? I thought you would be gone till late?"

"I just came home to grab my laptop charger. I forgot it this morning."

I stand up on the top step, and he stops a couple of steps below me so that we're face to face.

"Do you like it?" I ask.

I haven't really taken it all in myself, but the me that is reflecting in his eyes is the me that I want to always be. It makes me smile.

He says nothing, but he reaches up to wrap his arms all the way around me.

"My baby girl. You are so beautiful when you smile."

In his pocket, his phone pings and pings again.

He pulls back, and I look at his face. There's longing and sadness and pride all mixed together.

"Go, Dad."

He smiles and reaches up to pinch my nose. "Love you, Immy."

"I love you too, Dad."

I watch him turn the corner, and then I turn around to face my friends who've been watching and sniffling quietly behind me.

Brice is dabbing tears from the corners of his eyes. He plays it off and says, "I know you're the one wearing it, but I have truly outdone myself."

"Man, what a crybaby!" I say as I blink away tears.

We laugh loudly as my nervousness builds. I check the clock on the wall. I haven't heard from Grant, but I know he won't be late.

I walk past the two of them, admiring each other in the hall, and into my room where I make a beeline for my closet door and my full-length mirror.

My reflection is blocked off by so many pieces of paper taped to the glass. I've covered so much that it's mostly good for checking makeup and ensuring that my fly is zipped. I reach up and pull down the playbill covers for *Spring Awakening* and RENT. I pull down posters of ballerinas that I idolized as a kid. With the paper littering the floor, I can see clearly.

In front of me is a girl wearing a seriously killer dress. Her steely grey-blue eyes are ringed with shimmering shadows, and her cheeks look rosy and lifted, like she spends a great deal more time smiling than she actually does. Her hair is out of her face, as if she's got nothing to hide. She has delicate shoulders, and an hourglass figure peeks through the fabric. Her skirt almost meets the ground but stops short, granting a view of lily-white cankles perched on a great pair of hot pink sneakers.

She's not me.

Not entirely.

But maybe she could be.

"Gen, your dad let me in!" I hear Grant shout from the top of the stairs.

My head snaps to the side, and my doorway is almost completely filled with Grant, tall and spiky haired, dressed in cool black tux pants. A great tux jacket covers most of a slate grey T-shirt with hot pink hexagonal shapes and lines on it.

He looks awesome.

Really awesome.

"Gen. Wow."

He takes the few steps toward me.

"Oh. Hey." I physically shake his significant cuteness out of my head before saying, "How was the competition? How'd you do?"

He looks like he's having a hard time collecting his thoughts. "I got third place."

"Oh my God, Grant! You liar! You said you'd text with good news!" I take three steps and throw my hands up over his shoulders. I feel his hands wrap around my waist. I hear him smell my hair as he holds me. Being close to him and feeling beautiful, my gut feels like it's been shot through with a bazooka, and I pull away from him, sure that he can feel the pull of his gravity and the black hole in my belly tugging at him.

He's looking at me all over the place. His eyes are jumping from my hair to my eyes to my shoes, and stopping at a few other places along the way. Brice and Antonique are giggling and whispering on the other side of my room, but Grant and I aren't paying much attention to them.

"Hey, what's on your shirt?" I say, drawing his focus.

"Oh, this? Brice told me about your dress, so I went to my favorite tee shop after the competition."

I grin at him. His face looks so clean. I can still smell his hair stuff from our hug. I want to bury my face in his hair.

"So..." I gesture to the nonsense on his shirt. "What is it?"

He fidgets with his sleeves, his lapel, and his hair before finishing. "It's the chemical composition of serotonin."

I look at him expectantly, sure that he'll fill in the gaps for his less-than-scholarly best friend.

"It's the monoamine neurotransmitter that's commonly credited for feelings of satisfaction or happiness."

"That's what happy looks like," I say as I point to his shirt.

As I point to him.

"Yep. Pretty much," he says. His smile creeps up sideways until that dimple appears.

He's such a nerd.

"You look...really beautiful, Gen."

"Oh, shut your face." My chest flushes with heat as I speak.

I turn away from him a little, and he turns away from me a little. I find my fingernails incredibly interesting, while he's studying his shoes.

I clear my throat. "What I mean to say is, thank you. And thanks for taking me tonight. I think it might actually suck less than I originally anticipated."

He awkwardly shifts his weight on his feet, while smiling and reaching up to his hair again. "Yeah. Totally."

"Umm, if you two weirdos are ready, Antonique and I have a fierce quota to meet. I have a very cute boyfriend waiting for me at the dance, and we need to get a move on."

Brice links arms with Antonique and pushes Grant out the door, leaving me for just another second with the girl in the mirror.

"Come on, brain. Just make a little serotonin," I whisper.

I smooth my skirt before grabbing my phone and keys and setting off.

"Be happy," I mutter to myself. "Just for one night."

We arrive at the courtyard fashionably late, as the sun has fully set behind the west wall of the school. The sky is streaked with vibrant hues. Corals, violets, and navy patches smear across the bright open air, and the stars have begun to shine. The courtyard that sits at the heart of our campus has been transformed. Every tree has been tightly wound with twinkling lights, and paper lanterns hang in the open spaces between them. The mural serves as the backdrop for the raised platform, and steps are mounted on either side beside tall, heavy, black curtains. As we pass, my eyes automatically sweep over the blurs of color.

Refreshment stands create a boundary along the wall of windows near the cafeteria. The scent of popcorn and cotton candy swirl with the smell of fall leaves and waft all around us in the cool breeze. We're lucky. Sometimes it doesn't really feel like fall in the south until it's basically winter, but tonight is perfect. Crisp and bright.

Even though Grant and I usually treat the Rally as a joke, there's something really amazing about walking up to the dance and looking like I'm actually going to a dance. It's a combination of the best parts of a carnival and a prom rolled into one. The clusters of friends sweep around in great masses, and every fine arts group is represented. There are easily a couple hundred students already here.

As we enter and duck through the trees, Brice saunters up to Jonathan, who hands him a giant yellow daisy before giving him a sweet kiss. I watch as Jonathan takes Brice's outstretched hand without a moment of hesitation and then picks up Brice, twirling him around under the twinkling lights.

At the edge of the stage, people are taking turns stuffing slips of paper into cardboard boxes labeled with "King" and "Queen."

I smile as I remember a conversation at the cast party about the royal nominations. We finally figured out why theatre kids never win. Techies don't care enough to vote, and actors only vote for themselves.

On the floor, lots of people are already dancing. It looks moderately horrifying. But at the same time, putting on a dress is horrifying, too, and I did that just fine.

Antonique is already bouncing where she stands as the music sails over the crowd through the large speakers by the stage.

Grant looks at me, and I try to look a little less like the dance floor is a pit of lava. He gives me a little wink and then says, "What do you say, Antonique?"

Grant offers her his hand. She looks a little shocked, and her eyes flit from him to me and back before she stammers, "Oh, sure, I mean, yes. Thanks."

Grant turns to me with a laugh on his lips. "I know you hate dancing, Gen. We'll be back soon!"

He isn't wrong. I mean, of course he's not wrong. But I guess I thought that part of doing the dance thing right meant sucking it up and trying to play the game. I guess I should have mentioned that.

The two of them glide to the dance floor. They're both so tall and thin. They look like two well-dressed giraffes shaking around. Seeing them laughing lightheartedly should make me feel all warm and fuzzy inside.

Somehow, it's just made me feel stabby.

"Hey, Imogen."

I turn to my right and see Andrew. I'm instantly caught off-guard. All I can think of is how he ignored me in English during first period yesterday. He stood up for me when Carmella freaked out at the show and was handsomely rewarded by reading immature nonsense I wrote about him. I am trying to calculate how far I could run in the opposite direction before he'd catch me, but I decide that four steps probably won't be good enough. I brace myself for his blow.

"Wow. You look nice."

That was not what I expected. I let out an "uh" before I fall silent again.

He is smiling at me. Not full on shoe-salesman cheese, but sincerely, or so it seems. I'm speechless.

The fact that I'm staring at him like he's an eye chart has thrown him off.

"So..." He rocks back on his feet and takes a sip of his soda.

"Right, um. Andrew, I need to apologize. I wrote those things about you when I was in a really messed-up state of mind. I never intended for you or anyone else to ever see those private thoughts. It meant a lot to me that you stood up to Carmella...uh, Ella, and I hope we can be cool." I reach up and nervously tug at a loose lock of my hair.

"Don't worry about it. I was kinda mad at first, but then I realized you were just being honest. And I can't fault you for that."

"Uh, okay. So, yay."

I am the most awkward panda in the universe.

"What do you say? How about a dance? It will be like old times. I'll even do some of my sweet breakdancing choreography moves with you."

Passing out would be a bad idea, right? Because I'm pretty sure a boy just asked me to dance.

It isn't Grant, but I've known since Christmas that, at some point, I'd have to stop seeing him as the only boy in the world. I push my shoulders back and slide my small purse to the center of the table.

"Why not?" I say. "But I have to warn you, I require a larger than normal dance space. Mere inches cannot contain me."

"Well, I need a lot of room for my massive ego and fat head. At this rate, we'll take over the entire floor."

He laughs as he offers me his elbow, and we head into the crowd.

The lights swirl all around us as we make our way to our cluster of friends. I try to keep my movements small to minimize the sweat and heavy breathing, but I'm not being a stick in the mud. I'm moving—just enough.

"Gen? Andrew? What are you doing?" Grant is looking at me with an incredulous look on his face. His eyes dart back and forth between Andrew and me.

"Is it that hard to identify?" I speak very slowly for him. "I am dancing."

"I'm kinda just bouncing. I don't know if you'd really call it dancing!" Andrew is shouting over the din and continues his gyration a few steps away.

"But...you hate dancing! I mean, you don't dance, right?" Grant asks, loud enough to be heard over the music.

"Well, you didn't ask."

He looks down with what seems like shame on his face.

"Hey," I shout to him over the music. "It's no big deal. I'm just kidding."

"No, it is a big deal." He steps between some bodies, and I find Grant, my best friend, standing really, really close to me on the color-drenched dance floor. The heavy beat melts into a slow and soulful song about youth and love and forever, and I can't think of a single thing to say about how ridiculous it all is. I smell the breeze and the perfumes of girls mixed with sweaty teenage pheromones, and he's close. He's really, really close. I feel the lightest pressure of his fingertips at my waist as he looks straight at me and says, "I should have asked you to dance. I mean, I asked Antonique because I assumed you wouldn't, but I was obviously mistaken, and now I've nearly lost your first dance to Andrew, too."

"What do you mean 'too'?" I ask.

"Nothing. It's nothing."

"No, really, what?" I insist. I put my hands out and tug gently at his coat lapels.

"I just...I mean, do you like him or something?" he asks with his head turned toward the stage. Before I can even ask him to explain what his crazy brain is talking about, he continues. "I mean, he's got your first kiss, your first dance, I mean, Jesus, I just always thought your first..."

"Yeah, my first...?"

"Dance. Your first dance...I thought it'd be with me."

I can't breathe or figure out why his fingertips are on my waist or why my chest is so hot or why my heart is beating so hard it feels like I've got lava pumping through my veins. I bet if I look down, I'll see my dress has burst into flames.

"Well, then how about you ask me?" I furiously chomp down on the edge of my thumb.

"Can I have this dance?" He says it slowly. Right to my eyes. No jokes. No bowing and offering his hand. He just asks me.

"Won't Antonique mind?"

"I don't think so. It looks to me like she's already been swept off her feet."

He points over my shoulder, and I see Andrew shifting back and forth on his feet, very close to Antonique, who's timidly got her arms on his shoulders.

I turn back to Grant and say, "Well, seeing how the first girl you asked already ditched you, I guess I'll throw you a bone."

He grabs my hand and walks me deeper into the crowd, then turns me around to face him. He steps closer, placing his hands once again around my waist. I begin to reach up and place my hands on his shoulders, and at that very moment, the smooth rhythm is interrupted with a double-time dance song.

The bodies around us resume their frenzied pulsing to the up-tempo song, and the slow dance expires.

I start to pull away, but he holds my hand at his shoulder.

I look up at him, and he throws his head back in laughter. "Just dance, Gen!"

Our bodies pull apart, and I throw caution to the wind. I shake my booty and bob my head, my pulse races and my heart beats faster. Serotonin and sweat mix together, and soon I'm laughing as I'm jumping around for the first time ever on a school dance floor.

I t doesn't take long for me to become totally winded, and after several minutes of flailing, our group decides to grab some drinks and stand around talking for a bit. I resist the urge to raid the cookie table and shovel snickerdoodles in my face by the dozen just for the fun of it.

Grant has his back to the mural, and over his left shoulder, I notice a small shape on the wall that I don't remember seeing before. It's not like I have the whole mural memorized, but I can't take my eyes off of this patch of color that seems new. It seems familiar.

"Hey, I'll be right back," I tell Grant with one hand on his shoulder.

"Are you okay?" he asks.

"Totally. I'll just be a minute."

I tug at my lacy gloves as I press through the crowd and wipe the sweat off my forehead.

At the side of the stage, the rigging is easily twenty-five feet high. Huge black curtains hang down in narrow strips, blocking off patches of the wall from my view. As I duck behind one and climb the metal staircase, my eyes scan desperately for the shape that caught my eye on the wall. I can't even remember exactly what it looked like; my head is still sloshy from dancing.

The stars are bright, and the moon is illuminating the tiny backstage area, casting a snowy glow over everything. I turn and prop my back against the railing so that I'm facing the wall. I close my eyes for a second and let the breeze cool the sweat on my skin and cause the fine hairs on my arms to rise in tiny bumps against the lace. I open my eyes again and scour the rough surface, stopping suddenly on a delicately written block of text.

Being several feet in the air has lent me a different perspective. Everything looks different than it does from the ground.

Above me and to the right, about a foot over my head, I see neat words, written in what looks like a white cloud, outlined in various colors like a rainbow border. It's familiar. I know this shape. I know it like the back of my own hand. The lettering is justified on both sides, creating a perfect square.

I almost scramble up the wall. I extend my body, pushing up on my tiptoes to bring myself a little bit closer. From here, I can read what she wrote:

> *For a Happily*
> *Ever After:*
> *'The End' is just*
> *the beginning.*
> *Angela Baker*
> *May 2, 1982*

I read the words ten times in mere seconds, my eyes darting back and forth over them again and again.

There has to be something more. Something new.

I've been waiting for years to find this new pearl of wisdom. But this isn't new. It isn't a revelation. It isn't a desperate message from beyond the grave. It's just the same old inscription I've read on the inside cover of my storybook since I was five.

I slump to a seat on the top step and bury my head in my hands.

I was so sure that, somehow, finding this would be like finding the words, "Imogen: Do this." But it's just more of the same.

Except...for little, meaningless changes. A word and a colon and a date. I picture my book and the way it's inscribed. "For *My* Happily Ever After..."

For me.

It's always been for me.

She treasured it as a girl and then passed it on to her own.

If my mom could see me now, she wouldn't care about my weight. She wouldn't care about my psychological problems. She wouldn't care about my constantly sweaty palms and defensive snark. She wouldn't be disappointed that who I am isn't good enough for her.

She'd be disappointed that who I am *is* good enough for me. That I'm content to be miserable. She'd be so sad that I resigned myself at freaking twelve or fifteen or seventeen years old to the idea that happiness isn't in my cards.

I can see her in my mind. Her arms, her hair, her smile.

I can hear her voice, and I know that if she were here, she'd tell me that it's worth the fight, that I have to fight. And she'd tell me that I'm not fighting against anything or anyone, but that I have to fight for something. For happiness...for a happy ending.

She'd tell me that Dad was right. I have to make more room in my heart for something bigger and better than all that pain.

A surge of strength moves through my limbs as I stand up on the step and smooth my hair with my hands. I look down at my dress and my shoes and back up at the wall again. I raise my hand and place it on her wall. The cool of the concrete chills my fingertips and pulses with her words.

I drop my hand and lift my chin so that I can see the stars. As if on cue, in my peripheral vision, I swear I see a tiny star streak across a little patch of sky.

"Make a wish," I mutter.

I shake my head and giggle to myself while hitching up my skirt.

I'm done sitting and waiting for dreams to come true.

Shooting stars are for suckers.

"Gen?"

Grant stands at the bottom of the stairs, looking up at me with a confused expression on his face.

"How did you know I was just about to come find you?" I'm smiling so hard it hurts. "Come up here." I take a few steps down toward him and grab his hand. "I wanna show you something."

The heavy black curtains that surround the stage block the access stairs from view, and we're tucked behind them on the platform as the giant moon shines down and lights up the very air we breathe.

"Look. Up here." I reach up on tiptoes along the rough stone and point. "Right there, you can see her name. Angela Baker."

I stare up and slowly slide my hand down the wall.

"That's amazing, Gen! I can't believe you found it!"

I lower my heels and spin around to find Grant distinctly in my dance space. He's stepped forward to read over my shoulder, and when I turn, our chests are close together and my back is against the mural wall.

Close.

So close.

I'm grateful for the moonlight because it's making his eyes glow, but I hope it doesn't illuminate the fire that has spread up my chest again.

He stands there, looking down into my eyes, and I keep expecting him to step back. We're just standing there and breathing, and the moon watches from above us on one side and my mom watches from above us on the other. The sound of the dance on the other side of the curtain is muffled, and all I can hear is the sound of my heart beating.

His chin drops just the slightest amount, and he smirks at me and says in his softest voice, "You found it."

"I did."

I really did.

The space between us is filled with so many things I've always wanted to say. And when we're standing here and he still hasn't stepped back, my whole heart wrings out like a rag because it makes me feel like maybe, someday, he could make his heart big enough to hold me—all of me, too.

"There's my masterpiece!" Brice shouts at the top of his lungs.

The spell breaks.

Grant steps back and down the stairs, and I feel that familiar tug as he leaves. That gravity tugs at me, and it might be the moonlight or the wall or the dress, but I swear I feel him reaching for me, too.

"Ladies and gentlemen of the Crestwood High School Fine Arts Collective, please gather your friends and make your way to the dance floor! Your Fine Arts Council members have some awards and honors!"

My friends huddle together and stand around our tables near the rest of the theatre kids. I can see little clusters of friends all smiling and standing together just like us. The DJ turns down the music as the fine arts teachers take center stage.

"Good evening, students! I am Mr. Paulson, director of orchestra at Crestwood High and the department chair for fine arts. I'd like to take a moment to welcome all of you to our annual Fine Arts Rally!"

The open air in the courtyard fills with the sound of applause and shouts from hundreds of students.

We all watch and clap and sip on our sodas while the various departments honor some of their best and brightest. After the orchestra and band and choir awards, Mrs. Gild steps toward the microphone, and I watch her scan the crowd as she speaks.

"I have a special award tonight for a special person who stepped into an incredible situation and really saved the day for our department. This young lady has demonstrated bravery and talent on both sides of the curtain, and I am so thankful to her—as are the rest of the cast and crew of *Once Upon a Mattress*. We've decided to honor Miss Imogen Keegan with a special Rising Star Award tonight. Imogen?"

The crowd bursts into applause, and Brice pops up and whispers in my ear. "Sorry I ruined your moonlit moment, but I couldn't let you miss this." He makes a kissy face at me as I turn around and glance at my friends. They're all clapping, as are the rest of the kids in the courtyard.

Grant gestures for me to go up to the stage. "Go on!" he says, clapping.

I walk slowly as Mrs. Gild continues to clap and coax me toward the stage.

There are smiles everywhere, and the music is on so I don't have to walk in silence. The entire thing feels like slow motion, and I'm pushing through the crowds of people until I feel the toe of my left shoe catch on something and I trip forward.

Thanks to my sneakers, I don't fall. I just sorta hop onto the other foot and wave my arms to steady myself, but the applause never falters. I look over my shoulder and check the ground for whatever I tripped on. I see the platform heel first, but it only takes a second to follow it up to Carmella's sour face.

I honestly forgot she would be here.

Completely.

The crowd is still clapping for me as I start walking again.

I just have to keep walking. Everyone is waiting for me.

And honestly, I don't care about her standing there, sticking her foot out. I don't care that she's a bitter, sad girl who needs more attention.

I climb the stairs and take a big hug from Mrs. Gild, and she hands me a certificate. I look out across the smiling faces and see Carmella standing where she tripped me with her arms crossed. On the other side of the crowd are my friends. They're smiling and clapping, except for Grant, who's asking me with his eyes if I'm okay. I nod at him and mutter thank you to Mrs. Gild and the crowd and then take my place with the others on the side of the stage.

"And now, I'm excited to announce the evening's top honors. I want to thank all of you who came up to vote. The time has come to announce the Rally King and Queen! These students are being recognized for their dedication to their craft and for going above and beyond the call of duty. I'll start with the King of the evening." He shifts the crown from one hand to the other and pulls a notecard out of his pocket. "The visual arts teacher, Ms. Kipler, is proud to present the young artist behind the new sculpture in the front office, 'The Crestwood Tree,' Carson Miller as your Rally King!"

Everyone is clapping and cheering for him, and he seems happy as Mr. Paulson sets the simple crown on his head.

"And now, for the young woman of the evening, our Rally Queen! She helped completely restructure and choreograph the dance team's upcoming winter recital, your Rally Queen: Ella Cinder!"

Of course.

Honestly, who else would possibly be the Queen? I almost laugh out loud.

The dance team and their section start to applaud uproariously.

Across the courtyard, I see her. Her smile is so bright and perfect. She's hugging and air-kissing and waving like Miss America. She climbs the stage stairs and nearly introduces the front row to her lady bits before taking her place by Mr. Paulson.

I glance back to my friends, who are looking concerned and standing with their hands to their sides. Their faces are etched with worry.

The whooping continues as Mr. Paulson places the crown upon her head.

I'm watching as her head turns slightly to face me on the stage beside her, and our eyes meet in front of hundreds of cheering people. Her eyes squint almost imperceptibly, and her smile turns just cold and smug enough for me to notice.

Reading her face, I can hear her in my mind: "I am everything you'll never be."

It takes only a second for me to decide that she's probably right. And I'm gonna prove it.

I raise my hands to my mouth and take a deep breath. Into the funnel I've fashioned, I let out a celebratory "Wooooo!" before starting to clap.

I raise my chin and settle into my applause, breathing in the incredible feeling of cheering for someone, even her. Especially her.

Across the courtyard, my friends are looking at me with confused faces. They were perfectly prepared to stand in silent solidarity with Imogen Scorned.

But I'm not scorned. Not anymore.

Grant is the first to clap with me, followed by Antonique, Jonathan, and finally—reluctantly—Brice.

Carmella stares dumbly, and then her expression shifts from a scowl to a smirk to a smile for the crowd.

The music clangs back to life as the feverish dancing reclaims most of the students.

My body chemistry feels electrically charged, and I realize that I've never felt so good in all my life. Not on stage, not when I put on this dress, not standing next to Grant and the smell of his hair, not ever. I know that my endorphins are pumping and that the rush will fade, but for now, I'm here. Right here.

As the Rally swings back into action, Grant is the first person to claim my attention in the swirl of faces by our table. "Gen! That was awesome!"

He pulls me into a giant hug that warms me to my core and sets fire burning in the pit of my stomach.

I look up at the mural, at the block of text nestled in the white cloud ringed by rainbows. From here, it looks like a simple patterned square in a bubble. It seems strange that I didn't find it before. Now, it's all I can see.

The music is loud, and Grant grabs my hand and pulls me out on the dance floor. It doesn't even cross my mind to resist.

I am one hundred percent certain that I haven't burned this many calories in probably ever. As I twirl,

I find myself pulling up the black lace and flirting with the pink underneath. My friends and I dance until our faces are red and talk over the music until our voices are hoarse.

I notice Carmella and the King are over to the side of the stage so that the photographer can get a picture.

I excuse myself for a moment and walk over to the photo station.

"Excuse me. Sorry to interrupt." I grin.

Carmella steps away from Carson, places her hands on her hips, and rolls her eyes.

I walk over to her and step into Carson's place. With her heels on, I look like a five–year–old, but even that strikes me as hilarious in this moment.

I wave to the photographer and wrap my arm around Carmella's waist. I talk fast before she has the chance to punch me. "Could you go ahead and snap a quick pic of me and my sister? My mom mentioned she really wanted one."

Flash.

I can't wait to see the picture of Carmella's gaping mouth and angry eyebrows next to me, giving a thumbs-up and a giant wink.

"Later, sis," I say as I walk away, leaving her speechless, her crown sitting crooked on her head.

34

G rant and I are quiet on the way home.
I'm not quite sure why, but it feels like the words we're not saying are bouncing around in the car with us, creating a cacophonous roar that no one can hear but me. Maybe he's just tired or maybe I'm just too distracted by the smell of his jacket over my shoulders. Whatever the case, we're fine. We're always fine—we're just not actually talking.

"Gen?"

"Yeah?" I ask, surprised that he broke the silence just as I was thinking about doing the same.

"Could we...I mean, could you pull into the cul-de-sac and park for a minute? I got you a little something. A present."

"A present? Who's gonna turn that down?" I glance over and see him smile as he looks out the window.

I pull into our neighborhood, take the curves slowly, and pull all the way around past the last few houses into the darkened, circular bulb of concrete at the end of Grant's street.

"Okay," I turn to look at him, and he reaches under the passenger seat. "When did you hide that under there?"

"Oh, days ago." He smiles so hard that his eyes almost close. "I wrapped it myself. Only used one piece of tape!"

I laugh. "Well, you are a master of efficiency."

He hands me a flat sort of rectangle with a lump on one edge. I tear off the paper and see a notebook with a beautiful, swirly cover. And a lock.

"A lock?" I ask with a smirk.

"Yeah, well, you know. Creepers gonna creep."

"I love it. Thank you."

"Sure. It's not a big deal. I was just hoping you planned to keep journaling. You know, I thought it really made you happy, and I was just scared that her shenanigans might have turned you off from it or whatever."

"No, I get it. And I love it," I say. "Thank you."

Silence falls on us like a heavy snow. Bit by bit, we're covered with the soundlessness. The words we're not saying are back, floating around us and filling our lungs.

"So."

"So."

We laugh at the sound of our pitiful attempt, and I notice he's tangling his fingers up in his lap. He's so twisted together that I can't even make out which fingers are from which hand.

Without thinking, I reach over and stop him. "Why are you fidgeting?"

He separates his hands, and I look down and see that I'm only holding one. And he's holding mine.

We've held hands dozens of times. But tonight, with the moon pouring in through the windshield and with the sound of the breeze creeping through the slightly open windows, it feels different.

He inhales and then breathes out through pursed lips. His breath makes a loud rushing sound that reminds me of trying to learn how to whistle when I was little.

"Okay. You can't interrupt me or I'll never get this out." He gulps down air again. "Do you remember last winter? When you were...when you weren't doing so hot?"

I turn from him and look out the window. "You mean when I was in such a state that they almost admitted me? Yeah. I think that's vaguely familiar." I smirk and lower my chin.

"Well, you may not remember, but this one day, you were really out of it. And you weren't really yourself or thinking clearly."

"I remember that day," I say. I look back down at our hands. "I remember everything about that day."

"You do?"

"I do."

"Well, I've been thinking about that day a lot lately. And I've been...worried."

"You shouldn't. I mean, don't worry. It's in my top five most embarrassing moments, for sure."

He looks down and chuckles to himself. "No. I'm not worried about it happening again. I'm worried that it won't."

I know what it sounds like he's saying, but I've been wrong before. I want to feel joy, but I'm shrouded with doubt.

Our tangled hands are the only things I see, and then he's moving his thumb across my palm and then his fingers intertwine with mine, one on top of another on top of another. We're not "holding" hands anymore. We're capital-H "Holding" hands. I clear my throat to cover the sound of my heartbeat, which I'm sure he can hear from where he sits.

"God," I say. "I'm freaking out thinking that I'm misunderstanding something in a really major way because...you definitely pushed me away last December. So I'm obviously confused, and things are about to get really embarrassing."

He laughs at me, and I smile.

"Then I'll say this as clearly as I can." He grabs my knees and turns me even further around in my seat. "We were little kids and your mom walked in on us, all of six years old, playing on your kitchen table. Do you remember?"

I shake my head. "I don't think so. What were we doing?"

"You had begged me to play Sleeping Beauty. And you were lying on the table, it was so cute, and you were holding this clump of weeds like they were flowers. And I climbed up on the dining chair, right? And I'm looking at you, laying there with your eyes closed, and I'm just about to kiss you, you know, to wake you up, and your mom walks in."

"What?" I ask, with a breathless laugh. "Why don't I remember this?"

"Well, she comes in, and she scoops me up and tickles me and whispers to me, 'It's not time for her to wake up quite yet, Prince Charming,' and then you sat up crying and told her she'd ruined your game."

"Oh my God, no, I didn't."

"Oh, yes, you did. You had a flare for dramatics even then."

He's still looking into my eyes, and he reaches up and draws his finger down the top of my nose.

"So last winter, you're lying there, and you're such a mess. You're so sad and empty, and you'd spent so much time with your eyes and your heart closed to... everything. And I just kept hearing your mom's voice. And I knew that it wasn't time yet. I knew that I didn't want to be something that you just did because you were sad and didn't know what else to try. I didn't want that moment to happen while you were still...asleep."

My heart stops beating. The silence of it fills my head.

His thumb sweeps a rogue tear from my cheek, which causes me to breathe in abruptly as my heart thuds back to life. Slowly, sweetly, he brings his face so near to mine that our noses are almost touching.

"Grant." I exhale his name so softly, I'm not even sure I said it. "It's time for me to wake up."

My lips drift into a smile and brush against his, and then we're pressed together, and I feel heat and tenderness and hope rushing through me. My lips and my heart soften and melt. All I can smell is his hair and it's all over me and settling on my skin like dew. His arms lower, and soon, they're all around me, holding and comforting me as they have so many times before. And his lips on mine soothe my fears and assuage the ache that follows me around like a shadow.

The ebb and flow of his mouth and mine is the exact sort of thing that would inspire the stories I constantly resist.

But it's better than those stories because this one is real.

My whole body aches as I pull away from him.

"Gen..." He wraps his arms around me tighter, but I hold up my hand and stop him from speaking.

I reach up, run my fingers through his hair, and say, "I have never not loved you. Never."

I start to laugh because it's like neither of us considered that there would have to be a follow-up in a scenario like this one. He giggles too and brings his face closer to mine.

"But—" I start.

"No buts!" He keels sideways, feigning exasperation, and I pretend to punch him in his ribs.

"Who's being dramatic now?" I grin as he sits back up and envelops me in his arms. His nose is buried in my hair, and as he exhales, my skin catches fire and ice and I'm only flesh and nerves.

With his arms around me, it's hard to think, but I collect myself enough to whisper in his ear as I swing my arms around his shoulders and bury my head in the hollow of his neck.

"But...I'm scared," I say. "Like, tonight was a good night, right? And I've got all this makeup on and there was dancing and serotonin, but tomorrow's coming, and it really might suck."

"You're right. It might suck. And if tomorrow doesn't suck, then next month might or next year. Suckiness will probably be a part of life until the day that we die." He runs his thumb across the lace of my sleeve. He places his forehead on mine and continues with a grin, "But, I mean...if I'm too late, I understand. I guess, technically, Andrew got to you first."

"What?" I search his face for the glow that seems to be leaking like water down a drain.

"Well, I mean, he was your first kiss."

Just hearing Grant say the word "kiss" makes me feel like I am going to spontaneously combust. I sit up straight and say, "Well, according to the first kiss charter documents, there is a loophole that applies to delicate situations just like this one."

His eyes shimmer with mischief and fire. "Oh, is that so?"

"Yes. According to paragraph thirty-one, a first kiss is null and void if only one side does the kissing. And technically, Andrew kissed me. I certainly did not 'kiss him back' because I wasn't even paying any attention to him. I was trying to remember my next line. So it would seem that, in accordance with the law, his kiss must be stricken from the record."

"Well, I definitely want to uphold the law," he says.

"Definitely."

The breeze stills, and the quiet is floating between us again. Every molecule in the air shudders to a stop and time itself shrinks into this tiny, meaningless thing.

His hair looks almost blue in the moonlight, and I reach up and run my fingers through it again until my hand is on the back of his head, and those eyes—more green than brown, but definitely both—cut me and cure me so completely.

I lean forward, mustering every ounce of trust, bravery, and hope I have within me, and I push myself close to him. His eyes sparkle as I close mine just before I pour my lips onto his.

Kissing...even better than being kissed.

BREATHE
EASY

35

The sunlight warms my face as it pours over me through the window. My skin flushes as the heat creeps up my neck and covers my head.

For a moment, I allow my eyes to remain closed.

I focus on the softness of my pillow and the gentle hum of my ceiling fan. I stretch my legs out, tightening my muscles and bringing life to my sleepy limbs.

My lips are soft and filled to the brim with new memories. For a moment—just a second, really—I fearfully consider that it might have just been a dream. I reach up and touch the side of my face and feel a grin pull my cheeks higher, and I know—beyond a shadow of a doubt—that it wasn't.

My eyes open, and as I sit up in bed, I look around my room, waiting for the world to present itself in a completely different way...but it doesn't. I notice all the familiar shapes. The curve of my squishy chair and the angles of my bookshelf—these are the same. I take an inventory of my feelings, recognizing instantly the same ones that walk beside me every day.

A little bit of sadness? Check.

A little bit of fear? Check.

A little bit of anxiety? Check.
And something new.
A little bit of joy?
Check.

Looking in the mirror is a strange experience for me. It always has been. Today is no different. I still see the roundness of my face, the sagging of my arms, and the dimples on my butt.

I know that I'm supposed to love myself as I am, and I think that I understand what that is supposed to mean. The girl in the mirror in front of me is the same me I always see...and I know that. But it would be so great to look in the mirror and get even a tiny glimpse of what she might be like if she weren't self-imposing the weight of the world on her shoulders.

Would she still have dark circles under her eyes if she didn't spend so much time crying?

Would she have the wrinkles across her brow if she didn't do so much scowling?

Would she weigh two-hundred pounds if she weren't constantly trying to alleviate her anxiety by sticking her hand into a jar of pre-made frosting?

Would she have captured his heart if he hadn't watched her fall apart?

I don't think I knew it was possible to feel so totally different and so totally the same in a single moment.

Predictably, I hear Evelyn bustling around in the kitchen even before I pass through the doors. She's standing at the kitchen table sorting through piles of clothes that she's setting gently into a box perched on the glass top.

"Are you packing stuff up for Goodwill? I have some shoes I can't wear," I say as I head to the cabinet to grab my pills.

"I'm glad you're up. We have to talk."

With my back to her, I'm startled at the sound of her voice. I've never heard it so deep or somber. I turn around and see her lift the box off of the table. Under it are a half a dozen crumpled pieces of pink paper which have been flattened out. She turns them over, and I feel the blood drain from my face.

"Evelyn, where—"

"While I was cleaning Carmella's room last night, I found these as I was emptying the trash." Her skin looks slack, and as she sits at the table, I barely recognize her without a smile and an obnoxious glint in her eye. "When I asked her to explain these this morning, she said, quite frankly in fact, that she had violated your privacy, made these cruel copies, and posted them on your locker at school..."

I bring my hand to my chest so that I can keep my heart from poking through my skin. My heartbeat is so heavy; my eardrums are vibrating.

"So the only thing I can't figure out is why you didn't tell me about this?"

I look at the tile floor and my eyes follow the grout like a maze. "I don't know," I mutter like a scolded child.

"Imogen, this is a big deal. Do you know that?"

"I know," I say. I feel brave for bringing my gaze from the floor to the tabletop. "I shouldn't have written those things. And I'm sorry."

"No." She stands and walks around the table until she's standing in front of me. "Those thoughts are yours. What Carmella did was unacceptable. Do you understand that? It is not okay. I knew that things were strained between you, but honestly, I didn't know that things had gotten so bad because you never told me."

"She's your daughter. Why would I tell you? Why would you *ever* take my side over hers?"

"Imogen, I want you to hear what I'm about to tell you. When I married your father, I signed up for the whole package. That means that, if you'll have me, I want to make it my job to be a mother to you, just as much as I'm a mother to Carmella. That means that it is now my job to love you and protect you, even if that means protecting you from someone whom I love with all my heart." Her eyes gloss with tears, and she turns her back to me and returns to the cardboard box. As she sets it back on the table and resumes sorting the clothes, she says, "Carmella and I had a long conversation this morning, and we both agreed that she should return to Austin."

Oh my God. She's going back?

This is crazy.

Evelyn reaches up and runs a hand over her hair.

"Evelyn, please. Just so you know, I don't need her to go. I'm fine. I'm really fine." I gather my thoughts with a breath and try to speak more concisely. "She doesn't have to leave on my account. I know things have been really hard between us, but I've got to be stronger. And at least things are out in the open."

Evelyn smiles at me sadly, but she just keeps shaking her head. "That's nice of you to say. But Carmella is not going to come into this house and treat you with the same viciousness and cruelty that she's been on the receiving end of. And yes, she knows what it feels like. She has to be *better* than that. And if she can't find a way to be a loving and supportive part of this family, then she's going to have to decide if she's going to be a part of this family at all. She's not going to take her problems out on everybody else."

Evelyn's eyes are soft, but her words are intense. I can't believe what I'm hearing, and I can't remember ever hearing a parent speak so sternly to or about their kid. It almost makes me feel bad for Carmella. Almost.

"Wow," I say with my eyes averted. "That sounds kinda harsh."

"It is," Carmella says. She has entered the kitchen in silence and is standing in the doorway. "And I would appreciate it if you wouldn't talk about my problems in front of her, Mother."

Carmella's eyes are puffy, and I can tell, without a doubt, that she's been crying. Her face is bare and she looks tired, but she also looks like a lot of other things. Like angry and frustrated and scared. She's wearing a giant sweatshirt and her trademark tiny shorts.

It occurs to me that she has nobody to impress. Maybe she really does just like those shorts.

"Imogen is your family now," Evelyn declares.

"She is not my family," Carmella snaps. "*You* are supposed to be my family. And Dad. *My* dad. That's supposed to be my family."

I swallow and take a step back. I don't need to be in the middle of their squabble. It doesn't feel right.

Evelyn's voice is firm. "I believe you have some things you need to say to Imogen. Now."

"Fine." Carmella's voice sounds mostly bored, but also gritty and annoyed. She gestures to the sliding glass door.

I hesitate just a moment, choking on the word, "Okay."

We head out the back door and sit on the weatherworn patio furniture.

She sits across from me, her legs crossed in her seat, and she still manages to look like a freaking beauty queen. Even without makeup, it's obvious that she really is beautiful. It's not just a façade. She really is.

"Let's get this over with," she starts abruptly.

Touching.

"My mom wants me to apologize to you for the posters. So...sorry."

"Your sincerity astounds me."

It's strange to me that, all at once, Carmella is no longer a threat. I'm not sure if it's what Evelyn's said or if it was the picture at the dance or if it was my going back to school and moving on or what. But in this moment, I see that she is just a girl.

A very sad, very angry girl.

"Take it or leave it," she says.

I stand up from my chair, unwilling to sit and stress myself out on this beautiful post-kissing day.

"Carmella, I know this is going to sound weird, but I'm ready to move on from this. So, whenever you're ready, you just let me know, and we'll wipe the slate clean. Congratulations again on Rally Queen."

"You know," she says to me as I walk toward the house. "The first time I met you, I was so excited. I thought that maybe, just maybe, a sister would be the silver lining of my parents ripping our family apart. But that first day, I walked into your life, and I realized it would never be about 'us.' It would always be about you. The rest of my life as your sister would always be about you."

I pause for a moment at the open door, with one foot on the threshold. I turn slowly to face her. "You know, I'm sure you think that going through whatever you've been through all alone makes you stronger than me. I bet you feel so tough when you hide your feelings behind your makeup and mean words, but I can see through you now."

Carmella is looking out into the yard, her eyes so tired and sad, and even though she's been horrible, I feel bad for her. I really do.

"You said something once, and it stuck in my head like superglue. You told me that when people who don't have power pretend that they do, they lose. Sometimes they lose what they have. Sometimes they lose what they want. But they lose." I resist the urge to bite at my thumb, but take a deep breath instead. "So, when you're ready to stop pretending, you let me know."

I follow her gaze out across the mostly dead grass as the sun continues to climb over the houses behind ours. The weight of my own pretending causes my shoulders to slump. I take a deep breath and turn back to her where she sits cross-legged on the worn plastic chair. Her jaw is set like stone.

I hesitate for half a moment more before I speak. "I've got one question for you though." She doesn't move a muscle. "I've gotta know. Why were you 'Carmella' last year and 'Ella' this year? I mean, why did you get so adamant about this name change? I've been wondering since the day you moved in."

At first, I think she's going to ignore me. She sits there for so long, unflinching, that I wonder if I asked it in my head. And then she turns to me with a calmness and a sadness I haven't seen on her face since Christmas.

"I..." She stops, and I can see the words swirling behind her eyes. "I wanted so badly to not be me that, eventually, I made myself into somebody else." She closes her eyes for a second and then opens them again. "Okay?" She tries to snap back at me, but her words have none of their usual fire. "Is that what you wanted to hear, Imogen?"

My stomach drops at the familiar sight of pain, this time sitting behind *her* eyes. I know the look of it so deeply, I feel, for a second, like I'm staring straight at a mirror instead of at the girl I'll never be. She hugs her knees to her chest and drops her chin.

"Ella..." I wait a moment, and slowly, she lifts her head and turns her red-rimmed eyes to mine. "You can call me Gen."

I step inside and slide the door closed with a gentle click.

36

B ack in my bedroom I walk over to my shelves and see the photo of my mother lying on its face. I set it upright and look at us, smiling and beautiful.

Sometimes it's just as simple as wishing I could look at her and say, "Oh my God, Mom, you wouldn't believe the drama."

I think she'd eat it up.

My eyes slide over from the frame to the storybook, and I reach to pull it from the shelf. I run my hand over the cover and open it to the inscription she wrote.

The little rainbow frame and squared off words look different now. But they look the same too, I guess. I toss the words around on my tongue, tasting them, trying to figure out if they're any different now than they've been since I was five.

The shine of the blade looks lackluster and muted even in the bright sunlight. I hold it in my palm and let the cold metal shoot needles of chill into my hand.

I wonder, for a moment, if I really need to make such a gesture.

Handing it over to my dad for good will mean that—well—that it's been handed over.

My phone buzzes across the top of my nightstand.

My pulse starts to pound as I reach for what I'm sure is the first text from Grant post all the kissing.

"Hey you. Can I see you later? I need to make sure you're conscious after my amazing display of manliness and romanticism. Hope it didn't overwhelm you. ;)"

Oh yeah. This blade has got to go.

I pull my hand up into the sleeve of my hoodie and hop back down the stairs, passing Carmella's closed door.

Downstairs, I approach my dad's office door and take a deep breath.

I'm terrified.

Not at what he'll do or say or think, but I'm scared about what it will feel like to know that that little sliver of metal isn't up there hiding for me.

I lift my hand to knock just as I hear his phone ring on the other side of the door. It's muffled, but I hear him greet his agent and they dive into a discussion of rights and territories and plans.

The wind sucks right out of my lungs.

I lower my hand and spin the blade around between my fingers, hidden in my left sleeve.

Just then, I hear the sound of the oven timer.

Evelyn.

I close my eyes and try to remember the sound of my mom's voice. Just one word. I wish I could hear it again.

When I reenter the kitchen, my mouth drops open just a little because I'm embarrassed by what I need to do and what I need to say.

Evelyn sees my hesitation and immediately pushes back from the table. "Is everything okay?" she asks politely.

I pull my hand out of my sleeve and look at the blade lying in my palm. I grip it firmly, drawing from it the very last bit of "strength" it will ever give me.

With a breath, I set it on the table in front of her.

"Obviously, I didn't give all of them to my dad when I was supposed to. I mean when George made me hand them over. I don't know exactly why I kept one, but I did, and I didn't use it for a long time, until I did." I look up at the ceiling for just a second to recapture my resolve, and Evelyn takes my hand in hers. "I don't want to keep it anymore because I don't want to hurt the people I love in the moments that I hurt myself. I need to give this to someone I love. Someone I trust. So I need to give this to you."

My voice is a little shaky, and I'm looking down at her, seated at the table. The blade sits on the smooth wood between us. I don't know what else to say.

I start to pull away, but I don't really want to. I leave my hand lying lightly in hers. Slowly, she reaches over and gently tugs the sleeve of my hoodie up to my elbow and looks at my arm. The lines that stripe it are varied in their color and shape. Six are flatter and smoother, and one is newer, slightly raised, and pink.

She looks at me intently, and I feel my eyes begin to water.

She wraps her warm hands around my arm, her palm right on top of my scars.

"Every single one of these marks is a part of your story. But they're not the whole story," she says. Her eyes are glistening again, and she tugs my sleeve back down and pats my hand with hers. Then she stands, picks up the blade, sticks it in her apron pocket, and goes back to her packing and sniffling.

I pull away and head to the edge of the kitchen.

"I'm gonna head out for a little while. Is that okay?" I ask.

"With Grant?" she responds.

"Yeah." I nod. "Of course."

"Did you two have a good time at the Rally last night?"

In a surge of betrayal, my face flushes with heat. I'm so glad she's looking the other way. "Yeah. Sure. Totally."

"Well, have fun, but be back in time for dinner, okay? Grant can stay and eat with us if he wants."

"Okay, thanks. I'll tell him."

"And, honey?"

"Yeah?"

"After your dad saw you in your dress last night, he decided it's probably about time to make an adjustment to the current sleepover policy."

She giggles as she looks back at me and then shrugs her shoulder up and down in a phony, seductive way.

"Evelyn!" I squeal, before she turns back to her boxes.

On my way back to my room, my dad's office door swings open just as I reach the bottom of the stairs.

"Immy, give your old man a squeeze."

I walk over to him and wrap my arms around his waist.

He pushes back and looks into my face. "What is it? Is everything okay?"

I reach up to kiss him on the cheek before I turn and start heading up the stairs.

"It's okay, Dad. I'm okay."

When I open the front door, I see Grant sitting on the curb. With his back to me, I'm left to imagine what face he's making and wonder what he's thinking right now.

The door closes behind me, and he turns at the sound. When he stands up, he looks at me with an almost blank expression. I fear, for a moment, that he's disappointed. That he doesn't see the person he saw last night. Maybe when he sees me in the light, something will have changed.

His face slowly blossoms with a smile, and he stands in front of me with his hands shoved deep into the pockets of his jeans. He's still wearing the shirt from last night, and his eyes are swollen and sleepy.

I walk down the path, coming to a stop just a few feet from him. "Hi," I say.

"Hey," he replies.

He reaches out and grabs my hand with his.

"Wanna walk with me?" he asks.

"Yeah." I reach up to tuck a strand of hair behind my ear as we walk side by side down the sidewalk, deeper into our neighborhood.

We go on walking—without talking—for several moments, and every step seems to turn the gear one more notch, tightening the space between us. As we finally reach our unspoken destination—the cul-de-sac—I let go of his hand and turn to face him in the light.

"We're not talking," I say. "I mean, I know that's obvious, but I don't know what that means. Are you, like, okay? With everything?"

He smiles wide. "Okay? Are you asking me seriously if I'm okay? Gen, I'm always okay, but today, I'm better than okay. I'm home."

The urge to squeal like a six-year-old girl is almost overwhelming. I will not jump up and down like someone just gave me cheese fries.

I cross his path and make my way to the curb. I sit down, and soon, he's seated right beside me.

I pause for a beat before replying, "I need to say some things that you probably already know, okay?"

"Okay," he says.

"I've got a lot I need to work on."

"I know."

"And there are going to be times that I really need to be alone."

"I know."

"And I don't want things to be weird or whatever if I tell you that I don't want you there for whatever reason. I mean, usually, being around you is one of the things that makes me happiest but—"

"I know, Gen."

"Come on, now," I say. "You don't know everything."

"Well, I don't know everything. But I do know a lot. I mean, I am a third-place regional physics competition finalist you know." He places his hands on his hips in what is meant to be an impressive superhero pose. As he drops his hands, he says, "Honestly, I think things will be pretty much the same. Not that much is changing in this for me. I know that, despite my lack of skills in the subtlety department, this is news for you, but I've had plenty of practice caring about you and loving you and, well, quite frankly, wanting to kiss you pretty much all the time. So, yeah—none of this is new territory."

My face floods with embarrassment for the billionth time in twenty-four hours, and I avert my eyes.

"I don't completely understand it, Grant. I don't." I look at my fingers and pick at my skin nervously. "But I'm really, really happy."

"Me too."

He closes the small distance between us and leans over, planting a whisper of a kiss on my lips before putting his arm around me and drawing me close to his side.

"Walk?" I ask.

"Sure," he says.

He stands up and offers me his hand, which I use to pull myself from the curb. I shove my free hand into the pocket of my hoodie for warmth and feel a small knot of paper. I swallow hard as my body jerks to a stop against my will. I'm sure it's the little green Post-it from ages ago, scribbled with Carmella's cruelty. My fingers wrap around the crinkled object, and I pull it into the light. In my palm is the hot pink origami flower.

Maybe it's the shadows concealing words in the folds or maybe it's just this day, but the flower is gorgeous. I suppose it always was.

"What's that?" Grant asks.

"A present. Jonathan made it."

"Is that...?" Grant gestures at the bold black marks.

"Yeah. It took some work, but it's awfully pretty for something that started out so ugly, isn't it?" I ask, squinting against the sunlight.

"It is," he says, pulling my hand to his mouth and kissing it gently.

I place the flower back in my pocket and spare a thought for how great it will look at the top of my bookshelf.

We set off walking, and soon, in the shade of the trees and surrounded by cool autumn breezes, the laughter returns. And so does the ease of everything and the inside jokes. Oh, and some kissing. There's a little of that, too.

Edge of the Fall

37

Maybe they weren't lying. Maybe we're all just missing the point. In some cases, there's more to these stories than I thought. When I started thinking about the reasons why people do what they do—why they hurt others or act out of fear or expect other people to solve their problems—I realized that the storybooks emphasize the wrong things, like, all the time. The story with the old lady who poisons the pretty girl? It's about the old lady being afraid of not being seen as beautiful. A textbook self-esteem problem. In another story, a girl is bullied by her sisters and generally made to feel like nothing, and she believes them. It takes someone showing her—making her notice—she's special before she believes she's more than they told her she could be. At the end of the day, when the magic wore off and the clock struck midnight...she couldn't hide behind her ball gown. Like it or not, when things get scary, we've gotta be willing to at least try and make our own magic. I don't want to be a waiting-and-wanting girl. I want to be a believing-and-doing girl.

I put them on pedestals like every girl does, but maybe they're more than I give them credit for. Maybe I have more in common with them than I thought.

"So, Imogen."

"So, Therapist George."

He smiles a little as he gathers his pen and notepad from his desk. The room is a warmer shade of brown today, and his shirt is a brighter shade of blue.

It's a good day.

Just one good day. But that's enough for now.

"What are your cufflinks today?" I ask.

He looks down to his sleeves and back up to me with a question in his eyes. "You notice those?"

"Every time." I smile at him, and he squints his eyes before he answers.

"They're baseballs," he says with a grin.

He sits back in his chair and flips through some of his notes. The window behind him is already open all the way, and the sun is creeping across the rich patterned carpet.

"So I guess we should talk about what happened last week?" He uncrosses his legs and sits forward a bit on his chair.

"We will, but not today." I smile at him and scoot over, closer to the armrest so I can lean on the big brown leather couch. "Do you remember a couple years ago when I told you my mom wrote something on this huge mural at school and I couldn't find it?"

"Vaguely."

"Well, I found it at the Rally on Saturday night."

"Really? What did it say?"

"It was the very same inscription that I've been carrying around in my book of fairy tales since I was five. The very same."

I bring my middle finger to my mouth and start to nibble as TG jots something down in his notes. When he's done, he looks up and says, "Wow."

Yeah, wow.

I shake my head at him and look back out the window.

"So don't leave me hanging. What'd it say?" he asks.

I use my hands to shape the words in the space between us. "For a Happily Ever After: 'The End' is just the beginning."

"That's good," he says with a coy grin. "She's good."

She sure is.

My heart squeezes just a bit.

That ache.

The most familiar feeling I know.

"Yeah, I know. Of course, I probably should have 'gotten' that message a long, long time ago."

"When doesn't matter. The getting it matters. So what's it mean to you?"

"I guess just that, when it's done and you're done and everything has happened, that's when it's time to get up and start making things happen for yourself."

He smiles. "That's a really, really good start, Imogen. I'm proud of you."

His face is gentle.

"Thanks, George."

"So how do you feel now?"

I close my eyes for a second, and under the hum of the air conditioner, I can hear the answer echoing through my mind.

I feel like a door has been unlocked by a key that was in my pocket the whole time.

I've been broken, but I'm not broken.

That pain won't disappear anytime soon, maybe not ever, but it's not all I have.

As I inhale, my lungs fill completely before I speak.

"It made me feel like I am whole. I am more than just the pieces that I see. I am stronger than I seem."

I look out George's great windows and see the cloudless sky filling the wall of his office. The deep, vibrant blue spreads out before me, but I find myself looking up instead of down. A bird soars past the window, wings spread wide. Her sad song doesn't bring her down. She flies upon the strength and truth of her tune. I consider the rush and exhilaration of joy and feel certain that it's not actually a match for falling.

Maybe flying instead.

In a world of so many beginnings, it kinda makes me wonder if endings really exist at all.

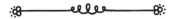

Acknowledgements

Unprepared.

I've used that word a lot lately. I was unprepared for how hard it would be to turn a pile of words into a book. I was unprepared for how scary it would be to hand over that book baby to the team that will help it enter the world. And I am unprepared for the overwhelming gratitude I feel for EVERYONE who has made this possible (especially those of you that I will inevitably forget in these paragraphs).

First, I want to thank Abby. My first "fan." You were the first person to make me feel—truly, deeply feel—like an author. I can never thank you enough for that gift.

My family has had so much practice upholding my crazy dreams. Mom, thank you for being my first true love. Dad, thank you for teaching me that aspirations are worth protecting. Clint, my weasel. Thank you for being so unapologetically enthusiastic right along with me. John, LaDonna, Thomas, Lawson, Grams, Art, and Mama Macke, I can't think of a day or a moment in my life that I didn't feel encouraged and uplifted by each of you. I am so grateful.

I am so humbled to have the most beautiful, wonderful best friends who make me better every day. Megan, you held my hand through every single step of the publishing process. I would have collapsed into a puddle of stress without your DAILY support.

Missy, my fellow mental health warrior, I am so glad I forced my friendship upon you. I'm all the better for it. Lola, my other half, my sister across the sea. Besos for always. AWWA-TIH. Jess, thank you for reading my first words, for dancing to '90s jams with me, and for sharing your gorgeous artwork with every reader of this book.

To my most faithful critique partner, Annie, you helped shape this story before it was even a story. Every time you read (and re-read) this story, I fell further into CP Love with you. You are an incredible teacher and friend. Also, huge thanks to Suzanne and Crystal for the early encouragement and critique.

Publishing is, in a word, CRAZYPANTS. Endless love to my darlings, my other sisterwives: Angi and Sarah B. And also to my sweetests, Tameka, Rachel G., Jessica L., Simon C., Dahlia, Mario, Febe, Smash, Katie (my Twinner), Summer, Hay, Emily H., Sarah G., Erin T., Alex T., Mikey, Jurassica, Jenn N., Candice, Mark O., and Jaye.

I have to thank my early readers (here's where I pray that I kept good notes): Jessica N., Dahlia, Mel S., Christine, Kari, Rachel S., Andrea H., Jennie, Jen (my Rev), Lola, Leah S., Marieke, Jacki, Sarah G., Mandy, Katie, Missy, Emily H., Rachel G., Ashley W., Jessica L., and Megan.

There are some people who will, I hope, indulge me for thanking them in groups: my debut group, We Are One Four; the OneFourKidLit community; my OBGirls; my Nestie Writing Group; the Wonderly family; the North Branch Critique Group; the Lasties; Nerdfighteria; the #Lufkin6; my friends in the DFW theatre community; my HMS and DISD family; and, of course, my incredible students (especially my Twitter angels and book club kids).

I have to thank the original members of my street team, my #OMGen crew. Thank you for being willing to champion someone and something you hadn't yet experienced: Jamie, Veronica, Jessica W., Emily, Ghenet, Rachel S., Tammy, Suzanne, Laura B., Lauren S., Carlos, Zoey, Kayla, Crystal, Tawney, Megan, Rachelia, Andrea D., Alana, Michael, Summer, Serena, Rosemond, Stephanie, Jenny M., Angi, Nik, Jessica C., Annie, Tyler, Tabitha, Antonya, Rachel, Liza, Lisseth, and Hazel.

To Jake and the team at NoStigmas, thank you for inspiring me with your endless dedication to people who are living with all kinds of mental health needs.

I can never thank my Spencer Hill family enough. Never EVER. Thank you to all who had a hand in making this book happen. Danielle Ellison, thank you for loving Gen as much as I do. Cindy and Meredith, my publicity team, thank you for helping me share this story with those who need to hear it. Kate and Patricia, thank you for your leadership and guidance. Also, I am so grateful for Briana, Asja, Lauren, Harmony, John, Becca, Sarah, and Jenny.

Thank you, Jenny Zemanek, for your incredible cover designs. They so perfectly symbolize what I could never put into words.

Jessica Sinsheimer, my agent and friend, I am so grateful for your guidance, protection, and creativity. Thank you for being collaborative, kind, and brilliant. Please give extra squishy hugs of gratitude to everyone at the Sarah Jane Freymann Literary Agency.

And to Daron, my best fress, my mame, my rock star, my partner in crime, my cutie-boy-with-the-heart-of-gold, I can only say thank you for never doubting me for a second. Thank you for telling the musical part of Imogen's story with me, and of course, for basically writing the whole book.

THE
HIT
LIST

NIKKI URANG

The Fine Art of
Pretending

Rachel Harris

Whisper Falls

Elizabeth Langston

BOOK TWO in the WHISPER FALLS SERIES

A Whisper in Time

ZABETH LANGSTON

BOOK THREE in the WHISPER FALLS SERIES

Whispers from the Past

ELIZABETH LANGSTON

Get lost in the past...

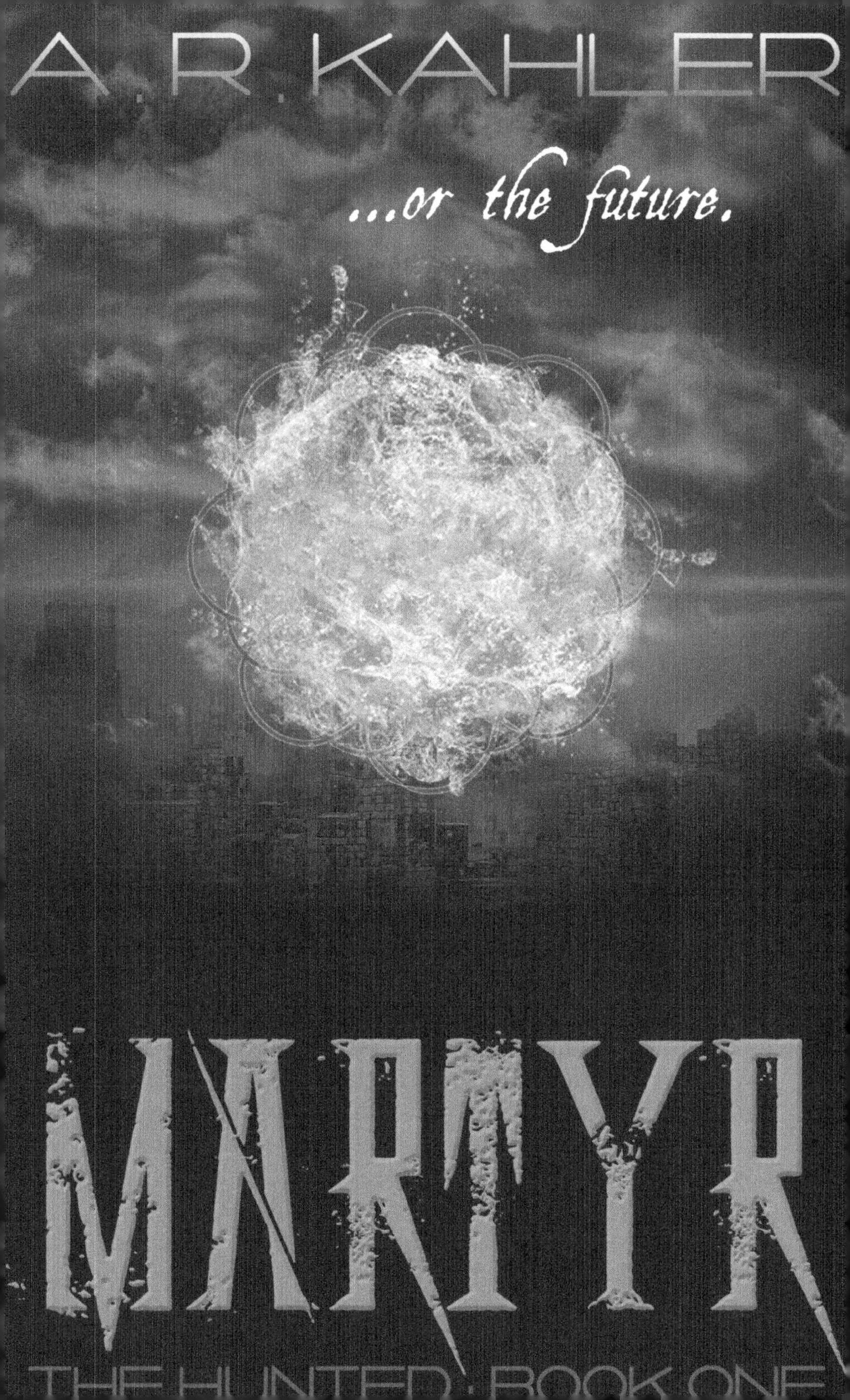
A.R. KAHLER
...or the future.
MARTYR
THE HUNTED . BOOK ONE

About the Author

Photo: Lindsay Van Meter

Kelsey Macke has been creative for as long as she can remember. Her formative years were spent writing songs and horrible poetry, and she mastered the art of drama queenery at a very young age. When she's not writing, she's usually working on music with her husband, Daron, as part of the folky indie-pop duo Wedding Day Rain. Her YA debut, *Damsel Distressed*, combines a powerful story with original songs in a mixed-media project that sets Kelsey's hyper-creative heart all aflutter. She is represented by Jessica Sinsheimer of the Sarah Jane Freymann Literary Agency.

CPSIA information can be obtained at www.ICGtesting.com
Printed in the USA
LVOW05s0152021114

411631LV00005B/6/P